Pat started to speak and had to clear her throat first. "I'll hold you, Kate. I'd love to hold you."

"And if I want more?"

"We'll see."

Later in the dim light of the bedroom Pat asked Kate how Gordie was. Kate replied, "Angry, sad, bereft but functioning. Except for being so thin, he doesn't look any different from last summer." Pat's arm was around her and Kate turned and kissed Pat softly, teasingly on the mouth.

Pat turned her head away. "Don't do that."

Kate kissed her cheek and neck. "Why not?" she whispered. She moved her lips over the skin, feeling, tasting, smelling — velvety, sweet, clean. Memorizing Pat with her senses.

"Because I won't be able to resist, that's why. Kate, what if this is a mistake? We're such good friends. I don't want to lose that."

"You won't, even if this is a mistake, but it's not," Kate replied, taking Pat's face between her hands, looking into her eyes and then pulling softly on Pat's mouth with her own, running her tongue tentatively around the inside of Pat's lips.

"Jesus," Pat breathed into Kate's mouth, "I'm not a saint."

"So stop acting like one."

Lifestyles

by Jackie Calhoun

Lifestyles

by Jackie Calhoun

The Naiad Press, Inc.
1990

Printed in the United States of America
First Edition

Edited by Katherine V. Forrest
Cover design by Pat Tong and Bonnie Liss
    (Phoenix Graphics)
Typeset by Sandi Stancil

Library of Congress Cataloging-in-Publication Data

Calhoun, Jackie.
    Lifestyles / by Jackie Calhoun.
        p.   cm.
    ISBN 0-941483-57-6
    I. Title
PS3553.A3985L54   1990
813'.54--dc20   89-48968
                                                                      CIP

About the Author

Jackie Calhoun Smith was born in Wisconsin and grew up there. She lived in Indiana for twenty-seven years and moved back to Wisconsin in 1987. She divides her time between her cottage and home. This is her first novel.

To Chris

Lifestyles

by Jackie Calhoun

I

Gripping the steering wheel tightly with both hands, her teeth locked together as if she were in combat, Kate glanced in the rear view mirror just before turning off U.S. 41 onto the access road. She saw herself in the dawn light, frown etched between her brows, and forced herself to unclench her jaw. The dentist had warned, "You'll grind your teeth down to stubs." She bared her teeth in a grimace and ran her tongue over the enamel.

None of the gas stations were open, so she turned the car west on County Road E as the sun outlined the landscape in the new day. Fog hovered above the ground and floated across the road. Forty-five minutes later, when the blacktop curved and the hills closed in on it, Kate sighed and visibly relaxed against the back of the seat.

The core of anxiety nearly always at the back of her throat vanished. Kate had never understood the words *You can't go home again* because she had always returned to the safety of her childhood retreat. She thought of it as coming home to her roots to renew herself — to the old farmhouse and small lake, the pine hills of her youth.

But never like this. The anxiety reasserted itself, and she swallowed a few times and breathed deeply to dispel it. The nightmare her life had become threatened to close in on her. She refused to think of it. She had turned it endlessly over in her mind, and there was no satisfactory solution. The best thing to do now was forget it, push it away from her, at least until she could get a different perspective on it. The only way she seemed able to do this was to remove herself from the source. Was she running? She shrugged in answer. At least she had somewhere to run.

The drive had seemed interminable as the ribbon of road had unrolled under the wheels of the gray Taurus, mostly through the dark of night. The Ford topped the last hill and turned into the narrow drive — hemmed in by towering white pines and ending at an old white house and red barn. The slope beyond led down to the sandy beach and circular lake.

Cramped from the long drive, she opened the car door and stretched, then let herself onto the back porch and unlocked the door to the kitchen. A closed and musty odor greeted her; no one had been here since the previous fall. She smiled as she went through the rooms — opening windows to let in the smell of pines and lake, occasionally running a hand over the furniture, touching her past. She sat in one of the front porch chairs and studied the lake, misty and quiet in the early morning, while the familiar feel of the place settled over her. Twisting her mouth at the irony, she recalled her wish to live here, now possible and now unwanted — not like this, not alone.

Then she hauled in her suitcases and unpacked in the front bedroom where she had always slept. With the quiet beginning to unnerve her, she put on her swimsuit and headed down the warm sandy path between Norway pines to the beach. Pier sections lay neatly stacked on the shore as if waiting for her. The lake glittered like a jewel in the early July sunlight. Dug by the last glacier to sweep over Wisconsin, it was similar to other lakes in the area, a product of glacial derangement — spring fed with no creeks leading in or out — and surrounded by pine-covered hills. A strange term for such beauty, Kate thought. She waded up to her knees in the cool water and stood surveying the expanse of blue-green before her. Cottages overlooked the water like silent watchers in the trees. When she was a girl, there had been only a handful of summer homes around the lake.

The sun picked out highlights in her reddish-blonde hair, styled to turn under but now pushed back behind her ears. Her eyes, squinting against the reflection of sun on water, were the color of the lake. A boat with a lone fisherman broke the flatness of the surface. Taking a deep breath Kate immersed herself to her waist and then dove in. Like a cool caress, the water enfolded her, and she swam out to the depths where she rolled over on her back and studied the shore. When the fisherman started his motor, she felt the vibrations in the water.

She'd put in a pier section today. That would do until someone visited. Her daughters? Anger threatened her, as their unjust accusations echoed in her mind. "What did you do, Mom? What did you say to him?" She shook her head to drive away the voices and concentrated instead on the flowers along the shore, which made her think of her mother. Feelings of grief and loss engulfed her as she remembered her mother's love for wildflowers. The place was full of ghosts. Perhaps it had been a mistake to come. Maybe she should have gone somewhere without memories, but she couldn't afford to do that.

After carrying one of the galvanized steel posts into the water, she inserted a rod in the matching top holes and began screwing the post into the sandy lake bottom. It went down easily. Pleased with herself she lifted the crossbar over the top to know where to start the second post. It fell to the bottom of the lake, which was all right since the water was so shallow. She screwed in that post and lifted and fastened the ends of the crossbar to both posts. Then she dragged a wooden pier length off the pile on shore and floated it between the posts, so as to know where to put the next set of posts at the deeper end.

A motorboat had twice passed Kate and created waves which rocked the wooden pier length, crashing it against the shore. Annoyed, Kate glanced at the boat as it rounded the lake and came toward her

4

beach a third time. There was no skier behind it. Why did it keep circling? She had never been partial to speedboats because of the smell and oily slicks left in their wakes.

The craft closed in on Kate's stretch of sand. "Need some help?" the woman in the boat asked after pulling the throttle back to idle.

Standing with a post gripped in both hands and frowning at the intruder, Kate was caught off guard. Who expected such a bold overture? How did you protect yourself against it? She felt the sun beating down, the cool water on her lower body. A slow smile curled the corners of her mouth.

The other woman grinned in return, displaying a perfect set of teeth. Her hair was a sandy color, short and curly, her eyes brown and friendly. Freckles were sprinkled across her nose, her cheeks were red, the rest of her very tan. She looked wholesome. "My name is Pat Thompson," she said as she clambered over the side of the boat and jumped into the water.

"Kate Sweeney," Kate said, alarmed by this unexpected offer of aid. How could she return such a favor? "I'm getting along," she protested, somehow knowing she wouldn't be able to fend off this woman and her good intentions.

Pat pulled the propeller out of the water and dragged the boat up on shore, then splashed out to Kate. "I've got nothing to do," she said with a shrug and another white-toothed smile.

"Well," Kate said, "if you'd driven past again, I might have thrown this at you." She indicated the pier post still clutched between her hands.

Pat laughed. "The waves don't help, I suppose. Tell me what to do and I'll do it."

Together they quickly set up the first pier section. "That's all I was going to do today," Kate remarked.

"We may as well do the rest," Pat replied and grabbed another post. "I need the exercise."

She didn't look it, Kate thought. The woman was maybe five foot-five, a little taller than herself, and in superb condition. Kate thought regretfully of her bike, which she had not brought with her.

They put in two more sections. The fourth section would be in the water over both their heads. They had had enough trouble with the deep end of the third section. "I'll have to save the last one for someone taller," Kate remarked as she stood on tiptoes and swayed like a weed, water up to her chin. "This was really nice of you."

Pat climbed onto the pier with Kate, and as they dried in the hot sun, Kate wondered why Pat had bothered to stop and help. Kate leaned back on her hands, feet dangling in the water, pleased at this apparent new friendship. Wanting to repay Pat's help, she asked, "How about dinner Wednesday?"

"How about it?" Pat asked. She lay on her back with one arm covering her eyes from the sun and one leg hanging over the edge in the water.

"That's an invitation." Kate turned to glance at Pat.

Pat stared at Kate and sighed. "I'm not alone. I'm staying with a friend," she explained.

"Bring your friend with you," Kate suggested.

Pat continued to observe Kate. "Thanks, I'll bring the wine."

"You don't need to bring anything. It'll be my thanks."

6

Pat sat up and wrapped her arms around her legs. "Have you been here long?"

"Just got here this morning." Kate felt as if she'd been awake forever and thought she probably looked it, too. She lay back on the pier and squinted at Pat. "How about you?"

"A week. We rented a cottage at the other end of the lake for a month."

Reluctantly, Kate was placing Pat in her mind. "Do you own a sailboat with a blue and green sail?"

Pat nodded. "Do you like to sail?"

Sitting up, Kate met the friendly brown eyes. She had only sailed a few times. "I wasn't hinting," she said with a smile. "I was just remembering you."

"Really? We've been renting for several years now. You've got one of the nicest locations on the lake," she added.

The dykes, Kate thought unwillingly. That's what Jeff had always called these women. Sometimes there had been four of them; maybe two others had visited. Suddenly afraid her thoughts might be readable, she glanced away from Pat. She recalled how she had watched them with fascination, when they were sailing or in their speedboat. The fascination had been tinged with fear. Fear of what, she wondered — herself? The easy comradeship with Pat was in danger of being dissolved.

Pat slipped into the lake. "Got to go," she said. "What time Wednesday?" She turned and met Kate's eyes.

"Cocktail hour begins at five-thirty," Kate replied as she returned the look and smiled faintly. She pushed herself off the pier and helped shove the motorboat into deeper water. She waved and thanked Pat again as the other woman started the engine and drove across the lake.

Gail lay sunning on the floating dock as Pat idled to it, cut the motor and grabbed the raft ladder to hold the boat in place. "Want to go for a ride or ski or something?"

Gail raised her head and looked at Pat through strands of blonde hair. "Not really. Where've you been?"

Pat considered the question. If she answered it, she knew the response she'd get. "Helping someone put in a pier."

"Is she attractive?"

Again Pat paused before answering. "Yes, very — nice, too. You'll like her," she added.

"I don't intend to meet her," Gail replied, nestling her head in her arms.

"We've been invited to dinner Wednesday night." The boat rocked on its own wake. Pat studied Gail's reclining figure, wondering what was happening to them and why. "You're burning, babe."

Gail sat up and clasped her legs, leaving white marks in the red. "*You're* invited to dinner, and I'll tend to my own body, thank you." She stood, dove into the lake and swam to shore.

Feeling that empty loneliness Gail once filled, Pat shoved the boat away from the raft. She wanted to push the throttle to full speed and slam into the beach. Instead she drove to a secluded spot, took her rod out of the bottom of the boat and cast until long

8

after dark. She hardly noticed the spectacular display put on by the setting sun.

Sipping wine and trying to read while the sun disappeared, Kate sat on the screened-in porch. The western horizon was engulfed in shades of purple, which faded to pink toward the east; the lake reflected the colors of the sky. A soft breeze, cooling Kate's sunburned skin, rippled the water into tiny waves. As darkness fell, it gradually blurred out even the lightest objects, until only sky and lake were discernible. Bats swooped over the water.

The next morning Kate drove to Waushara early, before the heat became too intense. She went to the grocery store first and then to the telephone company to request the phone be reconnected. Returning to the house with grocery bags in both arms, she heard the phone ring — stridently, insistently. How could it be hooked up already?

"Mom? Dad said you were at the lake. What's going on?"

Kate felt a twinge of irritation; she hadn't heard from Jeff for several weeks. She wrote regularly; he called occasionally, usually when he needed something. "I'll write to you, Jeff."

"Some woman answered Dad's phone, Mom. Who is she?"

Kate sighed. She couldn't believe Jeff's sisters hadn't told him. "I'll write, Jeff. How's Florida?"

"Hot. Tell me, Mom. I've got to know."

"Haven't your sisters told you anything?"

"They said you and Dad weren't getting along,

that you might separate. I didn't believe it, because you didn't write me about it." Accusing.

Why was she always to blame? Why didn't they lay the guilt at Tom's feet? But she knew she should have told him. "Jeff, I thought it might not happen." Kate struggled to keep the tremor out of her voice.

"Who is the woman?"

"Ask your dad or her. I don't know her." Kate tasted the bitterness again. She couldn't bear to talk about it, even to Jeff. It made her angry and then she cried and hated herself for crying.

"Are you moving to the lake for good?"

"Maybe, I don't know yet."

"What about our house?"

"It's for sale."

"I'm coming home, Mom."

The alarm in Jeff's voice brought out the mother in Kate. "I'll be here," she said, "and don't worry, Jeff. It'll all work out."

Would it? She reveled in self pity for a few seconds after hanging up and then jumped when the phone rang again, the sound piercing the stillness of the house. She snatched up the receiver.

"Kate? What the hell is going on?" It was her editor, Dan Mills.

"Ask Tom," she snapped.

"I did; that's how I got this number. What about your column?"

"I took it in before I left town. I told your secretary I'd call."

"How can you write a column from two hundred fucking miles away?"

"Why not? Just mail me the letters."

"We'll see about that."

Her heart sank. "That's okay, Dan. I know Tom got me the job, something to keep me busy and at home. I always wondered why you don't carry Ann Landers. Now you can tell me."

"Because we carry you. Why the hell did you leave like that?"

"I don't want to talk about it now. Ask Tom."

"I'm asking you, Kate."

"I had my reasons." Like not being able to face everyone.

"Tom's fooling around, huh? He'll come to his senses."

"I think I came to mine," Kate retorted. "Goodbye, Dan."

The day stretched before her. She turned on the radio and strains of Vivaldi's *Four Seasons* filled the room. She smiled, feeling the tension lines around her mouth relax. The music gave her new energy and she set up her typewriter. If Dan would let her keep her column, maybe she would maintain her sanity. Besides, she needed the extra income. She opened the first letter on the pile. As usual, she was amazed at the number of letters to be answered each week. The *Orion Town Chronicle* came out once a week but, since the paper was free, funded by advertising, the circulation was large.

Dear Jane,

I been married six months. My husband been real friendly with my little sister, pulling her on his lap and stuff like that. I come home the other day and they was coming out of the

11

bedroom all messed up. I told my sister, she's seventeen, to get out and not come back. Then my husband got all nasty when I asked him what was going on and he hit me with his fist and knocked me down. I love him and don't want to lose him.

Sounds like a winner, she thought, wanting to write: Pack your bags and run, don't walk, to the nearest door.

Dear Abused,
     What is going on between your husband and your sister could be statutory rape, a crime on his part. You didn't say whether he has physically abused you in the past, but if he's using his fists on you now, he probably will again. If you can't get him in to counseling, I advise leaving. He sounds like very bad news.

These letters had a way of putting her own problems in perspective. She opened another one.

Dear Jane,
     My husband never cuts his toenails. My legs are covered with bloody scratches from sleeping with him. I've begged him to cut them, even offered to do it for him. He says he wants to see how long they'll get. They make me sick to look at, and they're ruining our sex life.

Jesus. She wouldn't let the man touch her even if he did cut them.

Dear Scratched Legs,
Tell your husband if he won't cut his toenails you're getting twin beds or moving to another room. Then do it.

Two lulus. She tore open the third envelope.

I been looking for you. I'll find you, lady, and give it to you good.

Kate shivered involuntarily. There were always the creeps. She glanced out the window toward the lake and noticed Pat's sailboat sailing past the pier and heeling in the wind. Drawn by the bright blue and green sail, Kate went down to the beach. She had put her suit on.

Leaning so far back she was shaped like a bow, Pat sailed nearly into the wind. A gust caught the sail and overturned the boat, throwing her into the lake. She came up under the boat, ducked out from it, and appeared startled to see Kate treading water next to her.

"My turn to help," Kate said.

Pat grinned at her. "Let's get her upright and I'll take you for the sail of your life. It's a great day for it."

They grabbed the centerboard, pulled it down until they could brace their feet against it and took hold of the hull; slowly the Sunfish rolled over. Then, wet and laughing, they struggled in over opposite sides. Pat turned the rudder until the sail caught the wind and they were off. Pat wouldn't give slack to the wind. Together they leaned against the pull of the sail to keep the Sunfish from going over. The sailboat skimmed over the lake and came about with a tremendous spurt of speed as they just managed to duck the swinging boom. The warm spray washed over their straining bodies and they brushed the tips of the waves with the backs of their heads.

Kate sensed the wildness in Pat — a heedless need to escape from something or someone — and decided she was doing it in a wonderful way. All of Kate's concerns dropped away, too, in the exhilaration of the ride. A motorboat passed them, and Kate recognized it as the boat Pat had been in yesterday, when she stopped to help with the pier. There were three women in the boat. Pat turned her head away from it, even when it came within twenty-five feet of them.

Puzzled at first, Kate met Pat's gaze, noticed the troubled frown, and raised her eyebrows in question. Pat smiled wryly and Kate returned the smile with a like one. So someone else was hurting. What else was new, Kate thought. Maybe Pat's girlfriend had found someone else, just like Tom. She almost laughed at the irony of it and then with a jab of physical pain remembered the agony. Certainly, Pat didn't look amused; there was a fierceness about her Kate wouldn't challenge.

Pat tried to gesture the motorboat away as it came perilously close, but it was too late, and the Sunfish capsized, throwing Kate and Pat into the sail as it sank in the waves. When they came up sputtering, the speedboat rocked in the water nearby.

Pat shouted, "What the hell are you doing, Gail? You know you're too close."

"Fuck you," Gail yelled and took off, pinning her surprised passengers to their seats.

"Same to you," Pat hollered.

Wishing she knew what to say, feeling uncomfortable as if she were somehow the cause of Gail's anger, Kate looked at Pat.

"Sorry, let's get her up again. I'll take you home," Pat said.

"I'm having a marvelous time," Kate countered, spitting out a stream of water.

"So am I," Pat replied. "Let's not go in yet."

That night Kate ate a late supper on the porch, while the sun set behind clouds. Thunder rumbled and lightning flashed but as yet no rain had fallen. She was pondering what to have for dinner Wednesday, when the sound of the phone startled her. It was her older daughter.

"Mom, when are you coming home?"

"I'm not," Kate replied. "When are you coming here?"

There was a pause on Beth's end of the line. Kate visualized her daughter standing on one leg, the other bare foot resting on her calf, leaning against the counter in her kitchenette, fair hair hanging in her face. "This weekend Jeff will be here, and we'll come up for a few days. Sarah will be with us, too."

All three of her children. Great, as long as they got along and didn't criticize her too much. "Good. Will you be here for dinner Friday?"

"Should be. Mom, I'm sorry about what I said about you and Dad. It wasn't your fault."

Kate grimaced and bit her tongue. "It's okay, honey. Oh, and bring my bike up, will you please? See you Friday." When she hung up, she heard rain drumming on the house. Perhaps she'd sleep tonight. Sleep had been a casualty along with her marriage.

Wednesday morning Kate took the manila envelope with the letters and her replies in it to the post office. Dan would decide which to publish and which to mail to the writers.

At the grocery store she examined the fresh fruit while a man next to her studied the melons. He appeared vaguely familiar to her — ascetic looking, about six feet tall and skinny with a narrow face and wire-rimmed glasses. He wore a tasteful linen suit, unusual in this small vacation town.

"Pardon me." He turned toward her and smiled. Nice teeth and lovely brown eyes, Kate noted. She wanted to know him. "Can you tell me which of these is ripe?" He held a cantaloupe in one hand like an offering.

"That one looks good," she said and nodded at his hand.

He asked, "Are you here on vacation?"

Kate hefted a few melons, glad she had taken the time to brush her hair and apply a little make-up. "I have a place on Round Lake."

She caught him looking surreptitiously at her left hand. She had removed her wedding band in a fit of rage and transferred her engagement ring to her right hand. "What are you doing Friday night?" he asked. "I mean, would you like to go out to dinner with me?" Surprised, she stared at him, a cantaloupe balanced in each hand. "You look familiar," she said. "Do I? My name's Bert Holloway." "Holloway." She rolled it around on her tongue. It sounded familiar. She told him her name. "I'd love to have dinner but I've got company coming." Her kids were company? "Maybe another time." "Sure, how about next Tuesday?" Kate laughed abruptly. "I don't know how long the company's staying." She hoped he wasn't a murderer. "Why don't I give you my number. You can call on Tuesday, and if they're gone we can go to dinner." Perhaps she wouldn't be lonely after all.

Early Wednesday evening Kate sat on the pier with a can of insect repellent beside her, along with a small pitcher of orange juice with vodka in it, two glasses, and a box of Wheat Thins. She felt as if she'd been turned on a spit all day, even though she had worn a T-shirt to protect her fair skin from the sun. She knew her face resembled a sunburst with her eyes glowing like neon signs in contrast. She watched Pat's motorboat make its way across the lake toward Kate's beach. "Too nice to be inside," Kate commented when Pat cut the engine and grabbed a pier post.

17

"Come on, get in. Let's have cocktails on the water," Pat suggested.

They drifted in the center of the lake, slowly draining the pitcher of its contents and munching on the Wheat Thins. "Not very fancy but portable," Kate apologized.

"It's wonderful," Pat said. "Just great. Wish we could have dinner out here, too."

The sun turned the lake crimson and drew a red curtain along the western horizon. Feeling the warm current of air slowly pushing the boat back toward Kate's place, they floated in companionable silence.

If she wasn't so wrapped up in the latest round of battles with Gail, Pat realized, she would wonder what this woman was doing here all alone. She had asked Gail to come with her tonight, told her she was welcome, but silently hoped she wouldn't want to come. She needed release from the tension the two of them generated and didn't want to subject Kate to it.

"Well, the crackers are gone, the drinks are drunk, and the sun is nearly set. What say we go eat," Kate said, breaking into Pat's thoughts.

Kate had set a table on the porch. She brought out chicken salad, rye rolls and fresh fruit, while Pat uncorked a bottle of wine.

The light on the porch illuminated the table framed by the soft darkness around it. Moths beat frantically against the screens trying to incinerate themselves in the light. The darkness was like the unseen corners in their lives, Kate thought. Remembering Pat in the boat, she felt her unspoken distress and compared it with her own. "You must teach," Kate said, a statement.

"I do — eighth grade English. Good guess."

"What does Gail do?" She offered Pat the chicken salad.

Pat was startled at the sound of Gail's name. "She teaches, too, fifth grade." Then she met Kate's eyes, noticed her smile and raised eyebrows. She laughed, embarrassed. "I'm sorry about that bit in the lake yesterday. We're not getting along real well right now."

Kate wondered if she wanted to hear anyone else's troubles. But her interest was caught. Already she cared about this woman. She heard Pat's voice but not what she said. "I'm sorry."

"I asked how long you're staying?" Pat repeated.

"Oh, I don't know. Maybe for good." Kate took a bite of the chicken salad but didn't taste it.

Pat paused, fork in midair and studied Kate, wondering whether to inquire. Was this an opening? "Alone?" she heard herself ask.

"My kids will be here this weekend, but yes, basically alone."

"You're divorced?" Another impulsive question.

"No." Kate chewed and swallowed, set her roll on her plate, appetite gone. She drained her glass of wine and refilled it and Pat's. "Separated."

"Oh," Pat said and waited for something else to come unbidden from her mouth. "Are you a good poker player?"

It was the last thing Kate expected to hear. "I'm a good bridge player."

"Is that the same?"

"The ability to hide your thoughts, you mean?"

Pat nodded.

"I'm not so sure you're a good poker player," Kate said after a slight pause. She ate more chicken

19

salad to encourage Pat to eat hers. Besides, she needed to stop losing weight.

Pat began to eat again, her gaze still on Kate. "So it shows?"

Smiling slightly, Kate nodded. "That you're troubled, yes. I don't know what's wrong, but I think I could make an educated guess." She added quickly, "Of course, it's none of my business."

"And you're not troubled?" Pat countered in self-defense, to throw Kate off the track. After all they had just met. Did she want to risk scaring Kate away with the knowledge of her personal life, with the fact that she lived with and loved another woman?

"Oh, I'm troubled all right. My husband left me for a younger woman. My kids think I drove him into her arms. Actually, I didn't know she existed. It was a total surprise to me." Kate was amazed at this admission. Confession begot confession. She wondered how she had not known Tom was seeing someone else, was madly in love with her to boot. Had she been so wrapped up in her own world that she had completely missed seeing his?

Pat stared at Kate, wine glass part way to her mouth. "I'm sorry," she said lamely. "Where are you from?" As if that were relevant.

"A town outside Chicago called Orion. I've been coming here all my life. My grandparents used to farm this land. Vegetables," she added, as she thought of the acreage that stretched behind the house and barn. She and Tom had planted pines on most of it.

"You're fortunate," Pat said, wanting to get away from true confessions. To endure this month with

20

Gail she might need this woman as a friend, and she couldn't tell her she was a lesbian, could she? The woman was obviously straight as a line.

"Fortunate?" Kate asked.

"Yes, to own a place on this lake. I wish I did."

"There are some nice cottages for sale."

"I know, but teachers aren't well paid."

Kate realized she was indeed lucky to have this place. She was momentarily ashamed for ever feeling sorry for herself. "Where do you live?"

"Northland."

"And Gail?"

"She's my roommate," Pat heard herself say. She finished the chicken salad and started on the fruit. She noticed Kate's slight smile.

"I see. I'm sorry she doesn't like me more."

"It's not you, Kate. How can she not like you? She doesn't know you."

"Life can be a bitch," Kate remarked with a flippancy she didn't feel.

This observation seemed so out of character to Pat that it startled her. She looked at Kate and laughed.

21

II

The kids had made a beeline for the lake as soon as they'd arrived. Kate had known they would. They'd spent most of the afternoon in Beth's VW Rabbit. She watched them cavort in the water. They weren't kids anymore, she corrected herself as she put together potato salad. As soon as she finished, she would join them, but right now she was happy just listening to their voices and laughter. She had always loved watching and hearing them enjoy each other.

A hot breeze off the lake offered little relief from the heat. Kate had spent the day in and out of the water. Pat had been over earlier and they had gone for a short sail, both avoiding personal talk. Firecrackers increasingly shattered the quiet day.

Darkness descended on them as they ate, and a soft current of air touched them on the porch. "I nearly forgot how nice it is here," Jeff said.

"When summer school's out, I'll come stay with you, Mom," Sarah informed Kate.

Kate glanced from one to the other — Beth, tall and fair with gray eyes; Sarah, not quite as tall with reddish brown hair and Kate's blue-green eyes; Jeff, a carbon copy of his father with dark hair and eyes. Their height sometimes made her feel dwarfed. After eating and carrying in the dishes, they turned out the porch lights and sat and talked.

"You going to be all right here, Mom?" Beth asked.

The night was black and velvety, the air soft as a moth's wing. "I'm fine, really." Fine, what a meaningless word.

"Why didn't you tell Jeff?" Sarah wanted to know.

"I told him I thought maybe it wouldn't happen. What you don't know hasn't happened yet." Her own perverse logic. "And it wasn't like someone died or was sick." Something had died, though, or had it already been dead and she hadn't known it?

"How could he do that, Mom?" Jeff sounded vehement.

Kate smiled slightly in the dark. Always partial to

his mother. "Maybe he didn't mean to. Maybe he fell in love with her," she said, surprising herself. She couldn't believe she was talking this shit.

"Who is she?" Jeff asked the question Kate wanted answered.

"Her name is Nancy Kitkowski," Beth informed them reluctantly.

"Beth met her," Sarah explained, an accusation.

"She seems pretty nice," Beth said defensively.

"It's okay, honey. I wouldn't want any of you to ignore your dad. He's been a good father." But then why did she feel betrayed, and what was all this idiotic crap coming out of her mouth, these platitudes?

"Well, I'm not going to meet her. I hate her," Sarah said angrily.

Good, Kate thought, and then admonished herself for being spiteful. Besides, Tom still supported Sarah. She leaned her head on the back of the chair and breathed in the night smells. She knew she should say something like life was too short to waste hating, but she would gag on the words.

"Do you hate Dad, Mom?" Sarah asked.

"I don't know," Kate replied honestly, wondering whether she did anymore. "I don't like him very much right now." At least he wasn't dominating her thoughts; she was sick of thinking about him.

"Anybody want some pop or something?" Jeff asked, getting up.

"If there's any diet pop, I'll have one," Beth said.

"Me too," Sarah said.

Jeff stood in the doorway. "Let's hear the magic word."

"Please," the girls chimed.

Hoping it would help her sleep, Kate was finishing off the supper wine. She glanced at the glass and knew she would have to stop using wine as a sedative. Soon.

"What are you going to do here, Mom?" Jeff asked when he returned to the darkened porch.

"Well, I think I'll still be writing my column. Right now I'm just letting myself down." She longed to ask how old Nancy was and what she looked like but couldn't bring herself to do so.

Kate woke before anyone else and took her bicycle for a ride. The morning was filled with the sounds of birds, and she pedaled along the empty roads, her eyes watching for deer. Rounding a curve she nearly ran down Pat, who had stopped her own bike and was staring out over a field of wildflowers. Kate braked next to her, glad for a reason to catch her breath.

"What are those orange flowers?" Pat asked with a welcome grin.

"Hawkweed. Pretty, aren't they? Is that what you're looking at? They bloom all summer but they go crazy in June, turn whole fields orange."

"And the blue ones here?" Pat pointed at the flowers in the ditch.

"Spiderwort. My mother loved the wildflowers. She used to fill the house with vases of flowers. Do you ride often in the mornings?"

"Mornings or evenings, when it's not too hot."

"Gail doesn't ride?"

"Not today. Are your kids here?" Pat leaned on

her handlebars. She looked young in the morning light, her smile lighting up her face.

"They came yesterday. I left them sleeping. Maybe the coffee will be ready when I get back. Which way are you going?" Kate asked.

"Let me follow you. You know the area better than I do." She felt more together today. Last night Gail had wanted her, and the night had been spent curled against each other in a sweaty embrace.

They rode side by side along the deserted roads. Kate sensed Pat's feeling of well-being and hoped it was not temporary. "These hills are a challenge," Kate said, panting.

"Aren't they? Out of shape?" Pat glanced at her.

"Sure am."

"We'll have to make this a habit then. Every morning at seven."

A little bossy, Kate thought. Must be the teacher in her. She grunted in reply.

"Is that a yes?" Pat did not want to come across as pushy. She smiled faintly at Kate, who struggled along next to her.

"I guess," Kate replied. "I can't talk and ride at the same time."

Pat left Kate at her driveway and waved as she rode on down the road.

Sarah was pouring herself a cup of coffee. "Been riding your bike already?" She grinned. "You look terrific, Mom. Dad should see you now."

Kate didn't feel terrific. Her legs were limp weights attached to her body, which she thought unpleasantly sweaty. "Dad doesn't want to see me," she said, putting milk and sugar into her own coffee.

"How long are you three staying?" Kate's breathing slowly returned to normal.

"Tuesday. I've got classes on Wednesday, Jeff's plane leaves Tuesday night and Beth's got to get back to work."

"How is school?"

"Really tough." Sarah was in her last year of college. She lived in an apartment in an old house on campus.

"Dad taking care of the expenses all right?"

"Oh yes, the checks keep coming."

"Good, I knew he would."

"But you asked."

"I wanted to be sure, not that I could help much."

"Are you going to have enough money?" Sarah asked, sounding alarmed.

Kate nodded. "I'll have to be careful, but I'll have enough."

"Mom, I'm sorry I blamed you. I know it wasn't your fault. Beth said the woman he's living with doesn't look much older than she is."

Hearing this, Kate was surprised by the intensity of her pain. She looked away from Sarah, but when she looked back she saw the hurt in Sarah's face. "Oh honey, I wish I could help you. I don't know what to say. It happened."

"Maybe he'll get over her. She must seem like one of his kids."

"Maybe," Kate said, the thought intriguing her. Was that it? Did this other woman make Tom feel younger?

The day was even hotter than yesterday; the

thermometer climbed rapidly into the nineties. After putting in the fourth pier section, Jeff and the girls set up the volleyball net in the shallow water. When Pat sailed near, Kate waved her in and then had a moment of panic as she remembered Jeff calling these women dykes. She'd cut his tongue out if he said anything rude. Gail was draped across the front of the Sunfish. "How about some volleyball?" Kate asked.

Pat glanced at Gail, who shrugged. "Sure," Pat said.

Were they really gay? Kate wondered, looking at Gail — a long-legged, blonde, slender woman. Surprised at how attractive Gail was, Kate watched her slide off the sailboat. There was something vulnerable, almost defensive about her movements, and she didn't look happy. Kate felt Pat's gaze, met it, and grinned openly. She was only curious, after all.

They submerged frequently to cool off. Chasing the ball and getting to it in time was difficult. The water tugged at their legs, causing them to fall. Gail and Pat were especially good at the game. They teamed with Sarah against Jeff, Beth and Kate. Jeff didn't like losing, Kate could tell. After three games, he suggested changing teammates. He joined with Beth and Pat against the other three. The next two games his side won, and then Kate called a halt and fell back into the water.

"I'm quitting," she said. "Sorry but I'm beat. Why don't we swim for a while."

"Dykes," Jeff said, watching the sailboat catch the wind and lean as it picked up speed.

"Don't be so sure," Kate said sharply.

Beth lifted her shoulders. "So what? They're nice."

"You want a muff diver?" Jeff asked, leaping at her and pulling her under.

Beth came back up sputtering. "Hey, quit that, and I bet you do some muff diving yourself."

"You just didn't like getting beat by them," Sarah accused Jeff. He dove at her and she shrieked and went under in a trail of bubbles.

It was true, though, Kate knew, as she stared after the sailboat. She felt indignant at Jeff's arbitrary judgment but was unable to express the indignation without drawing more attention to Pat and Gail.

Playing poker, Pat watched Barb and Sandy with amusement. She had been relieved when they had arrived at the cottage, thinking maybe they would bring back some of the good times. They were made for each other, she thought — both avid bowlers and softball players, both physical education teachers. They probably never even thought about their relationship; it was just an extension of themselves.

Contrary to Kate's opinion, Pat was a good poker player and most of the money was piled in front of her, where she kept rearranging it into neat piles. "Can't you just leave it alone," Gail said with annoyance.

Pat met Gail's eyes. She remembered the flare-up of ardor the other night, recalled suddenly their early days, when it had been the passion between them that made others uncomfortable instead of the

29

tension. She took her hand off the money. "Sorry." But the apology was not meant for Gail; it was directed at Barb and Sandy because of Gail.

"Come on, ante, you two. We've got to win this dough back," Sandy said heartily.

"Anybody want another beer?" Barb inquired, getting up and going to the refrigerator.

"Sure, please," Pat said, "and you know you don't stand a snowball's chance in hell of winning this pile back."

Kate's eyes opened at six a.m., and she lay in bed until quarter to seven while absorbing the morning outside the windows. Baby blue jays muttered in the trees and squirrels chattered and dropped pine cones on the ground. Wondering if Pat would be waiting, she got dressed and started off down the road toward Pat's cottage. They should have clarified how to meet for these morning rides.

With a slight smile, Pat pedaled out of her drive. Kate returned the smile and unwillingly read Pat's face — the tiredness, the unhappy eyes — and wondered if her own face was a book for others to read.

"Nice kids," Pat said after they had struggled up a few hills and were on a long downhill coast.

Kate was panting, her legs already leaden. Maybe in a few days the agony in her calves and thighs would lessen. "Thanks."

Pat suddenly grinned at her and then laughed. "It'll get easier every day."

Kate shook her head. "It better," she gasped. "I don't know if it's worth it."

"It's worth it. It's good for you."

Easy for her to say, Kate thought, glancing at Pat who set the pace easily.

"I'm not the enemy," Pat said with another laugh.

"Who is?" A loaded question. There was no answer, just a quick look of pain.

"Would you like to water ski today?" Pat asked.

Kate shook her head. "Thanks, not me anyway."

"How about the girls and Jeff?"

Kate nodded. She still had trouble riding and carrying on a conversation. "They probably would."

"We'll come by for them."

Kate looked up from her paperback when the sail shaded her from the sun. "Great," she said, putting the book down and joining Pat in the boat. The wind was adequate, not an exciting day to sail, but a relaxing way to spend the afternoon. "Your friends are fun. It's really nice of you and them to take the kids skiing like this."

"They're having as much fun as your kids, believe me."

The wind caught the sail, pushed them along with a short burst of speed, and then died. "I'm sorry about Jeff," Kate said, trailing a foot and hand in the water to cool herself. She had been watching Jeff and was annoyed with what she considered show-off behavior.

31

"Why?" Pat asked, preoccupied with facing the anger she had been provoking in Gail all day. Sandy and Barb would be gone come evening, and then Pat would have to deal with whatever Gail threw her way. Maybe she was ready for the breakup.

Kate sighed, searching for the words she wanted. "He's a good kid. Well, he's not really a kid," she corrected herself. "But he's so . . ." She paused trying hard to find the right word. "Assertive, I guess. It's part of being young and male maybe. But he's not really like that — or he didn't used to be." Maybe this was just Jeff emulating his father, whom he claimed to hate, but Tom wasn't like that, was he? She remembered Jeff as a small boy bringing home baby rabbits to raise and turn loose.

"Don't worry about it." Pat grinned at Kate. "Maybe he'll get over it."

Kate threw her head back and laughed. "Think there's hope for him then? Mind if I take a dip?"

Pat shook her head, dropped the sail and the two of them slipped over the side and towed the sailboat to Kate's pier.

Tuesday morning Jeff and the two girls left. The house was strangely quiet, and Kate was at loose ends even though she had received a packet of letters from the paper on Monday. She would get to them later in the day. She was vacuuming when the phone rang.

"Hello, have a nice weekend?"

It was him, Holloway, she realized with a jolt. She had forgotten he was going to call. "Lovely. My kids were here. They left this morning. It's sort of quiet right now."

"You can go out to eat tonight then?"

"Sure, it'll be something to look forward to."

Clouds dominated the sky, threatened rain. Kate continued cleaning the place — changing sheets, dusting, knocking down cobwebs. After an hour of this, she went out on the porch with a cup of coffee. It was hot and muggy; maybe rain would clear the air. Pat rode in on her bike.

"Have a cup of coffee with me," Kate said, pleased to see her.

Pat accepted a cup and joined Kate. "You didn't ride your bike this morning. Everything all right?"

"The kids left early, so I didn't get a chance to." She smiled at Pat and sat near her, suddenly wishing she could do something for her. "Pat, I'm a good listener," she said.

Pat avoided Kate's eyes by looking down at her coffee. Her thoughts were in turmoil. "Gail's going to leave me," she heard herself say. Alarmed, afraid she would confess her lesbianism and Kate would be horrified, she got up.

"Sit down, Pat; where are you going?"

"You've got enough troubles of your own, much worse ones than mine." Pat set her cup down on the table between the two chairs and inadvertently met Kate's eyes. She noticed the slight frown etched between the eyes so intently focused on her. She felt trapped and, unable to escape Kate's scrutiny, sat.

"Maybe we can help each other," Kate suggested.

"So she leaves, so what? I'll get another roommate," Pat said, jutting out her chin.

"But you don't want her to leave, you love her, right?" Kate had a little trouble with the word love.

Pat felt panicky. She looked away from Kate and back again. Don't use the word love, she protested silently.

And Kate suddenly understood and wondered at her own density. How to tell Pat she knew she was gay, and it didn't matter? "I thought we understood each other," she said.

"What?" Pat asked, her eyes wary and frightened.

"Pat, I don't care. I mean, I care about you. I don't care that you love Gail, that you live with her." That you're gay, but she didn't say it.

You don't understand, though, do you, Pat thought. She transferred her fear of detection to a sure indignation that Kate couldn't possibly understand her depth of feeling for another woman.

Hoping she wasn't wrong, that Pat really was gay, Kate tried again. Did she have to spell it out? Wasn't Pat listening? "Maybe I can't help you, Pat, but if you want to talk, I want to hear it. I could use someone to talk to, too, you know."

Pat's eyes cleared a little as she recognized something besides her own pain. "I'm gay," she said quietly. "You know that?" And you think I'm not as good as you are, don't you? she asked silently.

Kate smiled uncertainly. "Do I have to hit you over the head with it?" she said suddenly.

"How did you know?" Pat asked a little belligerently.

How could Kate tell her she'd been watching her for years, ever since Jeff had started calling her one of the dykes? "I don't know. I was guessing."

"Jeff told you, didn't he?"

34

Kate was startled. "Does it matter? I don't really care. Now why is Gail leaving?"

"She won't leave until we go back home, but she'll leave then. I think I might even be relieved. All we do is fight." But she knew she'd be lonely. Maybe by then all the love would be destroyed. "How did you cope when your husband left?"

Kate thought about this. "Not well. I couldn't even talk about it, but it was so sudden. I must have been turned completely inward not to see it coming. I ran. That's what I did. Put the house up for sale and came here. A real coward." Had she really not guessed anything? Their sex life had trickled off to nothing. Her gaze met Pat's and they assessed each other silently. "It hurts, doesn't it?"

Pat's eyes clouded over again. She nodded and pursed her lips. "I don't want this to spoil my memories of the lake," she said. Why was that so important?

"You'll get through it," Kate said softly. "You're tougher than you look or feel right now, I'll bet on that."

Pat laughed a little.

"Guess what?" Kate asked. It was time to lighten things up.

"What?"

"I've got a date tonight. I don't know if I'll get through it. I haven't had a date in twenty-five years. I thought my dating days were over."

Pat smiled faintly. "You don't look old enough to have grown kids." She meant it. She found Kate's bright hair, intense eyes, and small figure attractive. Then she realized with a start that she had been only eight years old twenty-five years ago.

Kate grinned. "That kind of flattery will get you everywhere."

* * * * *

Kate tried on several outfits and heaped them on her bed as she discarded them. Maybe Tom had been embarrassed by her outmoded wardrobe? She eventually settled on a casual dress. Ready long before Holloway arrived, she mixed herself a drink to calm her nerves and forced herself to sit on the porch. Clouds hung low, but it hadn't rained yet. Hearing a car drive in, she walked to the back porch. A Lincoln yet, the man had money.

"Ever eaten at Hillcrest Country Club?" he asked as they drove off.

"No, I'm not a member."

Over dinner she learned that he had a son and a daughter, both grown. "What business are you in?" she inquired.

"Holloway Funeral Home." He glanced at her, a smile playing around his mouth.

If he was looking for effect, he wasn't going to get it. She played it straight, even though it came as a shock for some reason. Then she realized why he looked familiar. "My parents' funerals were at your place. That's where I saw you before." She felt the grief again.

"What were their names?"

"My mother was Elizabeth Jorgenson. It's been four years since she died. My father died nearly ten years ago. His first name was Gordon."

"I remember, but I don't remember you."

"I was there."

They sat at a table next to windows overlooking a

small lake, and she watched rain pepper the water. Bert seemed to know everyone. "Tell me about your kids," he said, nodding at someone across the room. On the way home she was nervous again. She couldn't decide whether to invite him in. It had been so long since she had done this sort of thing and the rules had changed. Since she had no intention of sleeping with him, would asking him in give him the wrong idea? As it was, he told her he had to get back to the funeral home; they were having a funeral in the morning. He asked her out again Saturday night and she accepted.

III

More than three weeks had passed since Kate's
arrival at the lake. She had taken on an advice
column for the local paper — the *Waushara News
Journal*. The previous week she had been introduced
in the column, and this week there were already
letters waiting for her to pick up. Deciding people
enjoyed reading about the problems of those less
fortunate as an outlet for their own, she still
wondered how qualified she was to answer these
troubled letters. Here she was with her own life in

shreds, her husband off with a woman probably twenty years younger than he was, and did she try to salvage her marriage? No, she'd run from it. But she could use the extra money. So many of the answers were common sense, and in a bind she could always refer the writer to a professional.

Holloway Funeral Home was on her way out of town. On impulse Kate stopped to see Bert, who was in his office. His face lit up when he saw her.

"I was driving past. I picked up my first packet of letters from the *News Journal*."

"The new advice woman for the county. Congratulations." Then he asked, "Would you like to go away this weekend?"

"Where?" she asked, caught off guard.

Hypnotizing her with his soft dark eyes, he lifted his shoulders. "Anywhere."

"Isn't it kind of soon?" she hedged.

"We've been going out for weeks now."

She had never cheated on Tom and now wondered, why not? "Let me think about it."

Pat was sailing. Standing on the beach Kate gazed at the boat and waved. The craft turned and headed toward Kate. Kate waded knee deep in the water, while the sailboat rushed toward her. A few feet away Pat let loose the sheet and the sail flapped. Kate grabbed the hull of the Sunfish and held it.

"I've been watching for you. Want to go for a sail?" Pat had been sailing back and forth in front of Kate's place, waiting for her to appear. This was her last week at the rental cottage, and she felt as if she was about to lose both Gail and Kate. Panic seized her when she thought of either of these possibilities.

"Sure do." Kate turned the boat, pushed it out and lifted herself over the side.

"Only a few days left," Pat said, attempting to sound casual.

Pat's words sunk into Kate's consciousness after a few seconds. She was pondering Bert's proposition, wanting to discuss it with Pat. "What? Oh, that's right. I'm going to miss you." More than you can ever guess, Kate realized. She glanced at Pat, who was wearing her poker face, hiding from Kate. "I mean that, you know. This is your last week, isn't it?"

Pat nodded and turned her face upward toward sail and sky.

"Will you come visit the weekend after you leave? Please? You can ask Gail to come with you."

"You know Gail won't come, but I will." Relief flooded her, knowing this friendship wasn't going to end abruptly. She welcomed the heat of the sun on her face.

"Bert wants me to go away with him this weekend."

"Well, it's about time, isn't it?" Pat asked, briefly surprised and a little resentful at the topic change.

"I guess, but I'm not sure I want to."

"Go and find out."

"It's not that easy, Pat. I never cheated on Tom. I'm not sure I want to get that involved anyway."

"Tom's cheating on you," Pat pointed out.

The wind propelled the little boat rapidly across

the lake. They leaned backwards to keep it from going over. "I'd like to just be friends and maybe we won't be friends afterwards." What if she hated sex with Bert? How would they remain friendly and not have sex once they'd done it? What if he got really serious? She'd never marry a mortician. This was dumb, she was already married, she told herself.

"Well, it's up to you," Pat remarked. What did she know about these things anyway? She'd failed miserably in her love life, hadn't she? "You're the advice lady."

"Why do you think I should?"

"I don't know, maybe you shouldn't. Seems like a good way to find out where you want to go with the relationship."

Ducking the boom, they changed sides of the boat, as it came about. "You know what he does for a living?"

"I know he owns a funeral home. Is that so bad?"

"I'm not going to be dressing bodies or fixing their hair or anything like that." Pat howled with laughter and Kate joined in at the absurdity of it. "I don't know what's the matter with me. I used to really need sex. Do you think it's my age?"

Again Pat thought she was not the one to consult. Her sex life had taken a dive into oblivion. "It's probably what happened to you. You need to get back in the habit again."

Maybe she did, Kate thought. She strained backward while she looked at the expanse of blue above and heard the water rush by. She would happily do this forever, sail back and forth across the lake, the warm breeze and spray washing over her.

* * * * *

Kate locked the doors to the house. She hadn't told her children she would be gone for the weekend, because she would have had to tell them with whom. She was nervous, more than she had been on her first date with Bert. "Well, I'm ready." She handed him the small suitcase she had packed. "Are we going far?"

"An hour's drive — Lake Greeling. I made reservations at a very nice resort."

How strange to leave this lake for another. Why not stay here? But she knew why.

Kate felt a sense of déjà vu as Bert unlocked the door to their room. Years dropped away to when she and Tom had spent a clandestine weekend together while in college. Beth's birth and Kate's marriage had been a result of that weekend. She noticed Bert was uneasy, too. He talked more than usual.

"Well, maybe we should get ready for dinner," he suggested as they stood at the end of the double beds.

Putting it off, she thought, which was all right with her. Then he turned toward her and put his arms around her, pulling her to him.

"Why do I get the feeling you'll run off if I get too close?"

"There's some truth in it," she answered, her body tensing at his touch.

"You are so elusive and smooth and attractive," he whispered.

By Sunday she was ready to return home. The farmhouse on the lake was home now. She yearned for her routine. Togetherness was wearing thin. On the drive back Bert asked her if she planned to divorce Tom, and she realized she could use her marriage to hide from anyone's serious intentions.

Lights shining from the windows of the house created shadows in the back yard. An unfamiliar car with an Indiana license plate was parked outside the barn. Kate wondered if it was her younger brother, Gordie, who had moved away twenty years ago. He had been unwilling to sell his share of the farm to Kate when she and Tom had offered to buy it. She hadn't seen him since their mother's death. She entered the house alone.

"Katie, how are you? You look wonderful, all tan and slim." He kissed Kate on the cheek.

She found herself smiling at his warm welcome. "Gordie, what a surprise."

Gordie grinned at her. He was a handsome man, tall and spare with nearly blond, graying hair and eyes like her own. With him was another man, short and dark and attractive.

Ah, Gordie, she thought, recalling his abrupt departure from home, her mother's inability to discuss it with Kate, her father's stony silence. Kate had already been married, with one child, another on the way and problems of her own, when Gordie had left for the University of Wisconsin, never to return home until their father died.

"This is Brad Newby, a friend of mine." Brad smiled and reached for her hand. She returned the smile automatically. "I should have called, I know. Where's Tom?"

43

"Tom and I have separated," she explained. There was no pain when she said it.

"Oh no, I'm so sorry. I've got some vacation time and thought I'd come for a visit. Are you living here, Katie?"

"Afraid so. There was no other place to go."

"The kids have been calling all weekend, wondering where you were. I can't wait to see them."

"Which of them called?" Damn, she thought, caught in the act.

"All of them. They were worried, especially when you were gone all last night."

She headed for the phone and called Beth. "Hi honey, you were looking for me?"

"Where have you been all weekend?"

"I was with a friend. You mustn't worry about me. Did you just call to talk or what?"

"I was scared when you weren't there. I told Sarah and Jeff. Want me to let them know you're all right? Where were you, Mom?"

She wasn't going to get off without some kind of explanation. "I spent the weekend with a friend, no one you've met yet." Would she always have to account for her activities?

"Sarah and I are coming up next weekend."

"Good, you can become re-acquainted with your uncle." She remembered that Pat would be visiting that weekend, too. She wouldn't be lonely anyway.

Gordie followed her into her room. "I put our stuff in my old bedroom upstairs. Is that okay?" He shut the door and lowered his voice a notch. "Do you mind Brad being here?"

Kate thought of Pat and Gail. "It's okay with me, Gordie. This is your place, too."

44

"What happened between you and Tom?"

She explained.

"Maybe he'll tire of her," he said.

"Maybe he won't." Did she even care?

Cedar waxwings, their high pitched keening a lonely sound, perched in the trees along the shoreline and flew over the water catching insects. Gordie and Brad spent their days in the water or on the pier, their skins steadily darkening. Kate answered letters, cleaned house for the weekend, rode her bike, talked daily to Bert on the phone. Fending off his verbal advances, she kept him at arm's length.

Pat arrived first on Friday. She was on the porch with Gordie and Brad when Kate returned from a lunch date with Bert.

"Well, I assume you've introduced yourselves," Kate said, as she sat down with them. "How are you, Pat?" she asked. One look at Pat answered the question: tense and tired.

"I put Pat's bag in your room, Katie. The girls will be upstairs, won't they?"

"Yes, thanks Gordie. Why aren't you in the water? You could fry eggs on the sidewalks in town." There was a nice little breeze on the porch. Kate felt it drying the sweat on her body. "I think I'll put my suit on."

A few minutes later, Pat joined her on the pier.

"I didn't know you had a brother."

"I nearly forgot I had one, too, it's been so long since I've seen him. I didn't know he was coming. How's Gail?"

45

"I think she's found someone else."

"I'm sorry to hear that." Kate sat on the edge of the pier. She cooled her feet in the water while the rest of her baked in the afternoon sun.

"I don't know if I am or not." To hell with it all. Fuck it. Pat lay on her back, one hand shading her eyes from the sun. The tension drained out of her body, and she felt as if she were melting into the pier.

"Why do you think she has someone else or shouldn't I ask?"

"I don't mind. I heard her talking to someone on the phone." In her mind Pat heard Gail's voice, honey-toned, speaking to another woman. Gail had once reserved that tone of voice for her. "She urged me to come here this weekend."

"I don't understand."

"She used to be so jealous."

"Why would she be jealous of me?"

"Why not?" Pat asked, teasing Kate. "I enjoy your company. Jealousy often has no logic." Pat decided she didn't want to think about Gail. "How was your weekend with Bert?"

Kate shrugged. It seemed ages ago. "It was okay, but now he keeps pestering me to spend the night with him." She lay back on the pier, her feet still in the water.

"Why don't you?"

"I just don't want to. I don't want any more ties, and I don't want to answer to him. Maybe I wasn't ready for it. One weekend together and he thinks he owns me."

Pat laughed. "I shouldn't have told you to go."

"I probably would have gone anyway. If he just

wasn't constantly after me now, it'd be fine — I think." She had always disliked being pursued by an ardent admirer, not that there had been that many, but she had never liked feeling cornered. She had wanted to push the enclosing arm off her shoulders after a few minutes. She watched Gordie and Brad walk toward the lake.

"Listen to those birds. They sound so sad," Pat remarked. The keening reached inside her.

"They're cedar waxwings. It is a lonely sound." Kate threw a towel over her face to protect it from the sun.

Gordie ran into the lake and dove when he was waist deep, then surfaced snorting, and splashed the two women on the pier. "Come on in, you two."

"Cut it out, Gordie," Kate said. "You're just as annoying as when you were a kid."

He lifted himself onto the pier, picked her up — despite her futile flailing — and threw her off the edge.

She was furious. "Goddammit, Gordie. I always hate it when you do stuff like that."

He just grinned at her, and when she got back on the pier and attempted to push him in, he grabbed her and dumped her off the end. She hung onto his arm and pulled him in after her. They swam to the surface, sputtering and blowing water.

"You're a son of a bitch," Kate gasped.

"Potty mouth," Gordie replied.

"Why are guys like that?" she asked, treading water. "Why do you always have to be so physical and show your strength?"

"Want to see more of it?"

"No."

47

"Is this your girlfriend?" Gordie whispered to her.

"What?" she asked, unable to believe her ears.

"She's nice. You've got good taste."

Pat and Brad were talking at the other end of the pier.

"You asshole, Gordie."

Gordie laughed, the maddening know-it-all laugh she remembered from childhood.

"She's a friend, Gordie, a good friend. Don't insult her," Kate hissed at him.

"I'm not insulting her. You're a handsome woman, Katie." He raised his eyebrows knowingly.

Kate gave up trying to convince him otherwise. What did it matter? Maybe she should try it. She glanced at Pat, seeing her as Gordie was seeing her. Interesting, she thought; maybe even exciting. She swallowed a smile, refusing to allow Gordie even a reasonable doubt.

The girls arrived late that night. They found Kate, Pat, Brad and Gordie on the porch playing Trivial Pursuit. Kate had three pies to the others' one apiece. She had heard all the questions at least once, but she hadn't let on.

"Hey, Mom, how are you?" Sarah asked, hugging her mother. "Good to see you, Pat."

Beth leaned over and kissed Kate. "Hi, Pat," she said when she straightened.

"You remember your uncle Gordie? And this is his friend, Brad Newby." Kate introduced the two men to the girls.

"You girls are gorgeous," Gordie said with enthusiasm. "You do good work, Katie."

Both girls were in sweats and without make-up,

but they were attractive young women. Kate looked at them with pride.

"So tell me what you girls are doing with your lives?" Gordie asked.

"Tomorrow," Beth promised. "Sorry to be a party poop, but I'm beat."

Sarah rummaged in the kitchen, making popcorn for those on the porch. Asking her mother to follow, Beth climbed the stairs to her room, took off her clothes and flopped on her bed.

"Were you with Pat last weekend?"

"No, I was with Bert Holloway," Kate replied defensively, annoyed because she felt she had to confess.

"Who is he?" Beth raised herself on one elbow and looked with interest at her mother.

"He owns the funeral home in Waushara, the one that had your grandmother's funeral."

"You slept with an undertaker?" she nearly shouted.

"Shhh." Why did she have to explain herself? "Did I say I slept with him? He's a nice man and he'll be here tomorrow."

"Mom, I'm moving in with Scott."

"Oh?"

"I wish you wouldn't do that."

"Do what?"

"Sigh like that. It always makes me nervous. I thought you liked Scott."

"I do like him. I didn't know you were that serious."

"Well, we are. We're just not quite ready for marriage."

49

Thank God for that, Kate thought. How would she handle a wedding right now?

Downstairs the game was over. Sarah grinned at her mother when she reappeared. "She told you, didn't she?" Kate nodded, suddenly exhausted. "I had my last final this morning. I can stay here now until the fall semester starts."

Kate looked around at the people on the porch. Three months ago if someone had told her to expect these changes, she'd never have believed it. "I'm going to bed," she announced.

She left a lamp on by the far bed for Pat. The windows were open and a tender breeze wafted through the room. She climbed between the sheets and lay there, unable to relax. Shit, she wasn't going to sleep tonight either. She was on her back wide awake when Pat entered the room an hour later.

"You all right?" Pat asked.

"I guess. A month ago I thought I might be bored here. Fat chance of that."

"Winter's coming," Pat remarked, undressing and getting into the other bed.

Saturday dawned lovely. Kate and Pat cycled through the early light. Kate now felt physically deprived if she couldn't ride every day. "You know, I missed you this week," Kate said, realizing how true it was. She glanced at Pat pedaling next to her and grinned warmly. The lake had been emptier without Pat and her sailboat.

"This is so much nicer than the real world," Pat

remarked. "Unfortunately, my salary comes from the real world."

"Come whenever you can get away, Pat. You're always welcome."

"How nice. I'll call before I show up, though." She added with a mischievous smile, "You look good on that bike, Kate, like you belong there."

"You just noticed that, did you? You don't look so bad yourself." She shot Pat an appreciative look, admiring the tan smooth legs moving effortlessly, and noticed a sheen of sweat on Pat's upper lip. "Am I wearing you out?"

"Are you serious?" Pat turned and studied Kate briefly, noticing the reddish hair dampened at the hairline. Her gaze took in Kate's length. "You are looking rather fit," she remarked with a smile, thinking Kate had a nice body.

In the afternoon, while they were all in the water batting the volleyball across the net, Bert strolled down the path to the pier.

"About time you got here," Kate called to him. "Where's your suit?" The ball whizzed past her and plopped in the water.

"I didn't bring it," he replied. He sat on the pier and removed his shoes and socks. He was wearing shorts and a polo shirt.

The game stopped for a few minutes, and the girls looked at Bert with curiosity. "I'll get you a suit," Gordie offered, starting out of the water.

"That's all right," Bert protested. He inserted his feet gingerly into the lake. "I'll just sit here and watch."

Kate wondered if he knew how to swim. He

51

certainly wasn't a tanning addict. "I'll get it for him, Gordie," Kate said, determined to get some sun on that pale skin.

Bert visibly brightened as she emerged alone from the water, and he followed her up the path to the house. She walked around to the back yard but the suit was not on the line. "It must be in Gordie's room," she said.

"I'm not wearing someone else's swimming trunks," Bert protested.

Kate glanced at him, frowned and turned to go back to the lake. "Why didn't you save me the walk to the house? What did you think I'd find? This isn't a clothing store."

He grabbed her arm. "Okay, anything to have you alone for a few minutes."

She pulled her arm away and went into the house with Bert close on her heels. "Don't be silly, Bert. You see me often enough."

For dinner that night Gordie and Brad grilled the meat because Gordie said he was good at that sort of thing, his eyes laughing at Kate's disgusted expression.

"Funny, Gordie," she said wryly.

"I won't let it get hard," he promised.

Kate shook her head and walked to the house, where the girls were preparing a tossed salad in the kitchen.

"When are you coming back?" Kate asked Pat, as the two of them set the table. She brushed against Pat in passing and smelled the good clean smell of her.

"I don't know. I'll have to see how things are

going at home. School meetings are scheduled for next week."

"Can you come next weekend?" Why was this friendship becoming so important to her? Maybe because she was so far from her old friends? Briefly, she thought of her Illinois friends, who had mostly been couples and who seemed to have gone the way of the marriage.

"I'll see. I'll call next week after I talk to Gail."

Evening set in. Kate wished she were out on the lake or the pier, because she could only see the sunset through the pines. The lake was blood red. Soon a full moon would rise to replace the light of day with its own mellow brand. "Excuse me," she said abruptly, finishing the last of her food. "I'll be back." All her life she had been constrained by polite conventions, and it took great effort to throw them off, even with these friends and relatives. She headed down the hill toward the pier.

Standing on the end of the pier, she wished she liked to fish. Then she could have something to do while watching the end of the day and the beginning of the night. She clasped her arms and hugged herself while enjoying the glory around her. How trivial everything became in this cosmic display.

Bert walked up behind her and stood close, carefully not touching her. "Everything okay?" he asked.

"Oh yes, I just couldn't miss this."

"What?"

"The sunset, Bert. How can you all sit inside when these glorious colors are outside?"

"Well, we didn't know what was the mater, you got up and left so suddenly."

So unlike her to do what she really wanted to do, to break the pattern of a lifetime of politeness. She smiled into the dusk. Other footsteps shook the pier. She turned to see Pat putting her fishing equipment into the rowboat. Kate asked, "Do you mind if I come with you?"

"I'd love the company," Pat said. "The girls chased me away from the dishes."

"I'll row. I don't have a fishing license. You don't mind, do you Bert?" she asked, knowing he would mind.

"I need to get back to the funeral home anyway. I'll see you tomorrow maybe."

"All right. 'Night."

Kate rowed away from the pier into the quiet crimson lake. Bats swooped around them. A whippoorwill called repeatedly from somewhere across the lake. Kate breathed deeply and the odors of lake and trees and wildflowers and grasses — the redolent smells of summer — brought a flood of memories. For a minute she was young again. "Where do you want to go?" Kate asked.

"Across the lake, out from that green cottage over there." Pat pointed.

"You got it. Maybe I should get a fishing license."

"Maybe you should."

Kate felt the muscles work between her shoulders as she rowed. Tom had loved to fish. Should she have joined him in more of his favorite activities? Did his young girlfriend? It didn't matter now anyway. Neither one of them probably knew what had really happened, when finally not even their love for their children, their joint friends and memories, their tangled finances, could hold them together.

"You okay, Kate?" Pat asked.

"Just fine," Kate replied. The crimson on the lake was fading. "I went out to see the sunset. That's all it was."

Pat nodded and cast, then slowly reeled in the line. Kate continued pulling on the oars, while bats flew so close sometimes both women instinctively ducked. The brilliant reds and purples in the sky paled to pink and in the east Kate observed the moon rising, red and enormous. "Look, Pat."

"I see," Pat said quietly. "Sometimes it's really good to be alive, isn't it?"

About one hundred feet out from the green cottage, Kate let the oars float in the water. She rested her arms lightly on them and felt a slight bobbing. A bass struck Pat's lure and she reeled it in. "Get the net, Kate, please. I can't reach it."

Kate held the net under the fish and brought it into the boat, where Pat unhooked it and put it on a stringer. "A few more like this and we'll have dinner tomorrow," Pat commented. Kate frowned at the fish as Pat hung the gill line over the side of the boat and the bass tried to swim away. Pat looked at Kate's face and laughed. "You asked to come," she reminded Kate.

"I know," Kate said, feeling foolish for imagining the fish's pain. What did she know about being a fish? She ate meat, didn't she? Someone had to kill what she ate. She just didn't see it done.

"What we need for bait are a few frogs," Pat remarked.

"Oh no, Pat. I won't let you fish with frogs," Kate protested.

Pat laughed again in the near dark, a husky

55

sound. "Just testing," she said. "I suppose this means you don't like to hunt either?"

"Do you?" Kate asked, barely able to make out Pat's face in the dark. She slapped at a persistent mosquito.

"Every fall I get a deer." Pat cast again and again the lure was struck. "This is my lucky night," she said, reeling in another bass.

Kate tried to imagine killing a deer, the large soft dark eyes dimming with death. She hated death in any form, and her mother's dying drifted unwanted into her mind. She recalled the astonishment of it, even when she had known it was imminent. Somehow she had never really believed her mother would die. It had been like a part of herself dying. When she had looked down at the sightless eyes — the light of life gone from them — and the mouth slightly open in a grimace, Kate had realized she too would look like that someday. Death had become a reality never to be shaken, only to be ignored. The death of one of her dogs, his heaviness, the smell of death on him — that, too, appeared unwillingly in her mind.

She stared at the moon rising above the pines, no longer red, casting a path of light on the water. The sky was close to completely black; a few of the brighter stars stood out. Her feeling of contentment struggled to return, to wipe away the pictures in her memory. She resolutely erased all but the present from her mind. Pat continued casting, the quiet between them comfortable.

Pat wondered what Gail was doing this weekend and what it would be like when the weekend was over. Would the distance between them be greater?

Nibbling around the corners of her mind was something she didn't want to hear: maybe her commitment to Gail was fading. Knowing she wasn't going to catch any more fish but unwilling to break the spell of the night, she glanced at Kate in the near darkness. Perhaps Gail wanted to throw her to this woman, to use Kate as an excuse to end their relationship. In truth Pat was a little confused about her feelings for Kate. Her life had been so clear these past few years, better to leave it that way. She reeled in the line and set the pole in the boat. "Want me to row?"

"What? Oh, you're through? But you don't have enough fish to keep. Maybe we better let these go."

Pat laughed. "No, we're going to eat them tomorrow. I'll fix them for you, and you'll love them. Let me row now."

Kate changed seats with her and leaned against the back of the boat while Pat rowed in. Neither wanted to leave the beauty of the night, and Pat took her time rowing across the lake.

The others were on the porch playing cards when Kate opened the screen door to the house. Pat went around to the back yard to kill and clean the fish.

"How long since you played bridge, Katie?" Gordie asked. "I'm surprised you haven't taught these young women. I thought Tom was a terrific bridge player."

"He is," Kate said. "The kids were never interested in learning to play."

"We're still not," Sarah said. Beth nodded.

The back door slammed, and Pat entered the kitchen to salt the fillets and put them in the refrigerator.

"Tell me you're a bridge player," Gordie commanded when Pat appeared on the porch with a can of Pepsi.

"Not a very good one," Pat said.

"You will be when we're through with you," he promised.

IV

Tired, the relaxing weekend already fraying at the edges, Pat unlocked the apartment and carried in her bag. With a determined smile Gail emerged from the kitchen. In her wake was a tall attractive woman. Heart lurching as she quickly appraised the situation, Pat frowned.

"Pat, this is Joy Anderson. She will be staying with us. Her things are in my room."

In the future whenever Pat tried to recall the rest of their conversation, it eluded her. The frantic need to escape the two women, to run from the pain, overwhelmed her. Her next conscious moment found her in the car with her forehead resting on the steering wheel. In a haze of pain so intense she felt like throwing up, she drove to Barb's house.

"What's the matter, babe?" Barb asked, her face crinkled in worry lines. She pulled Pat in the house and pushed her into a kitchen chair.

"This woman has moved into our apartment and is sleeping in Gail's room." Pat buried her eyes in her palms. The aching inside her increased as she talked. Barb placed a comforting hand on her shoulder. "I need a place to stay tonight." To her surprise tears rolled down her wrists. She wiped them away roughly.

Barb patted her on the shoulder. "Stay as long as you want to."

Ensconced in the extra bedroom, lying on the bed staring at bowling trophies on the shelves across the room, Pat felt a deep gratitude for old friends. She couldn't have spent the night in the apartment with Gail and Joy. She envisioned them wrapped together in the bed she and Gail had once shared. She should have exited months ago. Then she could have done it with class. Tomorrow she'd look for an apartment. She fell asleep with the light still on, an unread book on her chest, concentrating on her comment to Kate — something about it being good to be alive in the midst of all that unreal beauty at the lake.

The smell of coffee drifted into the spare bedroom wakening Pat. At first she didn't know where she was, and then her eyes focused on the bowling trophies. Her misery returned. She hadn't expected the ending to be this painful. Lying quietly, she relived the beginning, when her admiration for Gail had at first caused her confusion and then joy when it had been reciprocated.

"Hey babe, you awake?" A knock on the door. Barb, always an early riser, opened the door and peered in at Pat. "It's halfway to noon."

Pat grinned back. Such cheerfulness was contagious.

Barb came in and sat on the end of the bed. "Is it really over between you two? I thought you would last."

"She's got someone else." Someone gorgeous, she thought grimly.

"I'm sorry," Barb said with genuine distress. "You can stay with Sandy and me. We've got room for you."

Pat nearly grasped the straw and then thought of her furniture. "I've got too much stuff. It wouldn't fit in here. But thanks." Besides, she felt a need for solitude.

"Well, think about it. You could store your stuff in the basement. Now get your stumps moving." No moping allowed around Barb.

Barb and Sandy helped Pat move her belongings into their basement. Thankfully, Gail absented herself from the apartment during the move. The emptiness in Pat had slowly filled with a painful anger — at Gail, at herself, even at Kate. Would it have been different if she hadn't gone to the lake that last weekend?

"You know, we're just going to have to move these things again," Pat commented as they struggled out the door with a mattress.

"That's okay, babe. Maybe you'll decide to stay, and you need to get away from that woman. Out of sight, out of mind."

If that were only true, Pat thought. She had spent several nights in the spare bedroom. Finding an apartment she liked and could afford was not so easy. She tormented herself with thoughts of nights spent curled against Gail's long smooth body. Then she concentrated on the past few months, the fighting, the tension. She could stay here with Barb and Sandy and bowl on Mondays, play softball on Thursdays and poker on Saturdays, or she could find her own place.

Another Friday night and Kate still hadn't heard from Pat. Pat had called once and talked to Gordie, telling him she would call before Labor Day weekend, but she had left no number. Kate had experienced a frustrated anger. "Why didn't you get a number, at least?"

Gordie had backed off a couple feet. "Sorry, sis, I didn't think to. You really miss her, don't you?"

Kate had thought with amazement: I really need her.

Brad, Gordie and Sarah were playing hearts on the porch, while Kate curled up in a chair with a book. She listened with half an ear to their banter.

"Bert called," Brad said to Kate. "He's coming out tomorrow."

Sarah glanced at her mother. "Are you serious about him, Mom?"

"Not really." Kate considered her daughter. Sarah seemed quite happy here. She worked on her tan daily, read endlessly, exercised to tape every morning, helped Kate without complaint. Kate would miss her sorely when she returned to college next week.

Kate spent Saturday evening alone with Bert. They ate dinner at the country club. Staring out the window at the lake, the quickly setting sun casting a mauve halo in the western sky, Kate remembered their first dinner here and how nervous she had been. Had it only been a few weeks ago? It seemed like months. Later they went to Bert's home, a two story brick house next to the funeral home. Kate lounged on Bert's bed while he put a cassette in the tape deck. The phone's shrill ring startled her.

"Damn," Bert said, turning down the volume.

Sitting on the bed, he answered the phone. "I'm sorry, Mabel. Yes, yes, he's at the hospital?" His voice was gentle, kind. "I'll take care of it. Can you come in the morning? What time is convenient? Bring George's social security number and any clothing you might want to use. Are you alone? No? Good. See you in the morning.

Kate stood rooted to the floor. Someone had died in the middle of their evening, while they had been enjoying themselves. Well, it happened all the time. She usually just didn't know about it was all. "You have to go," she said.

"Not yet," Bert replied, heading her off.

* * * * *

63

"How long are you and Brad staying?" Kate asked. She and Gordie were waist deep in a field of goldenrod, the plumes waving in the soft August breeze. They were supposedly exercising Arthur but were actually using the puppy as an excuse for a walk. Gordie looked tired to Kate. She knew he had trouble sleeping. She had gotten up in the night more than once and found him sitting on the porch in the dark. He carried Arthur, who had nearly disappeared in the long grass. "He's too little for such a long walk and the grass is too tall for him," Kate commented.

Gordie had insisted on buying the dog for Kate. "For protection," he had said. They had gone to the county dog shelter. Kate's throat had ached over the plight of so many unwanted animals. It had seemed unfair to just take one. She had let Gordie choose.

Gordie had said, "He'll get large enough to scare intruders and he's got a good disposition." When she had inquired as to how he knew these things, he had said, "Look at the feet. He'll grow into them. And see how friendly he is." Arthur had been falling over his immense feet, sliding on his nose, scrambling up and down the dog kennel aisle, throwing himself with joyous and mindless abandon against the humans, while the other caged dogs had barked and thrown themselves against their bars.

"Labor Day weekend," Gordie replied to the question of his leaving.

"Are you losing weight, Gordie?" Kate asked, studying him critically and with a touch of worry. In the Sunday paper she had read a frightening article on AIDS.

"Maybe a little."

Sarah would be gone, Pat had already disappeared from her life, and soon Gordie and Brad would return to their real lives. Kate was silent as she thought about the coming fall and winter. "I'm so glad you came, Gordie," she said impulsively.

"I've been thinking about Mom and Dad, especially Dad," Gordie said, his mouth set, and Kate realized this was why they were walking alone with Arthur. "Being here brought it all back."

Kate steeled herself against the grief she always felt when her mother came to mind. Her father she remembered with startling clarity, but she hadn't watched him die, and his death had never been real to her. He was always alive when she thought of him. There was no one to ask about their past anymore, she thought. She glanced at Gordie's tanned face, at his eyes also seeing a time gone.

"I wish I'd made more of an effort. I wish I'd come back sooner, before Dad died."

Did he want her forgiveness, Kate wondered, or did he just need to talk it out of his system, if that were possible. "What happened back then, Gordie? No one ever really told me."

"Remember Junior Massengale?"

"Sort of," she said. Arthur had fallen asleep in Gordie's arms. Kate smiled. This friendly little animal was supposed to be her protector when Gordie left.

"Well, Junior's mother found us in bed together and snitched." Gordie grinned devilishly, watching her face for effect.

She sucked in her breath. "Jesus, Gordie, it couldn't have been funny."

The grin vanished from his face. "It wasn't. The roof fell in. Dad lost it and when he wasn't hollering

65

at me, he was deathly silent. It was unbelievably awful. He said things like he wished I hadn't been born and just to look at me shamed him." Gordie walked on, staring into the past. Kate had to take two steps to his one.

This wasn't the father she carried around in her mind. He would never have said things like that. He had always been so proud of Gordie and her. We both let him down, she thought, me by getting pregnant and never amounting to anything, Gordie by being what he was. "Gordie, surely he didn't mean those things."

"Oh, he meant them all right. You weren't there. Poor Mom, she tried so hard to make it all right."

"But they were said in anger." She thought her father would have mended the rift had he known how. "He read your letters to Mom."

Gordie turned to her, his eyes unreadable. "How do you know?"

"I was there visiting often," she explained, wincing as she said it.

His smile was twisted, painful to see. "If I could just go back, you know, Katie, and try. I never even tried. I was so angry and hurt."

So was Dad, she thought, but she didn't say it. It was too late. "You saw a lot of Mom, though, didn't you?"

"After Dad died. I'm not sure she forgave me for not trying to make it up with him."

"It takes two to do that, Gordie," she said, more to comfort him than out of any conviction. The sadness settling over them was almost unbearable. They had to struggle out of it.

"Katie, it seems like you've got all the time in the world and then it's gone."

They stood facing each other, the golden plumes swaying around them, the dog sleeping in Gordie's arms, tears running down their faces. It was a moment Kate knew she'd never forget. It was broken by Arthur who awoke and let out a sharp little bark.

While Gordie, Brad and Kate were eating pizza and listening to Bach's *Double Violin Concerto* on the porch the Saturday before Labor Day weekend, the phone rang.

"Hi, how are you?" Pat asked Kate.

Kate said the first thing that came to mind. "I thought maybe I was never going to hear from you again."

"You should know better than that."

What should she have thought? "When are you coming up? Where have you been? Why haven't you called?"

Pat laughed and Kate smiled at the sound. "One question at a time. I don't know when I can come up. I'm going to my parents' house for Labor Day weekend."

Kate felt a keen disappointment. "Gordie and Brad and leaving on Labor Day," she said.

"I know. Gordie told me. I'll try to come the weekend after. I'll answer the rest of your questions then. Okay?"

"Wait, Pat, give me your phone number." Then, after writing down the number: "Won't you tell me any more?"

"When I see you. We'll catch up on things then."

"All right, Pat, if that's the way you want it."

That was not the way she wanted it, Pat realized, hanging up. She wished she were going to Kate's for the holiday weekend. It had been nearly three weeks. But it had been longer since she had seen her parents and it was time she went home. Her mother had called asking if she was coming. Her brothers and their families would be there for Sunday and Labor Day. She could bring Gail if she liked. Did her father and mother know? She was certain her two brothers and their wives were aware she was not interested in marriage and had probably guessed why. At least they no longer asked when she was going to "tie the knot" with someone, as her father fondly phrased it. At one time, in the irrational happiness of new love, she had nearly told them she'd "tied the knot" with Gail.

She had moved out of Barb and Sandy's house last weekend and into this one bedroom apartment. Tonight was poker night, and Barb and Sandy were coming here with another friend for dinner and cards. She felt indebted to both of them but especially to Barb. Slowly her life was righting itself. At least she hadn't blown her head off, which had been a tempting thought a couple weeks ago. There had been no good place to perform the act. She hadn't been willing to mess up Barb's freshly painted walls with her brains. Anyway, as if reading her mind, Barb had confiscated her hunting rifle.

The difficult part was running into Gail and Joy,

as she had at the store today. The anger was still there, frightening Pat with its intensity. Recalling the besotted expression on Gail's face, she understood why people shot their ex-lovers.

On the drive to her parents Pat thought about Barb's pep talk on how to deal with her split with Gail. Worried that familiarity might foster discipline problems, Pat had always been a little standoffish with her students. Barb had encouraged her to change her tactics. She heard Barb's voice: "Throw yourself into your work. Bury yourself in it. Let these kids into your life." She and Barb taught at the same school. Pat resolved to try this approach after the weekend.

She parked next to her father's old Chevy pickup truck and sat in her car, where she gathered herself together to face the family, to hide her misery. Her dad emerged from his workshop behind the two-story house, a big grin on his face. Seeing how glad he was to see her, her heart went out to him, and in turn she was pleased to be here, to make him happy. She got out of her Honda Accord and hugged him.

As if on cue, her mother stepped out of the side door leading to the mud room and kitchen. She looked like an older version of Pat, which always startled Pat and unnerved her a little, like returning her own smile. "Hi, Mom, It's good to be home," she said, meaning it. In the past few years she had always been reluctant to leave Gail and begrudged time spent away from her. Too bad it had to take a breakup to bring her home.

Late Sunday morning Pat's two brothers and their wives and children made their appearances. The wives disappeared into the kitchen to help Pat's mother.

Pat had spent Saturday splitting wood with her father. Her muscles felt pleasantly overworked, and she sank into one of the back yard lawn chairs near her dad and brothers, while the kids chased each other, yelling when one caught up with another. Pat imagined what it must be like to have to live with this noise and was relieved it wasn't going to happen to her.

At ten-thirty the children were still up. The adults had moved to the back porch and were in two groups — the women together discussing children and food, the men and Pat talking sports and fishing and the coming deer-hunting season. Five-year-old Laurel had fallen asleep in her father's lap, and Pat wondered why someone didn't put her to bed. The boys were outside playing something that sounded like war, heard but not seen in the darkness.

When her brothers and their families left Monday afternoon, the sudden stillness was deafening. Pat stood under an enormous burr oak in the back yard and relished the silence. Her parents sat nearby in lawn chairs. Pat heard the welcome sounds of birds and insects, and she slid to a sitting position at the base of the tree. Looking up through the branches and leaves, she admired the blue sky littered with puffy white clouds. How could anyone ever think blue and green clashed?

"Ready for school to start?" her mother asked.

Pat nodded, unwilling to break the quiet with her own voice.

"Thanks for helping me split all that wood," her dad said. "Nice and quiet, ain't it?" he added with a grin.

Pat laughed. "I'm just not used to kids under

thirteen." They were bad enough at that age, she thought, but at least they were able to sit still.

"I love having them come, and I look forward to their coming again, but I enjoy the in-between time, too," her mother commented. "You've moved." It was a statement.

"To a smaller apartment," Pat said. "Less expensive. Nice neighborhood." Of course, it wasn't really less expensive, because she had no one to share the costs.

"Is it big enough for you and Gail?" her mother asked.

Pat studied the cloud formations. "It's a one-person apartment. Gail didn't move." Then she looked from one parent to the other and thought how nice it was they had each other.

V

Arthur had proved only troublesome so far, Kate reflected, taking him out for the third time Tuesday morning. "Piddle, for God's sake," she said in exasperation as he sniffed around the back yard. "I've got work to do." Tongue lolling, he wagged his tail and flopped down in the sand. She sat on the back steps for a few minutes to appreciate the cool day. The September light was mellow, not intense like the July sun. Gordie and Brad had left yesterday, Labor Day morning, after taking the pier down Sunday. Earlier in the day, knowing she would be coming home to an empty house, she had pedaled her bike slowly.

Her eyes were on Arthur, who was again padding around on those big feet with his nose to the ground, but she was remembering the weekend and Scott's first visit. The absurdity of whether Beth and Scott should spend the night in the same room (After all, this was 1986, she thought) had been solved when Beth had said she wanted to sleep with her mother so they could talk. And they had talked deep into the night Saturday. After discussing everything but Tom, Beth had finally brought him into the conversation. Kate heard her daughter's voice again, hesitant, worried. "Mom, have you talked to Dad at all?"

Startled by the question, Kate had replied, "No, honey, why?" Knowing at once Beth had been about to tell her something important and unpleasant, she braced herself for it.

"Just wondered is all." Beth's voice faltered.

Kate turned on her bed light and raised herself on an elbow to see Beth's face. Why should Beth have to be the purveyor of bad news? Surely Tom wouldn't have asked that of her? "Tell me, Beth," she ordered.

"He's going to marry Nancy," Beth had blurted.

"Oh . . . Did he ask you to tell me that?" Tom couldn't be that much of a coward.

"No, Mom, Nancy told me. I didn't want you to be surprised."

Kate emitted a short harsh laugh. She liked Nancy even less for imparting the news to Beth. Would she just get served with papers or would Tom have the decency to call her? "Why did she tell you, Beth?" Kate asked angrily.

"Scott and I were there for dinner, and I was

73

helping her clean up and she just told me. I'm sorry, Mom." Beth was crying.

Kate jumped out of her bed and into Beth's. They held each other silently for a few minutes, while Kate wondered what to say to comfort her daughter. "Beth, I won't say it's all right. I don't like her telling you and you thinking you have to tell me. I'm not terribly hurt, just indignant."

Stupid woman. Kate had been furious with her, and Beth had been sobbing, clinging. Kate had held her tighter, a few tears straying down her face. It was true she had been more indignant than hurt.

Now, sitting on the steps, she thought of Tom. He hadn't called yet, and there had been no official papers in the mail either. She hadn't wanted to marry him in the first place, she told herself resentfully. She had married him because she had been pregnant. More than twenty years ago you either married or gave up your baby for adoption. Abortions had been hard to come by and not safe. And it had been easier to stay married than get divorced. She had never been madly in love with Tom, she thought. Maybe that had been the problem. But it was easier to have a man around, she admitted to herself.

Arthur attempted to climb the stairs to reach her but he was too little to negotiate even the first step. After trying and failing several times, he whined and barked until she picked him up. What had Gordie saddled her with here? Arthur threw up in the car, wet and pooped on the floors, cried at night. She should have been answering her letter packet, not sitting out here with this animal. She looked at him closely. Gordie had thought he was a hound and

74

German shepherd mix, with medium length ears and hair colored white and brown and black. She couldn't tell. Playfully, he chewed on her hand with his sharp baby teeth. She carried him back into the house.

The phone rang just as she was tearing open the first letter on the porch where she had moved the typewriter. Growling with mock ferocity, Arthur fastened his teeth to one of her pant legs when Kate moved to answer it. She wondered if it was Bert knowing she was alone, wanting lunch and then dessert. She was not in the mood to be someone's cream pie.

"Kate? It's Tom." As if she wouldn't have recognized his voice anywhere. "How are you?"

"Good, real good. How are you?" Playing games, was she? She wasn't so good. She was lonely.

"Fine. I talked to Beth today. I'm sorry she heard before you did."

Kate was silent, relieved that the man she had lived with so long was not a complete skunk. "So was I."

Now the silence was on Tom's end of the line. He broke it. "I heard Gordie was there for a month. That must have been nice."

"It was." Kate wasn't going to help him with this.

"Kate, I'm sorry. I really am. I feel wrong about all this, but it happened."

Wasn't that what she had said to Sarah?

"I thought maybe you might want to initiate divorce proceedings," he said.

"I'll get a lawyer to take care of my interests, but you handle it, Tom. That's your profession." She wanted to make him uncomfortable, to punish him.

75

"Kate, I'll see you get your share, and I'll take care of the rest of Sarah's schooling. But yes, do get an attorney."

Kate said nothing. She only wanted her half of their jointly accumulated possessions.

Back at the typewriter, dog still attached to her jeans but losing interest now that the leg was not moving, she stared at the lake. It sparkled in the sunlight, empty except for a few fishing boats. A medium breeze stirred it restlessly, and Kate longed to be in Pat's sailboat. She recalled Pat losing herself in the excitement of sailing and hoped she would bring the sailboat this weekend.

Before Kate could read the first letter, the phone rang again and this time it was Bert, asking her to lunch.

Friday afternoon Kate feared Pat would change her mind and not come. The weather had turned, sending torrents of rain and dropping the thermometer twenty degrees in two hours. She had brought her typewriter back inside and shut the door to the front porch for the first time since her arrival. While Arthur drooped in the cold rain, Kate stacked wood outside the back door and readied herself for a cold spell. She then coaxed reluctant flames from the damp wood in the fireplace and settled in a chair with a book.

The week's letter packets were answered and disposed of, and her time was free until Monday. Pat hadn't called, so perhaps she would show up. Kate didn't know if she could bear this weekend alone.

Even Bert was gone to Milwaukee to visit his daughter. She thought of her friends from her life with Tom. She had lost touch with them, she knew, had only written to one of her closest friends and then only infrequently since she had come to the lake. It was as if she had run from them, too.

Pat negotiated the driveway through dripping pines, parked in the yard and jumped puddles to the back steps. Arthur met her at the door as she knocked, opened the door and walked in. Without so much as a bark the puppy threw his body at her in welcome. "What's this?" Pat asked. She removed her jacket and hung it on the back porch to dry, then picked up Arthur. "Oops, looks like I got him too excited," she said. There was a puddle at her feet.

"He leaks," Kate said, too happy with Pat's arrival to be annoyed at Arthur's lack of control. She cleaned the wet spot, then straightened and grinned at Pat with such pleasure that Pat laughed in embarrassment. Kate felt warmed by the dark eyes. She noticed the freckles, the sandy hair curling around the younger woman's face. Her gaze traveled down Pat's body, thinking how fit Pat looked, especially in a flannel shirt and jeans. Kate backed off a little, so Pat could move into the main room, and followed her.

The fire had taken hold and danced blue and red. It filled the house with warmth. "Nice, cheerful. Should I get more wood?" Feeling a little awkward, Pat turned to Kate.

"God, it's good to see you," Kate said. "You can't imagine." She had no idea how much she had missed Pat until now. Everyone needed a good friend, she thought, but had she ever cared for a friend like this?

77

Pat's presence had brought something into the house that Kate mentally tried to pin down — warmth, life, energy?

"So lonesome already?" Pat asked but she was glad to see Kate, too. Too glad, she thought, sure Kate's delight in her arrival was due to her isolation. Who wouldn't be happy to have company under the circumstances? Arthur chewed fiercely on her sleeve, occasionally biting through to her skin with his little incisors. "Ouch, the little bugger's teething on my arm."

"Gordie bought him for me for protection. You notice how he protected me from you, by lavishing you with affection." Kate took Arthur, set him on the floor, and he grabbed her jeans. "His teeth are either affixed to something or he's sleeping or fouling the floor," Kate said. "He's a pain in the ass."

Feeling a little silly because she couldn't stop smiling, she sat beside Pat on the couch in front of the fire. "I think I'd have lost my mind this weekend if you hadn't come." Then she shut her mouth and studied Pat so frankly and appraisingly that Pat turned her head away. "So what happened?"

Pat startled herself by laughing. "I can't hide anything from you, can I?" Maybe that was why she had stayed away this long.

"We've got the whole weekend. I'll start. Tom's divorcing me." Kate hadn't meant to say that, not yet. It had to have been waiting on the edge of her mind. "I wonder if it's his mid-life crisis." If that was the reason, then she understood that he was trying to recapture his youth through Nancy.

Jesus, Pat thought, and I'm supposed to tell her

about Gail? She'll think, so what? Pat gazed at the fire and absently rubbed her hands on her jeans.

Kate regretted her remarks as soon as they were spoken. She should have thought how Pat might react to them. "I didn't mean to blurt it out," she said. "I'm ready for a divorce." She touched Pat's hand briefly.

Pat jumped at the unexpected touch and met Kate's eyes. Liar, she thought, you're just trying to get me to talk. She'd forgotten how those blue-green eyes could reach into you, pin you to the wall. She looked quickly away to the fire. "I'm sorry," she said.

"I'm not. I'm just sorry I said it so soon. I haven't talked it out yet." She recalled her anger at Beth knowing first. "Are you hungry?"

"Not really."

Kate had never seen Pat so dispirited and unable to hide it. They sat in silence, listening to the hissing crackling of the fire and the drumming rain on the roof, the tapping rain on the windows. How to deal with this?

Pat was trying to deal with it. Somehow her defenses disappeared under Kate's eyes. She was afraid to open her mouth and sound like a whining wimp. Here was Kate, alone, with her marriage over. "How's Bert?" A logical, relatively safe question.

"He's visiting his daughter in Milwaukee this weekend, but he's okay."

Should she ask if he was still pursuing Kate? Maybe not.

"How's school?" Kate inquired.

"Different. I'm taking a new approach, getting a little closer to my students. It was Barb's idea." Pat's body language changed from dejection to assertion. She sat straighter, met Kate's eyes again. A mistake. "Don't look at me like that," she heard herself protest.

"Like what?" Kate asked.

"Like you can see into me."

"Is that how I'm looking at you?" Kate asked with surprise. "I didn't mean to make you uncomfortable. You seem so unhappy."

Taking a deep breath, Pat told Kate about the past few weeks. The pain, somewhat diminished, flared anew. Staring at the flames as she talked, she didn't look at Kate until she fell silent.

"It's no rose garden, is it? I wish I could make it right for you." Kate frowned slightly as she pictured Gail on the boat, playing volleyball. She wondered if she was happy. She hadn't appeared happy then.

Pat shrugged. "I'm free for the first time in years."

"So am I," Kate responded, "for the first time in my entire life." She reflected on this for a minute or two. "I think I like it."

I wish I did, Pat said to herself.

But the dam was broken and now they couldn't stop talking. Kate went into the kitchen to fix dinner, and Pat followed.

Kate related what Beth had told her regarding Tom and Nancy and then added, "I don't care if he marries her. If I'm going to be perfectly honest, though, I have to admit my pride does. I thought I knew him. You should know someone you've been married to for twenty-four years." She wanted to understand what had happened. Had it just faded away until there had been no commitment, until

80

there had been nothing? The fault had to lie with her, too, for failing to notice.

"You didn't say much about Bert. Is he still lusting after you?"

Kate smiled at the return of Pat's humor. "Yeah, I'm afraid he is. I just want it to be fun. I think he wants more." She speculated about what Pat did for sex these days.

"How are you feeling about what's happened between you and Gail?" she asked when they sat down to spaghetti and salad.

"I don't think about it if I can help it. I keep busy." She did, too, filling her evenings and weekends with activities. But that didn't keep her from waking in the night, remembering and wanting Gail with an intensity that would not permit sleep.

Pat suddenly looked so forlorn that Kate covered Pat's hand with her own. She meant only to comfort.

Pat turned her hand over and squeezed Kate's. A smile slowly turned up the corners of her mouth as she met Kate's eyes. The contact felt good, comforting, and she didn't want to let go. She felt such a surge of warmth toward Kate it frightened her. Her eyes strayed to Kate's mouth; she thought she knew how Kate's lips would feel against hers; she could taste them. She mentally shook herself.

Kate froze, barely returning the smile. Their relationship had taken an unexpected, unplanned turn, had added a new dimension, and she was paralyzed by the possibilities. Had Gordie been right about her after all? Confused, she let her gaze drop from Pat's and found herself focusing on the younger woman's throat, the pulse throbbing against skin so smooth she nearly freed her hand to feel it.

Pat released Kate's hand and leaned back in her chair. She reached for the wine bottle and filled their glasses. "To friendship," she said, raising her glass, still smiling.

Breathing deeply, Kate drained her glass. Conflicting feelings coursed through her, bumping into each other — relief, exhilaration, disappointment. "Did you bring the sailboat?"

"What? In the rain? No, but I brought my bike. We can ride tomorrow if it ever stops raining."

The rain ceased during the night. Pat slept little and awakened early. She made coffee and went outside with Arthur.

When Kate opened her eyes, she lay in bed for a while, hands behind her head, and listened to the blue jays screech outside the windows. Then she got up, put on a robe and followed the smell of coffee. She poured herself a cup and stuck her head out the back door. The sky was blue, the ground drenched, the air pleasantly cool.

She just wished she wasn't so tired and was temporarily annoyed with Pat for being the reason for her lack of sleep. She had heard Pat tossing during the night. Kate had fallen into an exhausted sleep only after her mind had refused to replay any more the events at the table last night. She took her coffee to the bedroom and dressed in jeans and sweatshirt, then stepped out on the porch, set the cup on a table and stretched while she breathed in the freshened air.

Pat and Arthur appeared around the corner of the house. Arthur's nose was to the ground and he ran in spurts. He suddenly stopped, emitted sharp yelping barks, took off in pursuit of some unseen prey. "Morning," Pat said, grinning at Kate, opening the

82

screen door to the porch. Pat's hair was a mass of unruly curls.

Startled, Kate ran her fingers through her tangled hair. "What the hell is the matter with him? Is he in pain or something?" The pup zigzagged through the pines.

"That's called belling," Pat explained. "It's the sound hounds make when on the trail of something." She had a coffee cup in hand and went inside to fill it. "Sleep well?" she asked, back on the porch. She looked at Kate appreciatively, at the small trim figure. Kate's cheeks were flushed from sleep; Pat wanted to warm her hands on them. Instead, she tucked them under her arms.

Kate glanced at Pat, noticed the dark circles under her eyes. "Nope and neither did you."

"Oh. Did I keep you awake?" Pat sat in one of the chairs, trying to keep the surprise off her face.

Kate noticed the dark eyes widening. She wanted to tame the curls that had gone wild around Pat's face, to run her fingers through them and put them in place, but, of course, she couldn't do that. She refilled her coffee and sat nearby, wrapping her fingers around the cup. She wouldn't play this game. "Yes, you kept me awake. Something happened at dinner last night."

Silence. Pat refused to meet Kate's eyes. She felt empty as she quietly said, "Nothing happened, Kate, and nothing's going to. So tonight we can both sleep. How about a bike ride?"

Amazed because she perversely wanted to argue with Pat, to insist something had happened, Kate looked toward the lake and told herself to say nothing.

The golden light slanting through the woods along the roadside, the sumac already turning red, the cool air, indicated fall had arrived. Pat watched as Kate rode effortlessly next to her. "Looks like you can talk and ride at the same time now."

"Hey, I bet I can outride you now."

"Wouldn't surprise me a bit, but I'll take you up on it. How far and how much?"

"To Waushara and back. Whoever loses cooks dinner tonight."

"You're on."

Kate lost, but by only a few feet. Sweat poured off both women as they pedaled down the drive, heads bent, bodies flattened. "Well, shit," Kate said, getting off her bike, her legs weak and trembling, her breath coming in gasps. But she was satisfied to notice Pat in the same condition.

"You didn't really think you could beat a jock, did you?" Pat placed a comradely arm around Kate's shoulders and squeezed.

"You're about as much of a jock as I am," Kate teased. She returned the hug with an arm around Pat's waist.

"Play racquetball with me sometime, and we'll see who's the jock."

"Swim across the lake and we'll see who gets there first."

Their arms fell to their sides, and a warm feeling radiated between them. Arthur barked frantically from inside the back door. "Guess I better let him out. He's probably already wet his tights. Why did Gordie do this to me? No doubt taking revenge for something I did to him as a child."

"Let's take him for a walk," Pat suggested. "It's

84

too nice to be inside." She sat on the picnic table in the back yard, wondering why she had promised Kate nothing would happen between them. She could have tested Kate's mind a little. She watched her carry a struggling Arthur down the steps, toss him, and return to the house. Maybe she should have put both arms around Kate, she thought, feeling again the yielding firmness of the other woman.

"Shame on you, Arthur," Pat scolded in a friendly voice. Arthur wiggled over to her, clamped his teeth on her Nike and, growling happily, swung with the movement of her foot. She thought about what it would be like to seduce Kate. Then she recalled her first seduction — only she had been the one seduced.

Ginny had been her roommate during her first year at college, and she had climbed into Pat's bed one night. Before Pat had been able to comment on this surprising turn of events, Ginny had taken Pat's face between her hands and kissed her on the mouth. There had been no going back from there. They had spent a lot of nights in each other's beds becoming proficient at lovemaking. Ginny had not returned for the sophomore year. During the next three years Pat had expanded her sexual experience to include two young men. They had failed to thrill her.

"What are you thinking about?"

Pat started. She hadn't heard or seen Kate. She grinned sheepishly. "Nothing much."

"Arthur crapped in the kitchen. I nearly stepped in it."

Pat laughed. "You could mail him to Gordie."

"I'd like to."

"You know, if you keep him outside until he's six months old, he won't go inside."

"Really? But that would be the middle of winter."

"Let him sleep in the barn. Maybe four months old will be old enough. It's just a matter of being old enough to hold it. You couldn't control yourself at his age either." She jumped off the table. "Ready to go?"

They walked single file through the pine woods behind the house, their footsteps cushioned by a blanket of needles. Sunshine created shadows of the tall trees and they moved in and out of the light. Arthur rushed away from them and than back as if dashing toward freedom and fleeing from it. "It's like he's on a rubber band," Kate said. She paused and turned as she spoke, and Pat walked into her.

"Whoops. Sorry." She gripped Kate's arms to steady herself.

Kate laughed, caught up in the pleasure of the day. "I'm the one who should be sorry." Looking into Pat's eyes, unable to read the expression, she added, "I wish you didn't have to leave."

"It would be a long commute," Pat said, caught mentally off balance.

Kate turned and walked on but not before saying, "It would be nice to have you around, though."

"It would probably be nice to have anyone around. It must be a little lonesome after the summer." Regret tugged at her as Pat stared at Kate's back moving away from her. She had missed the moment, but she wasn't sure she wanted to risk losing Kate's friendship by attempting to turn it into more. And did she really want something more anyway? Perhaps she was trying to replace Gail or maybe she was just plain horny?

In the evening after dinner and a few games of cribbage, Kate leaned against the back of the sofa and crossed her arms. "You were right when you said winter's going to be lonely."

Pat chewed on her lower lip as she shuffled cards. "You can come stay with me anytime, Kate. I get lonesome, too."

"Do you?" Kate replied, looking at Pat's forlorn smile, thinking of being alone. There was a difference between the loneliness when she had first arrived at the lake and now. In the beginning, just being outside had introduced her to others. Now that the lake was empty of its summer visitors it was a lonelier place. There was something about autumn that left her bereft.

Kate slept soundly that night. She was awakened once by a screech owl screaming outside. She glanced at Pat in the next bed, heard her steady breathing.

Agreeing that it was too windy to ride bikes Sunday, they walked — along the beach, through the woods. Arthur's tongue lolled and he flopped whenever possible. The women grew tired, too, and sat on rocks and logs when the sun emerged from the cloud cover. Their silences were as comfortable as their conversations.

Late that afternoon, Kate stood in the yard with Arthur sitting at her side and watched Pat's car until it was swallowed by the white pines.

VI

Kate read and reread Gordie's letter. There was something wrong about it that she couldn't pin down, could only sense. She called his home in Indianapolis. The ringing echoed in her ear.

Brad answered on the sixth ring. "Kate, how's it going?" He sounded genuinely glad to hear her voice.

"A little lonesome without you guys. How are you?"

"*I'm* fine, good."

An alarm bell went off in Kate's head. "Who isn't?"

Brad laughed and even the laugh didn't ring true to Kate. She zeroed in on him. "*You* tell *me,* Brad. How's Gordie?"

"Are you psychic, Kate?"

"Maybe." Her heart was sinking. It was impossible not to think of AIDS.

Brad lowered his voice. "He'll kill me if I tell you, Kate."

She could barely hear him. "Then let him tell me," she replied.

"He won't." His voice broke.

"I have a right to know." Did she?

"I'll tell you if you won't tell him I did. Promise?" He was crying.

Kate felt herself sweating, then turning cold. Did she want to know? "I promise."

"He tested positive."

Her heart beat in her ears. She rested her forehead against the door frame and for some reason saw her mother lying on the table in the emergency room.

"He woke sweating in the night even at the lake, and he was tired and losing weight."

"Why didn't he tell me?" She was angry. Why hadn't she been more observant?

"You know Gordie. He didn't want to spoil the fun."

She didn't know Gordie, she realized. "And you, Brad?"

"I don't have AIDS," he replied after a pause.

Not yet, she thought, as she banged her head lightly against the door frame. She chewed on her lower lip, refusing to break down and bawl. "Is he there?"

89

"Just a minute. I'll get him, but remember your promise."

"I remember. Thanks for telling me, Brad. And Brad, I'm sorry." Raising her face toward the ceiling, she blinked back tears. Jesus, not Gordie. Why did he have to die, too?

"Did you get my letter, Katie?"

"Yes, Gordie, there was something about it. I got the feeling something was wrong."

"Nothing's wrong."

Why wouldn't he tell her? "You sure, Gordie?"

"I thought I'd come for Thanksgiving. Think you could stand me?"

Would he be alive then? "That'll be great. That's a long time from now, though. Maybe you could show me Indianapolis."

"Love to, Katie. Any time."

"How about next weekend?"

"Is everything all right with you?" he asked, worry in his voice.

"Of course, I just got used to you."

"How's Arthur doing?"

"He's banished outside, where he's staying until he learns the house isn't a toilet. Pat said that would be sometime between his fourth and sixth months."

"Is he protecting you?"

"From what? Small animals? He's crazy about people."

"Let me give you directions here."

Kate hung up and pounded on the counter with both fists.

Arthur barked from the back yard. It was time to feed him. She had a date with Bert tonight. How good an actress was she? She couldn't let Bert find

90

her lying face down on the bed, a pillow over her head, which was all she wanted to do. As she filled Arthur's feed dish with puppy chow and carried it out to the barn, she saw Gordie's face, tanned and laughing, blue-green eyes bright against the glow of his skin. He had looked so healthy. How could she have guessed? An emptiness grew inside her. She wanted August back, wanted more Augusts, and knew there might not be many more.

At the restaurant Bert's puzzled expression registered on her wine-drenched brain. She had wanted to call Pat. However, she couldn't make herself say the words about Gordie aloud. That would make it real, and the words wouldn't come. What you aren't aware of hasn't happened, not in your mind anyway. Why had she dug it out of Brad? Besides, Gordie hadn't told her. How could she tell anyone else?

"Kate, what is it? What's wrong?" Bert asked, his face etched by a worried frown.

She'd been pushing her food around the plate with her fork. "Maybe you'd better just take me home, Bert."

"If that's what you want, but can't I help?"

"Not really."

"Why don't you come home with me tonight?" he asked as he started the Lincoln.

She reminded herself of her kids. She concentrated on them. After all, she had lived over twenty years without Gordie. She could get along without him. "Arthur is waiting," she said.

"Oh yeah, Arthur is coming between us."

Was there something to come between? She glanced at Bert's profile. Should she ask him to spend the night? Did she want to be held or be alone? The headlights caught movement and Bert slammed on the brakes as a doe leaped onto the road. Another followed close behind, took the blacktop in three bounds, and was gone into the blackness on the other side. Bert resumed driving slowly through the night. Many a car and deer had been destroyed on these roads. Kate's accelerated heartbeat subsided. She didn't want to see anything die. The Lincoln brushed the white pines along her drive.

"Wish you'd let me help," Bert said, putting the car in park and turning off the engine.

Arthur's bark filled the silence as he strained against the chain attaching his collar to the barn.

"All right, Bert, stay with me tonight. Just don't ask questions. Please?"

When Bert was sleeping quietly with one arm thrown over her, she slipped out from under the weight and got into the other bed. She wasn't sorry she had asked him to stay. She was aware her aggressiveness had startled him. She had been using sex to forget, to push Gordie to the back of her mind. She lay alone with hands under her head until exhaustion put her thoughts to sleep.

When Brad called Pat, she couldn't quite hide her surprise and the unease accompanying it. "Sorry I missed seeing you and Gordie before you left," she

92

said. Something was terribly wrong here, she thought, and as Brad talked a funk dropped over her like a blanket. Brad was worried about Kate's state of mind, her need to talk this grief out, her driving alone four hundred miles next weekend. "I can't get away next weekend, Brad, but I'll go see Kate today. Brad, I'm so sorry." How did you address something like AIDS to those who are afflicted with it?

"I know, Pat."

When she hung up, she sat quietly for a few minutes with the Sunday paper lying next to her. Then she sighed and picked up the phone to punch in Kate's number. If Kate didn't answer, she'd go anyway. She had to reassure herself of Kate's ability to survive this shock.

Hanging up after listening to twenty rings, Pat headed for the lake. She was having difficulty coping with one disaster after another. Her own problems were eclipsed by Kate's, and she was a little weary of it all. If this latest tragedy overwhelmed her, what must it be doing to Kate and Gordie and Brad? The thought of what Gordie faced was not something she wanted to think of right now.

The past week had been difficult enough. How did you get thirteen- and fourteen-year-old kids to want to read, to write a complete sentence? The real problem, if she admitted it, was having no one with whom to share the day or the food or the bed. She was growing morose and thin and horny.

Arthur greeted her frantically, and when Pat unsnapped the chain from his collar he fell on his nose in the sand. Panting and coughing from his efforts to free himself by self-strangulation, he jumped on her. She pushed him away two or three times with her knee. Then he sat at her feet while she told him what a good dog he was.

Pat noted the missing bike, walked down to the lake with Arthur exuberantly dashing before her, running back every few feet to be assured she was following. She climbed onto the pier sections. Still wondering what she could say to lighten Kate's burden, she waited for her return.

The lake, nearly empty of boats, fed her loneliness. Glinting in the sunlight as it had in July or August, still there was something different about it. Its abandonment by speedboats, sailboats, canoes and the summer people must make the fishermen jubilant. She should have brought her fishing equipment, should have left it here.

Arthur gamboled up and down the shoreline. She started down the beach with him, her footprints clear in the sand. It was one of those golden September days. Several cottages down the beach she heard Kate calling and turned back. Arthur raced past her nearly knocking her over.

"This dog needs manners," Pat said, studying Kate's face, attempting to read it.

"I couldn't believe you were really here," Kate said, examining Pat in turn. "What's up?" Why was she here on this Sunday afternoon?

Pat lifted herself onto the pier sections again. The sun offered a warm and soothing hand. "Brad called me, Kate. He was worried about you." Why beat around the bush?

Kate leaned against the sections. She met Pat's questioning gaze. "I'm all right. *I* don't have AIDS." The words were bitter.

94

"That means you're all right?" Pat asked sharply. How to break down this resistance? Should she? Maybe it was holding Kate together.

Kate looked at the lake. She didn't know how she felt. She didn't want to feel. "I'm going to see him next weekend."

"I know. Brad told me."

"You know everything then," Kate remarked in a low voice.

"He told me about Gordie."

"Did he tell you Gordie didn't feel well in August, but he didn't want to spoil the fun by telling me?" Her voice shook with emotion.

Pat paled at the intensity of Kate's words and tone. "No, he didn't tell me. I'm so sorry, Kate."

Kate contemplated Pat, and the anger drained away slowly, taking her defenses with it. "So am I." Smiling tensely, she touched Pat's arm. "Thanks for coming. I nearly called you myself yesterday."

Later, pushing around the food on her plate, Kate knew she had to eat. She took a bite, chewed until it turned into a lump and slid down her throat.

As Pat watched her, her own appetite shriveled. "You should have called me."

"I've always felt if you don't know something it hasn't happened. I realize that's stupid. I couldn't say it anyway." Her voice was so quiet Pat strained to hear it. "When my mother died, it was hours before I called anyone." Not Gordie, not Tom, not he funeral home. Bert, had it been Bert who had taken her mother from the hospital? "You know one of the things I felt, Pat?" She looked from her plate to meet Pat's dark eyes. "I felt humiliated for her, because she succumbed to death. I didn't want to tell anyone.

95

I didn't think she'd want them to know." Kate heard herself and it sounded crazy even to her, but she felt it again. "My mother was such a dignified person," she explained. "If there's any dignity in dying, she managed it."

"I haven't lost any family yet," Pat said into the quiet.

Kate resisted replying that she would soon enough. She said instead, "How have you been? How is school going?"

Pat launched into a monologue on the grammatical abuses of her students so clever that Kate laughed.

For a year after her mother had died Kate had tried never to let herself become too fatigued. She had drunk wine in the evenings until she'd slept, but if she became exhausted and wakeful, she relived the ambulance chase, the death scene. Now she opened a bottle of dry red Mondavi. Did one ever become comfortable with death?

Recalling how Kate had disliked even the death of a fish, Pat drank little and observed Kate carefully. "I wish I could go with you next weekend," she said.

"I wish you could, too, but I'll be okay. I'll stop and see the girls on the way or maybe on the way back."

"Will you tell them?"

"I don't know."

In bed, the room black and silent, both women lay listening to each other breathe. "Last night I frightened Bert," Kate said into the darkness.

"Oh, how?"

"I tried to forget it all and used him for that

96

purpose, but I couldn't tell him about Gordie. I couldn't tell him why I was acting the way I was."

"Did it work?"

"No, I just didn't want to be alone, I guess."

"Do you want to be alone now?"

Kate paused, listening to the rapid beating of her heart. "No."

Thinking only that there might be comfort in the contact, Pat slid into bed with Kate, put her arms around her and drew her close. She felt the soft curves, the smooth skin, smelled Kate's hair, and desire nearly buried her good intentions. She fended off the need to run her hands over Kate's body. She knew she wouldn't sleep tonight, not like this.

Kate tensed at first and then, as her heartbeat settled back to normal, the tension turned into relaxation. She'd held her daughters during their bad times. This wasn't so much different. Feeling the warmth emanating from Pat's body, she put an arm over her. How unlike a man she was, Kate thought — not bony or bristly like Bert, or heavy and muscular like Tom. A woman's body was more comfortable. She moved closer.

Pat tightened her arms around Kate, then lightly massaged her back with one hand.

"Mmm. Feels good. You can stop that in an hour or two," Kate murmured. Sleep was overtaking her. She liked this closeness, she realized, sniffing Pat's skin which smelled as fresh and clean as the outdoors.

Pat held Kate through most of the night, slipping out of her bed when she noticed the sky lightening.

* * * * *

97

Monday's batch of mail included her letter packet and papers for Kate to sign and return to Tom regarding the divorce. Two of the letters stuck in her memory long after she answered them.

Dear Jane,
*   I'm 16 years old. I know I'm gay, but I don't know what to do about it. My parents are prominent in the community, and they would never understand. I don't want to shame them. And I'm afraid of AIDS. I play a good game pretending with the other guys. I've even got a girlfriend, but I really want my best boyfriend. I can't talk to the minister, so don't suggest that. I've even thought of suicide. What can I do?*

Too bad Pat didn't have this kid in her class. At least he knew how to write. But the mention of suicide made Kate sit up straight in her chair. Too many kids killed themselves these days.

Dear Son,
*   Go to the local Department of Human services. You can receive free counseling there. Being gay isn't easy, but it's a lifestyle you can learn to live with. Perhaps someday your parents will accept it, too. But now it's imperative that you learn to accept yourself. Don't consider suicide. Please write again and let me know how you are doing. Use condoms if you have sex but know that condoms are not*

always safe against AIDS. It is important you do not exchange bodily fluids with someone else.

In the same batch was another letter from a woman who could have been the boy's mother.

Dear Jane,
  I think my son is homosexual, and I'm scared to death for him. He's such a bright boy with so much potential. I'm afraid of AIDS. I'm even afraid he might take his own life. His father will never understand. How can I help him?

There was hope here, Kate realized. The woman was tuned in to her kid.

Dear Mother,
  First you have to accept your son as a homosexual. Perhaps you can suggest counseling at the department of human services for both of you. With safe sex AIDS can be prevented. The boy's father would surely rather have his son alive and a homosexual. If possible get a dialogue going between you and your son. Let him know you accept him as he is, any way he is. And please let me know how it goes.

Why had all this information come too late for Gordie? She answered a few more letters and then took Arthur for a walk, before going for a bike ride herself. She had a lot to sandwich in this week if she was going to leave for Gordie's house Friday morning.

The leaves were turning, rustling in the slight wind, blowing across the road, crunching under her feet. She dawdled on the walk and on the ride. Within her was a core of serenity wrapped around her own core of determination that hadn't been there yesterday. The unselfish caring Pat had offered her last night would get her through the remainder of the week.

Nearly undone by her night with Kate, Pat sought out Karen, an old friend, and asked her to dinner Wednesday evening. During the days before Gail, Pat and Karen had been occasional lovers. In the darkened restaurant Pat studied this woman, whom she hadn't seen or talked to for at least a year. Karen was attractive, well built. For that Pat was grateful, but at this point she'd probably have jumped into bed with her no matter what she looked like.

Karen said, "I hear you and Gail broke up."

She wouldn't be here if they hadn't. Was that unfair? She'd been shit on enough in the past few months. "That's not news, Karen."

"I work with Joy, did you know that?"

Pat's heart palpitated, and her drink stopped halfway to her mouth. "No, I didn't."

Silence. Then: "I thought that might be why you wanted to go to dinner, to ask about Joy." Karen's voice sounded uncertain.

"No, Karen, that's not why." She was just horny

as hell was all, but she couldn't say that — or could she? She grinned slowly and saw the understanding in Karen's eyes. While they made love, Pat recalled the feel of Kate's body against her own. Had Kate known what she had been doing to her? And then, unwillingly, unbidden, Gail crept into her thoughts, and she made love to Gail through Karen. Her hands moved gently over the silky skin, caressing slowly. Softly kissing Karen's lips, running her tongue around the inside of her mouth, then moving to her neck and shoulders and breasts, Pat made love to three women through one. In return the rhythmic movement of Karen's fingers freed Pat from the terrible aching desire in her loins and she responded with long, shuddering spasms. Afterward she held Karen quietly, not wanting to talk, sorry she wished Karen were someone else but thankful for her willingness.

"Don't forget my number," Karen remarked the next morning.

"I won't," Pat promised. As the door closed behind Karen, it dawned on Pat that she had forgotten to ask about Joy. Good. Why torment herself? Humming while stuffing papers in her briefcase, she readied herself for school.

Barb passed her in the hall at school, stopped and pounded her on the shoulder. "How's it going, babe?"

Pat grinned at her, was glad to see her. She knew Barb would always be there if she needed her again — maybe not understanding but wanting to help. "Pretty good, actually."

"Glad to hear it. Poker at my place Saturday night?"

"Mind if I ask Karen Brown to come?"

"Why would I mind?" Barb's face broke into a big smile. "Things are looking up then?"

"Sometimes up, sometimes down," Pat replied, thinking of Gordie and Kate.

Thursday night Pat and Kate talked on the phone. They exchanged no real information, only small warnings. "Drive carefully. "Take care of yourself."

Gordie had restored an old house in Lockerbie Square, downtown Indianapolis. Kate was charmed by the house with its beautiful hardwood floors and bright rugs, Brad's paintings on the walls, the furniture comfortable and attractive. "I love it, Gordie."

"Well, it's what I do best," Gordie said immodestly. "I'm the best architect in the city and a damn good interior designer." He smiled faintly at her. He had lost more weight, but she noticed no other signs of ill health.

"Why are you looking at me like that?" He glanced accusingly at Brad. The secret was no more.

The three of them stood on the lovely oriental rug in front of the fireplace, drinks in hand to celebrate Kate's visit. They looked at one another and then away.

"She guessed," Brad explained after an interminable silence.

Gordie said, "Let's not discuss it tonight. Okay? We're going to have the best meal you've ever eaten, Katie. And tomorrow we're going to Brown County to see the hills and shop in the Nashville stores."

The food at the restaurant, a few miles north of

Indianapolis in Carmel, was everything Gordie had promised. Kate's vegetables were delicate morsels, the shrimp scampi prepared to melt in her mouth, the freshly baked rolls and croissants offered one at a time by the tuxedoed waiter. Truly elegant dining.

They laughed together as they had in the summer until Kate said, "You could have told me, Gordie. It hasn't stopped the laughter."

He smiled wryly at her. "I can always count on you as a good audience, Katie."

They sang during the thirty minutes it took to drive back to Gordie's. The years dropped away and Kate remembered their dad singing whenever he was driving, the rest of the family joining in. She and Gordie smiled at each other as they sang *Carolina In The Morning,* one of their father's favorites. He had sung it every morning when shaving.

The next day they traveled the back roads to Nashville, Indiana. Kate marveled at the hills that appeared south of Paragon. The road curved through the Sweetwater, Cordry Lake district — reservoirs with cottages lining their steep banks. When they were on Salt Creek Road with hills on both sides and a valley between, Kate wondered at the beauty. Salt Creek wound along beside them, buzzards circled slowly above the landscape. Their travels took them to Brown County State Park and the town of Nashville with its antiques and arts and craft stores. As they drove through the park, the tree-covered hills falling off steeply as far as the eye could see made Kate think they were in the Smokies.

"Thought Indiana was all flat, didn't you?" Gordie asked.

"I did, I really did. Why didn't you tell me about this? It's spectacular."

"Well, we didn't do a whole lot of talking as I remember," Gordie replied. "I don't know why exactly. Do you?"

Sunlight slanted through brilliant foliage. "I guess we were just too busy going our separate ways," Kate commented, thinking about the years past.

"A pity. I miss the water, though, the lakes of Wisconsin. This is pretty much a waterless state, and the northern two-thirds is nearly all flat farmland."

Later they had lunch at the Brown County Inn and toured the small shops of Nashville. The day was warm and sunny. Kate removed her jacket as they lounged on a bench in front of the courthouse to bask in the sun and watch people. She sneaked glances at Gordie. There were tired circles under his eyes.

"What do you want to do tonight, Katie?"

"Whatever you guys want to do."

"I'll stuff a turkey breast," Brad volunteered.

"Then we can smoke a joint and watch a tape or something."

Kate was startled. She had never smoked dope.

"What say we head back," Gordie suggested. "I've had enough people-watching. There's a cute guy over there, Brad." He nodded toward a young man in jogging shorts across the street. "Look at that ass."

Kate was also admiring that ass and she gave a short laugh. She and Brad exchanged smiles. She had taken a step into their world. It was interesting to be appraising the same bodies.

Relaxing that night after filling herself with Brad's good food, Kate sucked on a joint. A detached high took over her usual inner turmoil. Maybe she ought to do this more often, but where would she find marijuana in Waushara?

"Like this, Katie," Gordie instructed with a laugh. His cheeks caved in as he pulled on the reefer.

"Is this what you do every night?"

"We often share one before bed."

"I never smoked dope before," Kate admitted.

"No kidding," Brad said.

"Tom was a little straight and narrow," she explained.

"What's happening with Tom?" Gordie asked, exhaling loudly, handing the joint to Brad.

"He's started divorce proceedings. Didn't I tell you?"

"No shit. That's too bad, Katie." Gordie's expression turned into a frown.

She laughed. He had looked so happy a minute ago. "It's okay, Gordie. Remember, I didn't want to marry him in the first place." Did she really feel that little about ending twenty-four years of matrimony? Maybe she could use some therapy. There had to be deep feelings somewhere.

"It can't be that easy." He leaned forward, his forearms on his thighs, his hands hanging between his legs, his face a mask of concern.

"Let's not get serious about me, Gordie. My life isn't all that bad."

"And Bert? How's Bert? Are you still doing it?" The frown was replaced with a huge grin. The big "it."

"Yeah, we're still doing it, if it's any of your

business, which it isn't." Feeling carefree, she laughed again and inhaled deeply.

"And Pat? You been to bed with her yet? That's your best bet right there."

Kate exhaled and coughed. "Come on, Gordie, you big dope." But was it so far-fetched? "As a matter of fact, we did spend one night in the same bed."

"I knew it," Gordie said with satisfaction.

"She was just comforting me, nothing happened."

"You gotta be kidding," Gordie said.

"Nope, I'm not."

Brad smiled sadly. Kate raised her eyebrows and offered him a wry smile. He shrugged.

"Must have driven her nuts," Gordie commented, glancing from one to the other. "No tears tonight, you guys. I don't have time or energy for tears."

Driving to Beth's apartment Monday, Kate reflected over the weekend, the miles flashing by unnoticed as she relived conversations. They never had discussed anything serious for long, and Gordie refused to talk about himself and how he felt. She had never been alone with Brad long enough to talk about Gordie either. She would see Gordie at Thanksgiving, he had promised, as he hugged her before she left. She had asked Brad to come with him for the holiday, but Brad had said he always spent that day with his family. Funny, she hadn't thought of Brad as having a family separate from Gordie. She had asked Gordie if he objected to her telling the girls, and he had asked her to wait.

VII

Intermittently over the weekend, Pat thought of Kate and wondered how her visit with Gordie and Brad was progressing. She played poker with Barb and Sandy on Saturday night, taking Karen with her, and Barb jokingly threatened to ban Pat from future poker games if she didn't lose occasionally. Karen spent the weekend at Pat's apartment.

While stocking up on sale items Sunday, Karen and Pat ran into Gail and Joy at the Target Mall. Pat was throwing paper products into her cart when she glanced up and met Gail's eyes. She felt a jolt akin to an electric shock and made her face go blank. Gail looked at Karen and then Pat, while Pat gripped a four-pack of Northern toilet tissue.

Pat spoke first. "How've you been?" She searched Gail's face for signs of unhappiness.

Gail glanced at Joy, smiled slightly, then turned back to Pat. "Real good. And you?"

"Wonderful," she lied. "You remember Karen Brown, don't you?"

"Sure." Gail nodded at Karen in acknowledgement. "I don't think you've met Joy, have you?"

"No. Karen says she works with you," Pat said to Joy. She saw Joy close up for the first time. If she just weren't so damn good-looking. A picture of Joy and Gail in bed together in a tangle of limbs suddenly appeared in Pat's mind. She felt a twist of pain like a knife being turned. Her vision temporarily blurred. Goddammit she had to get hold of herself. She couldn't let Gail know how much it hurt.

Until then Karen and Joy had only nodded. All four were wary, like dogs stalking carefully around each other, waiting for the first snap of teeth. Pat forced herself to concentrate on what she was doing, which was crushing the toilet paper. As she threw it in the shopping cart, Joy stepped forward and extended her hand. Pat stared at Joy's hand as if it were something alien, then shook it firmly and met her eyes. Her eyes were hazel, the color of a trout stream, with flecks of gold. Were they mocking? She didn't think so. Joy was smiling, a friendly smile with a wonderfully sensuous mouth. Did she really think they could possibly be friends? Pat took her hand away, no longer disliking the woman.

108

She hadn't heard what Joy had said to her. "I beg your pardon?"

"I've been wanting to meet you." Joy looked amused. "See you at work Monday, Karen." Gail and Joy moved to another aisle.

Pat sighed, feeling sweat in her armpits and between her shoulder blades. Her muscles were so tight they were cramping. "Let's get out of here. Okay?"

"You all right, Pat?" Karen asked once they were back in Pat's Honda. "Want me to drive?"

"No, I'm all right." She studied Karen for the truth. "It showed?" she asked.

"No, you were terrific," Karen reassured her.

It had shown, she knew. Alone in her apartment that night she kept jumping up from the table where she was correcting papers. She couldn't let this affect her work, she told herself. She thought of Kate and started for the phone, then remembered Kate was in Indianapolis. When would she be home? She couldn't remember. Concentrate on Gordie, think of someone else's pain. Hers could be worse. What if she were dying? Maybe Gail would take care of her if she had a terminal illness. Fuck it. She finished grading papers, took a shower and went to bed, burying it all in sleep.

Arthur was thrilled to see Kate. He appeared to have grown in her absence. In the car he tried to crawl in her lap, and she held him back with a restraining hand on his collar. He smelled like the kennel and soon so did the interior of the Taurus.

His hair stuck to the plush upholstery. Choking but still struggling to reach her, he threw up on her arm. "Goddammit, Arthur." Letting go she reached for the Kleenex on the dash, wiped her arm and nearly drove off the road in the process. Arthur licked at the arm and wormed his front half under the steering wheel. "God, you stink."

Pat had said he needed to learn some manners. Maybe she ought to consult her on how to instill some into him. She'd call Pat tonight, see how things were going, let her know how Gordie and Brad were, ask when she could visit again for a few days.

She was anxious to be home. She had forced herself to stay with Beth two nights. Those two nights Sarah had stayed over, too, and she had tried to persuade Sarah to forgive her father, because she knew Sarah was miserable hating him. "What's the point, Sarah?" she had asked Monday night in bed. "You're hurting yourself so much, and in the end you're going to forgive him anyway. Don't let too much time go by." How did you tell someone so young how quickly time passed? "He could die accidentally, and then how would you feel? Guilty, that's how."

"Why are you defending him, Mom?" Sarah had asked sullenly.

"I'm not defending him, Sarah. It's you I care about. I know you love him, and he loves you. He didn't want to hurt you, you know that." For the first time, Kate had envied Tom's passion for this woman. It had to be powerful to have caused him to risk alienating his children. She would have liked to feel such a passion for someone. "Look, I think you need to talk this out."

"You mean a shrink?"

"Some kind of therapist. Will you go?"

"Who's going to pay for it?"

"Don't worry about that. I'll see to it." She'd ask Tom to pay, of course. It would be the least he could do.

With mindless joy Arthur dashed around the yard. Perhaps he had feared she wouldn't return for him. The humming refrigerator greeted Kate when she entered the house. She had picked up both letter packets on her way home. Because of Arthur, she hadn't stopped at the funeral home. She didn't feel like talking to Bert right now anyway. She would really like to talk to Pat.

The radio filling the house with a Brandenburg Concerto, Kate walked out on the porch, left the door open, sat in one of the chairs. The lake was the color of pewter under a cloudy sky. A cold rain was in the offing.

Pat was delighted to hear Kate's voice. "I wondered when you were getting back."

"I was hoping maybe you could come visit this weekend."

"Why don't you visit me? It's your turn."

"You've forgotten Arthur."

"How could anyone forget Arthur? Bring him with you. What is he now — eleven or twelve weeks old? He can sleep in the kitchen. How was your visit with Gordie and Brad?"

"I'll tell you when I get there. Okay?"

When she talked to Bert later, the dismay in his voice annoyed Kate. "But I thought we could spend the weekend together, Kate. You just got back and you're going away again?"

"Yep." Did he think their occasional intimacy gave him first dibs on her time? But of course he did. That was the nature of man. He'd driven four stakes around her. He just hadn't registered the claim at the courthouse yet. And he wasn't going to, either. Then she relented. "Maybe the following weekend, Bert." She had never thought she'd be in such demand after having been discarded by Tom.

"Can we go out to dinner tonight?" he asked.

If dinner would be just that, if she could come home and get some things done afterwards, but he'd want bed and something had happened to her desire. She hadn't known it was so fragile. Tell him. "Bert, if we just could eat and talk and then I could get back here and do some things. I have so much to do this week. Stacks of letters to answer."

His disappointment made her sad for him. "Sure. Whatever you want, Kate. Dinner is better than nothing."

"Oh Bert, don't play the martyr."

He laughed. "I'm not getting anywhere, huh?"

Parking outside Pat's apartment building, Kate grabbed Arthur's leash before opening the car door. He was growing rapidly to match his feet. His appearance hadn't changed, just his size. He tangled the leash around her legs as he tried to get out of the car.

Pat appeared at her side and took the leash from her hand, gave it a jerk, then two, accompanied by a reprimand. *"No,* Arthur." Arthur sat at Pat's feet. "Good dog," she praised him.

A little disconcerted at the discipline, Kate turned to watch her. "That's how you do it? A jerk and a praise?"

"Well, only if he does what you want him to do. We'll work on it." She grinned at Kate. Arthur started off, only to be hauled back by Pat. A cold raw wind tunneled down the street, a harbinger of winter. "Let's go inside."

In the warmth of the apartment Pat removed Arthur's leash and handed him a rawhide bone. "Something to keep him busy while we talk." Arthur tried to dig a hole in the carpet to bury the bone. "No," Pat rebuked him and to Kate's surprise, Arthur dropped to the floor and chewed on the bone.

She and Pat moved to the kitchen. "Smells good," Kate commented.

"Just chicken in wine with some vegetables."

"Sounds good."

"Are you eating again?" Pat asked casually.

"I'll eat tonight."

Pat turned from the stove to appraise Kate, who had lost weight and looked tired. She had hidden her excitement at Kate's arrival by taking control of Arthur. Now she concealed her pleasure in the other woman's presence with her concern. "Are you okay, Kate?"

"Yeah, I'm fine. It's just that I've been so busy. You look good." Kate spoke impulsively. "How about a hug. I could use one."

Pat hesitated, then held Kate to her for a few

seconds. "You always smell so good," she murmured, her face in Kate's hair. It was an effort to keep her fingers out of it.

"So do you," Kate replied. "You usually smell like fresh air."

Pat laughed a little. She stepped back, still feeling Kate's warmth against her.

Kate touched a curl that was wrapped around Pat's ear and smiled. "I like your hair. Did you get another perm?"

Pat nodded, her eyes fixed on Kate's. She said nothing, recognizing the attraction here for what it was. It was no longer just friendship for her. She wasn't sure about Kate's feelings. She doubted Kate would acknowledge more than friendship right now even if she felt more.

Kate broke the tension. "Let me help." And as she set the table, she talked. "I couldn't get Gordie to tell me anything that mattered. He's ignoring it, I think. Maybe that's the best way to go on with his life." Her voice broke on the last words.

Pat leaned against the wall next to the stove with arms crossed. "Maybe," she said after considering the thought. "You can't just lie down and die, and you probably don't want to. Instead you probably want to do all the things you never had a chance to do."

Kate poured the wine and drank some. She studied the liquid, swirled it in the glass. She was drinking too much, she knew, still using wine to sleep. "I like your apartment," she said. "It's a perfect size."

"For one person," Pat added, smiling wryly.

"How is it going for you?"

Pat faced the stove, dumped some vegetables in with the chicken, covered the pan. She leaned against the wall again and looked at Kate. "I've been seeing an old friend, keeping busy at school, and spending time with Barb and Sandy." She reached for her wine glass and drank half of it.

"And?" Kate encouraged.

"And then I saw Gail with Joy in Target on Sunday. I nearly came unglued, Kate. I can see why Gail wants Joy, too. That doesn't help." But she didn't really want Gail back, did she? Not the way things had been between them. She just wasn't ready to see Gail with someone else.

Why couldn't people be happy with what they had, Kate wondered. Tom wanting Nancy when he was married to Kate, Pat still wanting Gail when Gail wanted Joy, Bert wanting her when she didn't know what or whom she wanted. Jesus, everything was so complicated. People were so damn perverse.

Pat removed the pan from the heat and uncovered it for a few minutes. The rice was still cooking. "You're looking thin, Kate."

"I don't know why. I was well fed, certainly at Gordie's." Kate's smile was teasing, lighting up her face and eyes, taking away the tiredness. Pat wore jeans and a sweater that outlined her body, and Kate's scrutiny was frank and admiring. "We can't all look like you do."

"What does that mean?" Pat was taken aback.

Kate shrugged. "You have a nice figure." Especially the breasts, Kate thought, watching the sweater rise and fall and wishing she were as large. She had always wanted to be bigger than she was.

"Sometimes I worry about you," Pat said, rattled by the compliment. She turned back to the stove to escape Kate's eyes.

"You have enough worries of your own, it seems to me."

Arthur ambled into the kitchen, the rawhide bone in his mouth. He dropped it on the floor and whined.

"I forgot to feed the poor animal," Kate said, getting Arthur's dish and dog food out of the paper bag she had brought with her. "I keep wondering why Gordie forced this dog on me. He doesn't have a dog."

With rude noises Arthur gobbled his food.

"When we get through training Arthur, you'll be glad you have him. You'll see."

"It's a little like having a child again. I'm not sure I want that."

Pat set their food on the table and they sat across from each other. "I'm glad you're here, Kate."

"Good. That makes two of us."

Three hours later they were still drinking wine and talking. Arthur had had his evening walk and was stretched at Kate's feet, his feet twitching in a dream. "Creepy looking, isn't he? He sleeps with his eyes open." Kate stared down at the dog.

"He's dreaming of chasing something, I'll bet. Wouldn't you like to have the life of a dog? So uncomplicated." The wine must be getting to her, Pat mused.

"So boring, you mean. Imagine not being able to read or write or talk."

"No agonies, only adoring love for one's mistress or master. Think of that."

"You know, my life before I moved to the lake

116

seems eons ago, almost like it never was. I keep wondering if there's something wrong with me that I don't feel more of a sense of loss." Kate's smile was bemused.

"You were feeling it when I met you," Pat reminded her.

"That's true but now it's like I've always lived this way. Maybe it's because I haven't seen Tom or my old friends or where we lived for so long. They don't seem real anymore."

"I wish Gail didn't seem real," Pat commented dryly. Then, trying to be honest, she added, "I think maybe I just miss having someone around to share things with. I know it takes time. I just wish the time would hurry up and pass. Knowing you has helped, Kate."

Kate had questions she wanted to ask but had never known how to work into the conversation. Now was not the time, though, to ask Pat what it had been like when she realized she preferred females to males, how that realization had changed her life, and if it had made it very difficult. It was none of her business, of course. Her curiosity had always gotten her into trouble. But how could she understand Pat and not know her past? She couldn't. "I guess we've helped each other then. You were like a life jacket last summer when we met." She finished off her wine. "I have to go to sleep, Pat. I can't stay awake any longer."

"So do I. You take the bed. I'll sleep out here."

"I'm not going to take your bed. Why can't we both sleep in it? It's double." Kate raised her eyebrows in question, interested in this turn of events.

117

"Don't ask or argue, Kate. Just let me sleep out here." Pat wouldn't meet her eyes.

"I promise to stay on my side of the bed," Kate said.

Pat only shook her head. She recalled that sleepless night spent holding Kate and the desperate longing she had felt. "My apartment, my rules," she said.

Kate shrugged. "Okay, but you make me feel unwanted."

Pat snorted, knowing Kate was teasing her. "Look, I didn't sleep at all that night we spent in the same bed. I want to sleep tonight."

Amused and a little unnerved, Kate stared at her. "I'll consider that a compliment," she said, "but if you change your mind, feel free to climb in with me."

In her dreams that night Kate's mother made a rare appearance to tell her Gordie was dying, and Kate was so glad to see her she said it was all right if that was the only way she could talk to her. She tried to put her arms around her mother but couldn't feel her. She awoke and lay in the dark, not knowing where she was at first and feeling as if she had betrayed Gordie somehow. She missed the nights when her mother came alive in her sleep. She was forgetting her face, her voice, her laugh.

On the couch Pat slept restlessly. Her dream was the same variation on being caught and trying to think up excuses for why she was in bed with another girl, and she made herself wake up. After all these years why was she still dreaming like this? She never had been caught in the first place, but it must have been a valid fear when she had been living at home and at college.

She threw off the blanket and padded to the kitchen to drink some water, her throat parched from the wine. The gap between the bedroom door and the floor was lit. She knocked and stuck her head in. Kate was reading.

"Hi, come on in." She put her book face down on the bedspread. "You can't sleep either?"

"Bad dreams," Pat explained, sitting cross-legged on the end of the bed.

"Me, too," Kate said. "Only mine were good and bad. I got to see my mother again. I can never touch her, though. I either can't reach her or she doesn't feel like anything to me."

"That was the bad part?"

"No. I was so glad to see her I didn't care that she came to tell me Gordie was dying, if that was the only way I could see her. I suppose it means I would rather she were alive than Gordie, and that's not right."

"What? That you loved your mother more than your brother?"

"No, because she lived her life and Gordie should have a lot more years left." Kate thought about this for a short time. Was that what it really had meant? Probably not. She put it away to consider later. "And yours?"

Embarrassed, Pat laughed. "You don't want to hear mine." Meaning she didn't want to tell hers.

"Come on. Turnabout's fair play."

Pat flushed.

"Okay, you don't have to tell," Kate said, smiling.

"I often dream I'm a kid again and being caught in bed with another girl, and I can never think of a reasonable excuse to tell whoever caught me — my

119

parents or dorm counselor. This time I told my dad there was a snake in the other bed." She laughed softly, her eyes on the bedspread as she talked. Then she met Kate's eyes.

"Did you ever get caught?" Kate asked, curious.

"No, never, but it must have worried me."

Here was the opening Kate had been waiting for. "What was it like, realizing you were gay? Was it very difficult?"

To get comfortable and to avoid eye contact, Pat stretched out at the end of the bed. She cradled her head in her hands and stared at the ceiling. There was a cobweb in one of the corners.

"You don't have to answer that," Kate said quickly. "I shouldn't have asked."

"I don't mind answering it," Pat replied quietly. "I'm not sure I can give an accurate answer, though. The older kids I admired and had crushes on were always girls. I should have guessed when I was thirteen. When I was eighteen, my college roommate climbed in bed with me." She had taken to it like a dog to a bone, Pat reflected, but how had she felt about it? Had it been easy? No, it wasn't an easy way to live. "I haven't come out except to my friends. I can't afford to lose my job. I don't even know if my parents know. They've stopped urging me to marry, so maybe they do."

She felt anger grow as she talked and had to remind herself Kate was not the enemy. Neither, of course, were her parents, but she knew how they would have reacted had she ever tried to tell them how much she had loved Gail. Imagining the expression on her mother's face, she nearly laughed. Then she sobered. Being gay wasn't funny or fun.

She'd like to raise a fist to society, if she only could. Why should she have to hide her sexual orientation from anyone? Why was it considered queer? Now she was so agitated she'd never get back to sleep.

Kate leaned back on the pillows as she watched Pat. She wanted to know what she was thinking. She asked.

Pat sighed. "How can you understand, Kate?"

"Try me."

"I don't feel I'm different from other people. I resent having to hide being gay. If the school board suspected, they'd find a way to throw me out on my ear. I don't like being thought of as a pervert. I'm not a pervert." She heard the anger in her voice.

"You're one of the finest people I know," Kate said quietly.

The anger was spent and Pat turned, propped herself up on an elbow, and grinned at Kate. "I wouldn't go so far as to say that."

"I would," Kate said with a gentle smile. "Friendly, helpful, kind, thoughtful and intelligent, to boot."

"I sound like a Girl Scout. You're embarrassing me."

"Maybe it's time someone did."

"I'm going back to my couch."

Kate slept late the next morning. Pat and Arthur were gone when she got up. She looked out the window at another gray, windy day and wondered what they would do with it.

But Pat had plans for the weekend. She and

121

Arthur returned full of energy. Arthur jumped on Kate and Pat jerked him down and scolded him. "Put your knee into his chest or face or whatever is handy when he jumps on you, and tell him no."

Kate was momentarily annoyed. Whose dog was this anyway? Then she remembered her resolve to turn Arthur into an obedient dog.

In the afternoon Pat showed Kate Northland and they drove to nearby Andersen to do some shopping. Afterward they returned home to feed and walk Arthur before going out to dinner.

"Want to play poker?" Pat asked, looking up from her salad, noticing Kate eating, not toying with, her food.

"Sure, why not?" Kate replied. "I haven't played often, though. I have trouble remembering whether three of a kind beats a straight."

Pat swallowed a laugh. "I'll make a note with combinations in their winning order. Remember Barb and Sandy?" Kate nodded. "Well, I usually play poker with them on Saturday nights. It's kind of fun, but we don't have to do it."

"I want to," Kate said eagerly. She found the idea fascinating, so different from playing bridge with her friends in Orion.

In welcome Barb slapped both Pat and Kate on their shoulders and handed each a Miller Lite. "Good to see you, Kate. Watch out for the poker queen here," she said, gesturing at Pat. "I warned her she can't play if she wins all the time." If Barb was surprised by Kate's presence, she hid it well.

Sandy came down the hall and urged them to sit at the kitchen table. "Anyone else coming?" Sandy asked, setting bowls of potato chips and pretzels on opposite corners of the table.

Kate had only seen Barb and Sandy at the lake. Then as now, she had been struck by their resemblance. They both had short, straight, dark brown hair; they were tall, large-boned and athletic-looking. She thought they looked like sisters, dressed as they were in jeans and flannel shirts.

"I don't know," Pat said, when she realized Sandy was addressing her. "I didn't ask anyone. Did you?"

"No. I thought maybe Karen might come."

"Oh, not tonight," Pat replied, flushing slightly. "I should have asked her. I just didn't think of it."

Kate was aware of the polite curiosity of the other two women. It amused her, but appeared to embarrass Pat. She wanted to reassure them that she and Pat were only friends, if just to relieve Pat's discomfort.

After a few hands, the money started stacking up in front of Pat. Kate observed her closely to see how she did it. She decided Pat played cards the way she sailed, recklessly close to the wind, and the winning edge was her ability to make her face expressionless. She recalled thinking last summer that Pat's face could be read like a book. Had she wanted it read?

Pat turned and grinned at her. She questioned Kate with her eyes, her eyebrows elevated slightly. Was Kate having a good time?

Kate nodded and smiled wryly.

Barb said, "Well, you're doing it again, Pat, taking all the money. Why don't you stop teaching and turn pro? Why do we play this with her week after week, Sandy?"

123

"Habit?" Sandy suggested.

"Stupidity," Barb concluded.

"You beat me at bowling," Pat said, her face flushed. A smile tugged at one corner of her mouth, her eyes glowed with warmth and humor.

"That's true," Barb said, pointing at her with a pretzel, "but you're a terrible bowler. Are you comparing my poker playing to your bowling?"

"I wouldn't have the nerve," Pat said. "We can play something else if you want. How about Authors or Old Maid?"

"Whose deal?" Barb asked, snorting.

Kate's insides were swimming in beer. She'd spend the night beating a path to the john. She decided to try Pat's game and bluffed with a pair of nines and won the pot.

"See, I don't win all the time," Pat commented. But when the evening wrapped up, she had won most of the money. On the drive to her apartment she asked Kate if she had been bluffing when she cleaned up the few pots she had.

"Were you?" Kate asked in return, glancing at Pat in the darkness of the car, remembering how happy and at ease she had appeared at Barb and Sandy's.

"I can't answer that," Pat replied, flashing a white grin.

"You mean you won't, so neither will I." Then she added, "You play cards like you sail."

"What does that mean?"

"You know what *that* means."

Kate left Sunday as the sun set, smearing the western horizon with faint reddish-yellow colors. She watched Pat become smaller in her rear view mirror, missing her company already. After packing Arthur in the back seat, she had given Pat a hug and felt Pat's arms tighten around her. Pat had murmured something. "What?" Kate had asked.

"It's nice to have you around," Pat had repeated, her eyes solemn.

"We'll have to do this again soon," Kate had suggested, the corners of her eyes crinkling. They looked dark blue in the fading light. The wind parted her reddish hair and blew it in her face. She brushed it away absently and gave Pat a parting smile.

Pat crossed her arms against the cold, rubbed the sole of one shoe against the curb and glanced down at it. She hated to see Kate leave.

VIII

Three weeks later Gordie called on a Tuesday night near the end of October. The leaves were gone from the deciduous trees, except the oaks which stubbornly clung to shriveled russet leaves rattling in the fall winds.

Kate had been reading in front of the fireplace, actually enjoying an evening alone with a good book. "Gordie, how are you?" she asked, not alarmed. He often called just to talk.

"Not good, sis. I had to talk to someone. Sorry."

"What's wrong?" Now she was alarmed.

126

"I got caught."

"Caught?"

"With my pockets stuffed with ties."

"What are you talking about, Gordie?"

"I have to confess, Katie. I'm a shoplifter."

"Jesus, Gordie, you called to tell me that." She didn't really believe him. "What happened?"

"The store manager offered to let me go if I re-designed the inside of his office and gave him a blow job."

"Gordie," Kate said threateningly, laughing in spite of herself. "You're lying."

"Me lie? Actually, I thought you might want to come down for Halloween."

"Why? Have you got something different planned?"

Gordie sighed. "Brad tested positive a week ago, Katie. I can hardly stand this shit. It's so goddam unfair."

"How is he handling it?" Her brain must have been numb. It resisted this new information.

"He's weird, Katie. He sits in front of the TV and stares at it. He never watched much TV before. He was always too busy painting when he wasn't working."

Why did he want her to come, she wondered. But she'd go any time. All he had to do was invite her. "Okay, Gordie. It'll be good to get away. How are you? Really."

"I'm stuffing my face with vitamins, getting lots of sleep, not drinking too much. I'm doing all right. I haven't even had a cold yet."

"That's next weekend, Gordie," she said, glancing at the calendar next to the phone.

127

"I know. Bring your broom. We're going to trick or treat."

Gordie's idea of trick or treating was to go from door to door with an empty glass. When asked if he wanted candy, he said, "Hell no." Then they were invited in and everyone shared a drink.

Kate begged off the liquor after the fifth house. Her mind off in left field, she said whatever came out of it. Gordie and Brad were raving drunk, laughing and stumbling when they rounded the block and found themselves in front of Gordie's house. The night was nasty, cold and drizzly, and Kate was worried about both men. They were too vulnerable to colds, to flu, to anything.

Gordie and Brad fell asleep on the couch in the living room. Hoping the room wouldn't spin when she lay down, Kate left them there and went to bed.

The morning sun streaming in the bedroom windows wakened her. Brad and Gordie were no longer in the living room. After she'd consumed a cup of coffee, she went out into the bright morning. She walked to Monument Circle and back. Sodden leaves were piled along buildings and in the gutters, testimony to last night's rain. Gordie was shuffling around the sunlit kitchen when she let herself back in the house.

"How do you feel?" she asked.

His hair stood in spikes, framing a wan face. "Don't shout, Katie, for God's sake," he whispered. "I feel like shit. Why do you look so good?"

"I feel good, that's why. Want me to fix you something to eat?"

He made a face. "You want me to puke?"

"Not really." She sat at the glass-topped kitchen table. "Why did you ask me to come, Gordie?"

"I don't know. I just wanted to see you, get a little perspective on everything."

"How do I give you perspective?"

"Don't ask so many questions. I'm worried about Brad."

"He didn't seem strange to me last night. But I thought you were taking such good care of yourselves, and then you go off on a drinking spree."

"Yeah, he did act like himself, didn't he? And we *are* taking good care of ourselves. It's just once in a while you can't stand it and go off the deep end." Gordie perked up a little, then slumped in a chair across the table from her. "Maybe a piece of toast without butter," he said.

She fixed the toast and kept her advice to herself. Why warn him against a repeat performance in any form similar to last night? He knew.

He sneezed. "Shit." He grabbed a paper napkin and blew his nose.

Her heart had leaped at the sneeze. A cold could lead to pneumonia, then death. She should have stopped them before they started last night. But how could she have done that? She'd never been able to tell Gordie what to do.

Brad appeared. Just like a play, Kate thought, each making an appearance. His hair was standing on end, too.

He smiled thinly. "Why did we do that?" he

129

asked. "I just retched endlessly. All my life I've been tying one on and throwing it up." He sat at the table and put his head in his hands. "Must you eat in front of me, Gordie?" he inquired.

"Toast settles the stomach. Try it."

"Okay. I'll try anything." Brad's voice was muffled by his hands.

Kate put bread in the toaster, poured herself another cup of coffee, and joined them at the table. The sun pouring into the room warmed them. But all Kate could think of was Gordie's sneeze. Maybe it had meant nothing. He hadn't sneezed again.

Brad returned to bed. Gordie moved to the living room and stretched out on the sofa. "Sorry, Katie. It's going to be one of those eventless days."

She sat in a chair near him. Just don't sneeze anymore, she begged silently. She picked up the morning paper. Gordie had fallen asleep.

Sunday both men were recovered enough to take her to Eagle Creek Park and walk the trails around the reservoir. A pair of ospreys had stopped on their way south. Sharing binoculars Kate and the men watched the ospreys fish. It was a thrill for Kate to see one of the big birds dive and come up with a fish in its talons, then perch in a tree with its catch. Brad and Gordie rested on every available tree trunk. Full of energy, Kate quickly wore them out.

That evening she fixed dinner. Gordie kept her company in the kitchen, while Brad watched TV.

"See, he's watching the tube again."

"It was the news, Gordie, and now *Sixty Minutes*. Is that unusual?"

Gordie nodded.

"Well, maybe he's too tired and dispirited to do what he normally does."

"Maybe," Gordie replied.

"Will you still come for Thanksgiving?"

"Of course. Maybe Brad will come, too."

"I thought he always went to his parents."

"Maybe they won't want him."

She turned to stare at Gordie, who was sitting at the table with his chin in one hand, his eyes fathomless. "Why wouldn't they want him?"

"Don't be naive, Katie."

"Don't they know he's gay?"

Gordie shrugged. "They've never talked about it, I guess."

Kate was silent a minute. "Is he going to tell them he has AIDS?"

"Sooner or later he'll have to, won't he?"

"What are they like? Have you met them?"

"Middle class WASPs. I met Brad just after Mom died, you know. I was really in the depths of despair, feeling I'd failed both parents and it was too late to do any repair work. He was like a branch to grab in a wild river. He's ten years younger than I am, Katie."

Kate turned back to chopping onions. That would make Brad thirty-one. It was too sad to dwell on. She couldn't think about what was happening here for too long a stretch. "You could come home with me, both of you," she heard herself say.

"Maybe I'll have to, Katie, but not yet."

* * * * *

131

Walking Arthur Saturday morning, Pat reviewed the past week at school, thinking of one particular girl in her class whose intelligence was exciting. But communicating with this kid was like trying to have a conversation with Arthur. Thirteen had been a rotten age in her own life, she reflected, with puberty beginning to take hold.

Karen arrived early in the afternoon while Pat was reading. "It's a nice day," Karen commented.

"Let's go to the park by the lake, take Arthur with us."

Pat slid a blanket over the back seat to protect her upholstery. Arthur jumped inside and steamed up the window with his hot breath.

"Whose dog is this anyway?" Karen asked.

Pat glanced at her, smiled slightly. Karen's hair and eyes were dark. It crossed Pat's mind that she really was attractive. "Kate's. I'm taking care of him for her while she's at her brother's."

"Oh, I haven't met her, have I?"

Pat shook her head. "No, but you will one of these days. I met her at the lake. She's a good friend." Would it be nice if she were more than a friend? Kate sitting on the pier became a picture in her mind — sunburned, blue-green eyes bright, a grin on her face. She smiled at the image and it vanished.

Arthur was ecstatic about another walk. Pat kept him on the leash. He made friendly lunges at the few dogs they met. It was not surprising so many people were out enjoying the day, and it shouldn't have been a shock that two of them were Joy and Gail. But seeing Gail was not the jolt it had been at their chance meeting in Target. Weeks had passed. Pat absently drew Arthur close to her side.

"Nice dog," Joy remarked. "Is he friendly?"

Pat gave a short laugh. "That's one of his shortcomings."

Joy bent over and stroked Arthur's head; the dog licked her face and hand. Again Pat found herself liking this woman in spite of herself. Pat reached down and patted Arthur's side, then looked at Gail.

"How are you?" she asked Gail. The intense pain had been replaced by an ache for something loved and irretrievably lost, a sadness for what was gone and could never be again.

"Okay. Got yourself a dog, huh?" Gail raised her eyebrows and smiled.

"No, he belongs to Kate. You remember Kate from the lake? I'm dog-sitting."

"I remember her," Gail replied, the smile gone.

Joy was now standing near Karen, talking to her. "We'll have to get together sometime," Joy said.

Pat breathed deeply once Joy and Gail were gone. She smiled reassuringly at Karen. Promising silently she'd never lay herself open to that pain again, she wondered if that meant she'd never fall in love again. Had that been love?

Late Monday afternoon Pat parked her Honda next to Kate's Ford outside the apartment building, picked up the bag of groceries she had stopped to buy, spotted Kate and Arthur walking toward the building a block away. Locking her car she leaned against it and waited for them in the cold sun of the windy November day. Arthur pulled Kate toward every tree. When she jerked him back, Pat smiled

133

approvingly. As she watched the woman and dog, she was not altogether pleased with the feelings Kate generated in her. They were too strong. She was a little too happy to have Kate back. She shrugged and dismissed these thoughts. There was no going back and she didn't want to anyway. She walked to meet the two. Arthur saw her coming and, nearly pulling Kate off her feet, charged toward Pat with delight.

"Maybe you'd like to keep him," Kate suggested as she regained her balance. "He's crazy about you."

Magnetized as always by Kate's eyes which glowed in bright contrast to the high color of her cheeks, Pat wondered how someone so small could generate such large feelings in her. She thought with wary astonishment that she was crazy about Kate. She grinned. "Want me to walk him?"

Kate brushed the hair away from her eyes and mouth and shook her head as she dragged the dog to her left side. She sensed what was going on here, the attraction rearing its head. Some day it was going to surface. She studied Pat, who was standing just beyond the length of Arthur's leash — arms around the grocery bag, brown eyes shining in the sun, hair curling around her ears, grinning. She felt as if they were in a vacuum, enclosed from the outside world. She couldn't do this, could she? She heard Gordie saying *Pat's your best bet.* Kate laughed softly. "You look good, Pat."

"Come on, let's go in. It's cold."

They walked the short distance to Pat's apartment and let themselves in to the welcome warmth. Arthur had a way of breaking down the awkwardness

134

separation built between them. Kate fed him, while Pat emptied the grocery bag.

"I'm taking you out to dinner tonight," Kate said.

"You don't have to do that. I picked up something for dinner."

"Save it. You have to let me thank you for taking care of Arthur."

"All right. How are Gordie and Brad?"

Kate told her about her weekend, her face growing more troubled as she talked.

Pat, mixing drinks, noted the worry Kate was too distracted to hide. "So what now?" she asked.

Kate had been watching Arthur gobble his dog chow. Her expression was grim. "You tell me," she said. "Can you spend Thanksgiving with us?"

Pat shook her head sadly. "I have to go home, but I can come over Saturday. I'd like that. How do they look?"

"Like they did last summer, maybe a little thinner. Pat, I don't know how good I'm going to be at this."

"At what?" Pat set her glass down. She knew what.

Kate stared at her drink and stirred it absently with a spoon. She suddenly felt like crying. The back of her throat ached. She sighed and sniffed. "Never mind. We'll talk about it later."

Pat reached across the table and lifted Kate's chin so she could see her eyes, then wished she hadn't. They were swimming with tears. She sighed too, and ran her hand over Kate's cheek.

Kate laughed a little and sniffled again. She was

not going to bawl. She grasped Pat's hand and squeezed it. "Let's go to dinner."

On her way home the next day Kate stopped in Waushara to pick up the letter packets at the newspaper and the post office. Arthur sat on the back seat, his nose pressed to the window.

The day was gray and cold, a drizzle in the air, and the house felt damp and chilly and unwelcome. She turned up the thermostat, started a fire in the grate and huddled on the couch until the heat warmed her. The radio played Beethoven's *Fifth Symphony,* and Kate rested her head on the back of the davenport while the music flowed over her. She closed her eyes and forgot there was any future, because why would she want to contemplate it now? When the symphony ended, she reluctantly left the sofa and opened her letter packets, ready to immerse herself in the problems of the populace of Orion and Waushara.

Bert called late in the afternoon. That evening they shared a pizza at Kate's house. They sat at one corner of the table, Arthur under their feet. Kate knew he shouldn't be under the table while they were eating, that Pat would have made him lie elsewhere, but it was easier to just let him be for now. Kate slid her feet under his warm body.

"Kate, maybe this isn't the time or place but I love you. I'd like to marry you."

Oh God, why did he have to ask? "I'm not divorced, Bert." She was stalling, her mind searching for a kind refusal.

"You soon will be." His eyes were dark pools reflecting the firelight. They should have belonged to a woman.

"I want to be just friends," she explained, putting her hand over his, which he covered with his other hand. "I'm not ready for anything permanent again. I'm just recovering from the first marriage. I like being single and independent." She understood this to be true.

"You don't love me, do you?"

"I love you as a friend," she replied.

"I'd like to be married again," he said after a pause. He searched her eyes, a slight frown between his own eyes.

"I don't want to marry, not now, maybe not again." She thought of Gordie. How could she commit herself to Bert when Gordie might be coming back any time? But she could, she knew. She just didn't want to.

"I was at my daughter's while you were gone," Bert remarked, his eyes still fastened on hers.

Kate waited.

"I met someone there, took her out a couple times."

Kate silently examined her emotions. This was an either/or, she guessed, and she felt sadness threatening her. Another relationship was drifting away. This one she could hold onto, but only by giving her future to him, and she couldn't do that. "I'm happy for you, Bert." Was she? Not really. She would like to keep things as they were. "Are we saying goodbye?" she asked when he didn't reply.

"I don't know, maybe in a physical way. But not as friends. God, I'll miss you."

137

"Tell me about her."

"You'll meet her." He asked, as Kate poured more wine into their glasses, "Aren't you lonely, Kate?"

"Sometimes I am, of course." She would miss him, but she didn't say it, not wanting to encourage him. If he wanted to move on to something permanent, she wouldn't attempt to stop him.

She went to bed alone with only Arthur lying on the rug nearby where she could fall over him in the night. The drizzle had turned into a heavy downpour, and the wind moaned around the house splattering rain at the walls and windows. In an ache of loneliness she curled into a ball under the covers. There was no reason not to cry; no one was around to see or hear her. Arthur put his paws on the bed and whined at the sound. "So that's why you're here. This is what Gordie had in mind."

She laughed a little and snuffled, shoved Arthur's paws off the sheets and forced him to lie down next to the bed. Her hand rested companionably on his large head. She had read somewhere that an animal could dispel anxieties, offer solace with its presence. Arthur emitted a deep sigh and stretched out on his side under her touch. They fell asleep like this, and Kate awoke in the night, her hand and arm numb. She drew herself together under the blankets, tucking her hands between her legs.

IX

Thanksgiving was one day away. Kate carried in bags of groceries, half expecting someone to drive in any time. She had thought Gordie would be here by now. The sky spit snow out of sullen gray clouds, and a bitter wind whipped waves into whitecaps on the small lake. She made hurried trips from the car to the house and back again.

Arthur ran out briefly, sprinkled a tree and wanted back in the house. He padded around behind her on his large paws, toenails clicking on the floor. Whenever she turned she bumped into him. Finally she told him to lie down and he did so in front of the dying fire in the fireplace. She knelt next to him and added logs until the fire crackled and gave out so much heat the dog moved away from it. She thought he must be nearly full-grown, but he still had a lean and growing look about him. His shoulders were now above her knees. She patted him, then turned on the radio and went into the kitchen to put away groceries.

She glanced out the back window every few minutes, but it was Arthur's deep bark and rush to the back door that alerted her to Gordie's arrival. She opened the door and the dog galloped down the back steps to greet Gordie, who was unfolding himself from behind the wheel of his car. Arthur planted two huge feet on Gordie's chest. Hugging herself to ward off the cold, Kate followed without a jacket.

"Where are this animal's manners?" Gordie pushed Arthur off his chest, brushed himself. "My, he certainly is getting big, isn't he?" he observed. "Jesus, it's cold up here. Must be the Round Lake effect." He put an arm around Kate and squeezed her, got his suitcase out of the car, and they headed for the back door. "Lost your tongue, Katie?"

Kate reached over Arthur's back to open the door. The dog was standing in the way, as usual. She grinned, delighted to have Gordie back, if only for a few days. They walked through the kitchen and Gordie set his bag on the living room floor. "Nice fire."

Kate watched him as he removed his jacket. He looked thinner. "Brad went home?"

"Yeah, he decided to break the news to his family. It'll be a thrilling Thanksgiving for all of them." He

140

met Kate's eyes and smiled slightly. "I thought maybe you'd been alone too long and forgotten how to talk."

"I talk to Arthur."

"So he's good for something?"

Arthur sat between them and fixed his gaze on Kate, waiting for the customary dog treat, his reward for returning from outside. She knew he sometimes went out just so that he could come back in and get a treat. "I have to get him altered soon."

"What? Castrated?" Gordie eyed Arthur with sympathy. "Isn't he kind of young?"

"The vet said he could be cut when he was six months old."

"Is that what they call it — cut?"

"The vet does."

"Is he chasing females already?" He shook his head. "No taste."

Kate laughed. "Sometimes he disappears." She moved to the kitchen to give the dog his snack. Arthur nipped the tips of her fingers and took his reward to the rug in front of the fire. "So how are you anyway?" She had been sauteing onions when he had arrived. She put some celery in with the onions.

"Smells good," Gordie commented.

"Hungry?"

"Kind of." He opened the refrigerator door and stared into the interior, then removed some cheese and milk. "I thought you'd be inundated with company, at least the girls."

"They'll be here pretty soon. You haven't told me how you are."

"Pretty good. It's amazing. I even forget I have it some of these days."

"How's Brad?"

"Not so good, Katie." Gordie leaned against the counter, a scowl on his face. "He had a seizure about a week ago. Scared the shit out of me."

"What did you do?"

"Called the rescue wagon, but he was all right by the time they arrived and wouldn't go to the hospital." Gordie looked angry, jaw set, mouth in a straight line. "The doctor says he has AIDS dementia, to expect more seizures." His voice dropped to a whisper. "He probably won't live long, Katie."

Kate froze inside. She stirred the onions and celery, added some of the bread she had cut into cubes, blended it together, then scooped it into a large bowl with more bread crumbs and seasonings and mixed it with her hands. Strains of chamber music, the radio playing Corelli or Vivaldi or maybe even Bach, filled the quiet space. Lovely, she thought, wondering what composer it was. Too much was happening in her life. It was becoming difficult to cope. She wanted to dump the bowl of stuffing on the floor. Thanksgiving indeed. What was there to be thankful for?

"I don't know what to say, Gordie. Words sound trite." She turned toward him.

He ate the cheese and drank the milk, his face solemn. He shrugged and sighed. "There's nothing to say. Here's a guy who never hurt anyone on purpose, who minds his own business, who tries to do the right thing, and what happens to him . . ."

He could be talking about himself, Kate thought, as she listened. She used to tell her kids that life wasn't fair; sometimes they would be dealt with unjustly. But back then, perhaps from her Christian upbringing, she had believed deep down there would

142

be justice in the end. It was bleak to feel there was no fairness to the scheme of things, just a disturbing impartiality.

"Can you come in and settle now?" Gordie patted the cushion next to him and Kate joined him on the davenport. The fire pulsed and glowed with a life of its own. "We can't talk this way, Katie. You can't think about this too long or you'll go crazy, you know."

She nodded and stared at the fire. She didn't want to think about it, she wanted to put it out of her mind. There was a real need to escape reality here.

Arthur startled them both by jumping to his feet and running to the door, his bark deep and resonant. The girls had arrived.

"His voice has changed," Gordie said.

"Hasn't it," Kate agreed, getting up and going to greet her daughters. She missed Jeff but would see him at Christmas, and Scott thankfully was spending the holiday with his parents. It was time to tell the girls about Gordie. That would be difficult enough without any added company.

The wind rocked Pat's small car back and forth on the drive to her parents' home. She concentrated on keeping the vehicle in the middle of her half of the road. She was grateful for a few days vacation.

She would really have liked to go somewhere alone and hibernate, to hide from the outside world, to curl up by a fire with a good book and shut everything out, to listen to quiet. Instead she'd

143

probably go deer hunting with her dad and brothers. That she enjoyed. Maybe they could go Thanksgiving morning and escape from the children and dinner preparations.

She had never understood spending most of the day preparing more food than anyone could or should eat, sitting down to dine for an hour, then devoting the rest of the day to cleaning up. She ended up drinking too much at these get-togethers — maybe from frustration at not doing what she wanted to do. She promised herself to limit her intake of wine to two glasses this time, but she knew she'd drink more.

Her parents were in the kitchen, the heart of the house. Pat hadn't been home since Labor Day weekend. She was reminded how cozy the kitchen was as it enclosed them in a pool of warm light from the cold outside. After the usual greetings, she slid onto a chair next to her dad at the large round table.

"You ready to go hunting, kiddo?" her dad asked, patting her on the leg.

"Sure am. Cleaned my rifle yesterday. When are we going?" Tomorrow morning, she silently pleaded.

"How long are you staying?"

"I have to leave Saturday morning." She had promised that day to Kate.

"Mind if we go tomorrow morning, Mom?" her dad asked. He called her mother Mom more than he called her Eleanor.

"We probably won't eat until three or four in the afternoon. I'll have plenty of help when the boys' wives get here."

The next morning she and her dad and brothers

144

moved quietly in the kitchen, where they drank coffee and ate a quick breakfast before slipping out into the pre-dawn cold. This was a scene Pat remembered repeating every year since she had turned thirteen. An inch of snow coated the ground and more was coming down, large flakes falling thickly in the silent, windless morning.

They took her brother's Jeep and headed north and west out of the city. The talk was light, jocular, teasing — memories of other years and hunts and bets on who would get the first deer and the largest.

Leaning against a twisted oak, blending in with her surroundings, eyes alert for movement in the swirling snow, Pat waited in the ankle-deep powder. Her father was off to her right, she knew, but she couldn't see him. Her two brothers were walking the woods toward them, supposedly moving deer their way. Even encased in wool socks and boots, Pat's feet were cold. Her rifle rested in the crook of her arm ready to raise and aim in one movement. She wished she were in a blind, where she could sit and move a little. The world around her was hushed, the temperature hovering around thirty degrees. Soon she would be covered with snow, a living snow woman.

The deer, two prongs on each antler, moved hesitantly into the clearing, picking its feet up carefully and putting them down cautiously. Its ears pricked forward, large eyes casing the area, it was tuned to sense danger. Pat's heart beat faster as she slowly lifted the rifle into position. She took sight just behind the forearm. The buck made a futile, frantic leap before she heard the shot. She lowered her rifle as the animal pitched forward in the snow. It was her dad's deer. She walked toward the dead animal, her father joining her.

"A little slow on the draw, ain't you, girl? You used to be faster."

"You're just too quick for me, Dad," she said. "Nice buck, not too big. He'll make good eating."

"You and me can haul him out of here, Pat."

They had the deer out by the road when Jim arrived with the Jeep. Tim walked out of the woods toward them as they were sliding the animal through the snow-covered ditch.

After tying the buck on the overhead rack, they drove down the road several miles. Now it was Pat and her dad's turn to work the deer toward her brothers. It didn't look like she'd get a deer this year, but she didn't care much for some reason; it had always been a matter of competitiveness. All of that seemed unimportant now in the cold tranquil beauty around her and the companionship of her brothers and father. Experiences like this made memories, she thought.

The fallen branches and trees were snow-covered and Pat walked carefully through the deepening cover. Out of the corner of her eye she glimpsed her father walking. The woods were mostly pine trees and the snow and needles cushioned their steps. She saw her dad falling and thought he must have tripped over a log. But he didn't get up.

Her heart pounding, she ran toward him. She heard herself calling his name over and over and felt as if she were running in slow-motion with weighted feet. He was turned on his side and attempting to rise when she reached him. The color was gone from his face except for his lips which were pale blue. There was fear in his eyes and he clutched his left arm with his right hand. His breath came in gasps.

"Don't move, Dad," she ordered, dropping to her knees next to him. What now? What should she do? Her mind was paralyzed with the same fear she read in his eyes. Should she go after her brothers? How could she leave him here? He might die. Panic seized her; she pushed it away. Don't let him die, she begged soundlessly. Let us get him out of here somehow. She shot in the air twice. It was the call for help her dad had told her to use when they had first started hunting together years ago.

Her father smiled painfully as she cradled his head and shoulders in her arms. "Good girl," he said.

"Don't talk, Dad. Jim and Tim will come soon and we'll get you out of here."

She shot the rifle again every few moments until her brothers appeared. The younger men locked hands and carried their father out of the woods to the Jeep. He protested at first, said he could walk, but then he was silent. Pat walked in front of them, her feet testing for obstacles hidden under the snow. She frequently glanced back at the worried faces behind her.

The visitors' room in the intensive care unit of the hospital was pleasant: carpeted and furnished completely, with plenty of reading material and a television set. Pat could only sit for a few minutes and then found herself out in the hall or pacing the room. She was unable to concentrate on any of the magazines, picking them up and throwing them down.

147

Pat's mother was in the intensive care unit with her husband, and Pat and her brothers were waiting for another bulletin on his condition.

"Guess we shouldn't have gone hunting," Tim commented.

Pat stopped on her way to the door. "How could we know anything was wrong?"

"Do you think he knew?" Jim asked.

"I think he knew something. Maybe he thought it was just indigestion." She had read that heart attack victims often told themselves it was just heartburn. Sometimes they lost their lives by ignoring symptoms. She was angry and frightened. Why hadn't he said he didn't feel well before it happened? There they had been tromping through the woods while he had been having a heart attack.

She called Kate Friday. Gordie answered the phone. "How's it going?" she asked.

"Good. How are you? I understand you're coming over tomorrow morning. It's been a long time since I've seen you."

"I don't think I'm going to make it."

"Has something happened?" There was concern in his voice.

Pat took a deep, shaky breath. "My dad is in the hospital. He had bypass surgery this morning. Yesterday he had a heart attack."

"I'm sorry, Pat. Let me get Katie. She'll want to talk to you."

Pat leaned her head against the wall and corralled her emotions. After all, her dad's condition was fairly stable now.

"Pat, Gordie told me." Kate's voice sounded worried. "How's your dad?"

The urge to cry was gone. "Better. I think he'll be all right."

"And you?"

"I'm okay." Pat's voice was quiet.

Kate said, "Would you like company for a few days?"

"How did you guess?"

"Psychic, remember? Arthur and I'll be there Sunday evening. Around what time?"

"Eight, unless I call." Pat brightened at the prospect of seeing Kate. She hadn't seen her since the first of November.

Sunday Dr. Hiller said recovery would take time and James would just have to reconcile himself to letting others do for him. That would be difficult, but her dad had been frightened enough by the face of death not to protest the indignities of physical dependency. His wife had just fed him a soft lunch. Tubes and wires sprouted from his body. Pat intensely disliked this image of him.

No more cigarettes, Dr. Hiller also cautioned. "That's why you're here, James," he said.

Her father scoffed, a brief display of his former intransigence. "My father smoked all his life and lived to be seventy-eight."

"Well, you're not going to make another year if you don't quit smoking,' Dr. Hiller warned bluntly. "Your father might have lived to ninety if he hadn't smoked."

She stood next to the bed listening to the doctor.

They were all there — her brothers and mother, too. Pat studied her father's pale face, the former strong man in her life. The role reversal disturbed her, as she knew it would torment him. He was not a man who knew how to relax for long.

Arthur panted and whined in anticipation when Kate parked in the visitor's slot next to Pat's car. Did he really know where he was? Was he anxious to see Pat? Who knew what lurked in his mind — or if he even had one? Maybe he just wanted out of the car.

The black, cold night sky was littered with stars. Opening the back door she grabbed Arthur's leash as he bolted for the bushes. The wind was fierce, bearing down out of the northwest, and it didn't take much persuading to get Arthur into the building.

Pat looked tired.

She *was* tired. Kate hugged her, and Pat found it difficult to let go as she returned the hug. "Am I glad to see you," she said. "Want something warm to drink?"

"Sure." Kate followed her into the kitchen.

Pat handed Arthur a rawhide bone, which he snatched and carried into the living room. Kate said, "No wonder he's crazy about you. How's your dad?"

"Better." The weekend remained a nightmare in her mind. She felt as if she were waking up and wished it had been only a bad dream. "His arteries were blocked. He smokes, and he's always eaten whatever he wanted without a thought about his health. If you could just control the lives of those you

150

love." She shrugged helplessly. "How was your weekend?"

"Better than yours. Gordie and I started teaching the girls bridge, and the girls and I went for long walks. But Gordie couldn't go far, and he couldn't tell the girls what was really wrong with him, so he faked a pulled muscle. Then he had to limp all weekend. He didn't want to spoil the holiday." It really had been a nice, relaxing weekend, one to remember when things went bad. "I'm truly sorry about your dad, Pat, but bypass surgery does prolong life."

"I know. Let's go into the living room," Pat said.

They sipped coffee in companionable silence. Then Pat asked, "What was it like when your dad died?"

Kate recalled her mother's voice on the phone in the night, so alone and lost. "It was his third heart attack, not exactly unexpected, but no matter how you prepare yourself for death it always surprises you — or me, anyway. I was worried about my mother. I tried to make it easier for her. I stayed at the lake with her for a week or more and then I had to go home to my family. You just keep on living. I know she was lonely, but she was too independent to live with us."

"It's nice of you to come, Kate." She meant it. She had needed Kate, and she wasn't going to analyze this need tonight. She was just going to accept it.

"You were there when I needed you," Kate replied, looking at Pat. "You're tired."

"I am that. And I've got a full day ahead tomorrow. What will you do while I'm at school?"

"Walk Arthur and maybe shop. Christmas is

151

coming. I'll pick up something for dinner tomorrow night, too. Why don't you get me a blanket?"

Pat looked away and then back at Kate.

Kate felt herself smiling. "You're going to let me sleep with you. Right? You need a little comfort tonight?"

Pat nodded and looked away again. Was she so easy to read?

Kate reached for Pat as if she were Sarah or Beth and held Pat's head against the soft curve of her shoulder, her face in Pat's hair. She noticed again the good clean smell, the softness of the curves, the smoothness of skin. Pat's body relaxed against her own, its heaviness increasing as she drifted into sleep. Kate, too, fell asleep and awoke in the night on her side with Pat tucked up behind and against her. This was nice, she thought, but not something she should be doing. She couldn't stay awake long enough to think what to do about it.

Kate rose early in the morning. While Pat showered and got ready for school, Kate ventured into the cold. Arthur dragged her from tree to tree, until she decided enough was enough and led him back to the apartment.

Thinking about last night, wondering what would happen tonight, she poured herself a cup of coffee and sat for a few minutes at the table with Pat. Pat looked rested. The dampened curls were darker, their tips no longer bleached by the sun. Her freckles had faded along with her tan, but her cheeks were ruddy.

"Thanks, Kate. I slept like a baby." Pat smiled a slow, mischievous smile.

"I slept well, too," Kate said, drinking her coffee, speculating on the meaning of the smile.

"You're as safe as you want to be, Kate."

Kate gave a short laugh. Regretfully, she decided she'd sleep on the couch tonight.

Monday, after shopping, Kate ventured into the Human Services building and stood uncertainly before the receptionist's desk. The woman smiled at Kate. "What can I do for you?" she asked.

Kate fumbled for words. "Well, I was just wondering whether you have counselors, therapists here. I wanted to know about availability, costs, that sort of thing."

"Would you like to talk to one of our psychologists? Dr. Jane Blevins is in and can talk to you."

Before she could think of a good reason for not seeing this woman, she found herself in Dr. Blevins' office. After all, she had only been making inquiries. A tall, gray-haired, smiling woman with eyes as blue as Kate's mother's eyes greeted her. Kate sensed she'd gotten the rush. Did they need clients?

"Please call me Jane," the woman said, clasping Kate's cool hand in her warm one. "Sit down and I'll answer your questions." She indicated a chair in front of her desk, then moved back to her own. "You look a little perplexed. This first talk costs nothing. Were you asking about therapy for yourself or for someone else?"

"For myself," Kate said softly, looking down at her hands.

"This time is for us to become acquainted and decide if we're right for each other and if this is what you want."

"Jane is my pen name," Kate said irrelevantly, intimidated by being placed in what she considered an inferior position. "I write an advice column for two papers and here I am needing help. I think," she added.

"How interesting. What is your real name?"

Kate told her.

"A nice name. May I call you Kate?"

"Certainly." After all, she was supposed to call this woman by her first name. Kate was relieved the woman was older than she. It would make it easier to talk to her. But what to tell her?

"What made you seek us out?" Jane asked, leaning back in her chair, hands in her lap, attention riveted on Kate.

"I was standing outside here this morning with my dog. I was realizing I don't know how I'm going to get through the next few months." Not to mention the next few years. She met the other woman's eyes. "Can you help me?"

"That's why I'm here," was the reply. "Tell me something about your life."

"It's a mess. I'm not sure I can cope with it," Kate said bluntly. She breathed deeply, expanding her small frame. It had been such an ordinary life. "Maybe I should make an appointment and come back another day?" she asked hesitantly, suddenly backing off.

154

"No, go ahead. Tell me."

"Well, it's probably not so bad compared to some of the other people you see." Everything's relative, she told herself. It could be worse. She might be poor or sick or dying.

Jane smiled enigmatically. Kate took the plunge. "Gordie, my brother, has AIDS. His lover has it, too. My husband is filing for divorce because he fell in love with a younger woman. The man I was seeing is now seeing another woman because I won't marry him." She paused, thinking her life sounded like an afternoon soap. It made her want to laugh crazily. "You want to hear more?"

Dr. Blevins nodded, her eyes meeting Kate's.

"I've got three grown kids who know little about what's going on in my life except for the impending divorce. Still we're very close. I live alone on a lake. It's kind of isolated in the winter." She decided against saying anything about Pat, thinking she wouldn't muddy the waters with her feelings about Pat, not until she understood them better. She waited for Jane's comments.

Jane was silent, probably sorting her thoughts. "How do you feel about what you've just told me?"

"Overwhelmed. I no longer control my life, maybe I never did. I drift with events, and I certainly am an unwilling participant in the future. I can't even think about Gordie dying." Her voice cracked. "I sort of feel like a non-person, you know, reacting to other people and things that happen. I wouldn't stop the divorce if I could. I miss Bert but not enough to marry him." She glanced out the window at the traffic without really seeing it. "Well, what do you think?"

"It sounds like a lot of major changes in a relatively short time. It ought to help to talk them out. What is important is what you think."

"Yes, well," Kate said, looking around the room for the first time, noticing a beige, soothing room, with landscape watercolors on the walls and green plants in the bay window behind the desk. For some reason she felt incapable of rising.

"Would you like to start today?" Jane asked after a few moments. "Or would you like to think about it?"

Kate glanced at the older woman, noticed the warm blue eyes, and her heart lifted at the possibility. She hadn't even realized she had been depressed. "We can start today?"

"Why not? I have an appointment in an hour but none now."

"I don't know where to start," Kate said, frowning. There were so many places to begin.

"Tell me about yourself, a little background."

"Well, I'm forty-four. Gordie is three years younger. I went to college, got pregnant, got married, had three kids in five years, raised them. The usual stuff. My husband was or is an attorney; the divorce isn't final."

"That is brief." Jane laughed. "What about your parents?"

"Good people. My father owned a small tool and die company. My mother helped in the office. She died nearly five years ago. My dad has been dead almost eleven years."

"You got along all right with them?"

Kate bristled. "Yes, they were good parents. They tried. I know they loved Gordie and me. Most parents are just people trying to do their best. They're not perfect. I found that out when I became a parent."

Jane smiled at these words which came out as a reprimand, and Kate felt a little foolish. "You find it difficult to find fault with them," Jane commented.

"Yes, I do. They weren't flawless but neither am I. Do we have to talk about them?"

"We can talk about anything you want."

"I'd like to talk about Tom, my husband, if he still is my husband. I want to know what happened and why I don't feel anything anymore. I thought I loved the man, not when we first married but later. I certainly respected him, until he told me he was in love with a woman nearly as young as his kids."

"What did you do about that?"

"Nothing. I went to the lake and tried to forget it all. And now I don't care. I did at first, and I was certainly indignant after I thought about it some."

"Were you happy being married?"

Kate mentally chewed on this for a while. "I don't know. I didn't want to marry him. I was pregnant. That's how so many of us ended up married in those days."

Dr. Blevins smiled a little. "I know. Abortions weren't safe, birth control pills were just coming into vogue but for married women, and only the destitute raised a child alone. Times have changed."

"Now my daughter lives with her boyfriend and no one thinks anything about it. But now we also have AIDS." She wanted to get things in order, though, and Tom leaving her came before anything else. "I wonder why I didn't know he was seeing someone else. We didn't have sex toward the end. I should have guessed."

157

"I suppose you had other things on your mind?"

"Just the usual things I'd had on my mind for years — the kids, my column, friends, meetings, what to have for dinner. The sex just sort of tapered off; maybe that's why I didn't notice. I guess I didn't want to save it — the marriage, I mean. The kids wanted it saved. Perhaps that's why it lasted as long as it did. It's a common story these days. But why didn't I see it coming?" Her voice stopped as she considered this. "Well, perhaps I should be glad I care so little."

"If you care so little, why is it the first thing you brought up?" Jane sat back in her chair.

Kate licked her lips and shook her head. "I don't know. During all those years I never even cheated on him." Was that relevant to anything? She couldn't recollect more than a couple men who had even interested her, and they were husbands of friends. You didn't cheat on a friend. She didn't anyway.

"Have you talked to him since you left?"

"Weeks ago. I was angry with him. But, you know, there's still something comforting about his voice," she admitted. "I know he'll take care of things — if not me, the kids. He loves his kids. Perhaps that's what bothers me — the gray area."

"What is the gray area?"

"I can't really place blame. There's no right or wrong. It's just something that happened. It's like I lacked something — compassion, interest, empathy."

They were quiet for a few moments. "You have a lot of insight, do you know that?" Jane asked.

Kate made a sound halfway between a snort and a laugh.

"Would you like to make another appointment for next week?"

The hour must be over. "Yes. Monday would be best."

"Tell Julie on your way out."

Dr. Blevins came around her desk and walked Kate to the door, again shaking her hand. Her eyes and smile were so warm, so friendly, Kate felt she had found a haven.

Pat's dad was eating dinner when she entered his room. He had some color in his face but looked thinner than when she had seen him a week ago. "You look good, Dad," she said. It wasn't a total lie; he did look better than he had after the surgery, which wasn't saying much. She kissed him and her mother, who was in a chair next to the bed and appeared as pale and thin as her husband. Pat wondered briefly how her mother would get along without her father, if it came to that. "Mom, you look like you could use a little sleep."

"She won't stay home," her dad said, looking fondly at his wife. "She thinks I can't get along even here without her."

"You're always up doing something when I'm gone," her mother complained.

Oh boy, Pat thought with a sinking heart. She had known he wouldn't take care of himself.

"I want to go home. I'll rest there."

"You're going home next week."

"That's not soon enough for me."

159

"Are you, Dad? That's great." She recalled him wanting to go home before the bypass surgery. She had seen the fear in his eyes and realized with a start that he had thought he might not live, that he had wanted to go home again before he died. She had patted his arm and told him bypass surgery was routine these days, but there had been panic in her heart.

"I feel like a new man," he said with a grin.

"You still got the same heart," her mother pointed out.

Pat sank into an empty chair. "That's true, Dad," she said.

"Oh, don't be such a worrywart. Just like your mom."

Pat met her mother's eyes, read the resigned apprehension in them, and didn't envy her. "It's your life, Dad," she started, but she found she couldn't add to the statement. She wanted to tell him it wasn't fair to worry her mother and the rest of them, that he was responsible for taking care of himself. But she had never spoken to him that way, as if he were irresponsible.

X

Stepping out of Gordie's car into the December
wind, Kate pulled her coat collar around her ears and
shivered as the cold wind whipped up her suit skirt.
She glanced at Gordie over the top of the car. His
head was turned toward the funeral home, but she
had been looking at his eyes since she had arrived
yesterday afternoon. They were streaked with red and
underscored by dark circles. His thin face was etched
with bitter angry lines, his body taut with emotion.
Brad's death had been quick, leaving Gordie
unprepared. The disposition of the remains had been

left to Brad's parents. Kate wondered if she and Gordie were welcome here at the funeral home. She braced herself to meet Brad's family. But Brad's friends, those now filling the parking lot, would be here too. Gordie smiled tightly, a smile as frigid as the day. He was unwilling to enter the funeral home until it was time for the service.

The men and women getting out of their cars greeted Gordie with handshakes and regrets, and cast curious glances at Kate. The hushed atmosphere associated with death folded around them once in the funeral home. Someone laughing in the next room startled Kate.

A woman stood inside the door, her face tired and sad. Kate assumed she was Brad's mother. She smiled at Gordie and Kate and walked toward them, taking their hands. "I should have called, Gordie. I was afraid you wouldn't come." Tears filled her eyes, already puffy from crying. "Is this Kate?"

So Brad had mentioned her to his family. Kate fought back the terrible urge to cry. Her throat ached with it. She glanced at Gordie, who appeared remote and stiff. He was removing himself from this in order to cope with it, she realized.

But then he smiled sadly at Mrs. Newby and placed an arm around her, hugging her. "Katie, this is Sue Newby, Brad's mother."

"Thank you for coming, Kate. Brad thought highly of you."

Kate said she was sorry, she had thought a lot of Brad, too. With Herculean effort she kept her voice level; the ache had nearly closed down her throat.

Don Newby appeared and was not as friendly as his wife. Distant and polite, restoring control over the situation, he shook Kate's hand and then Gordie's. Kate was grateful there would be no unpleasant scenes today. She would be so relieved when this was over, when they could return to Gordie's home and she could cry.

The back rows were filling with Brad's friends. There was a gap between those chairs and the front section, which held Brad's family and their friends. Kate and Gordie sat in the front row of the back section, waiting for the service to begin, waiting for it to end. She was indignant that Gordie had not been invited to sit with Brad's family.

There was no casket, no body. Brad had been cremated and his ashes would be buried later. There was just this brief remembrance of Brad's life by a minister who had barely known him and certainly hadn't understood him.

Then they were filing out of the funeral home, escaping into the bitter day. What a terrible way to meet a new year. She and Gordie said nothing in the car driving to his home.

Brad and Gordie's friends started dropping in and Kate attempted to put names and faces together. The friends brought food and Kate set out plates and offered drinks and made coffee. She was on the fringe, watching Gordie anxiously, waiting for him to lose that distant control, but he didn't. How many of these people had or would have AIDS, she wondered, as she stood in the living room doorway, and then she put the thought away. Wanting to be alone, she returned to the kitchen. She longed to sneak upstairs to her bed and did so as discreetly as possible. No one seemed to notice.

Staring at the ceiling, she thought of Christmas.

Gordie had spent that day here with Brad. Had it been barely a week ago, when she and her children had celebrated the holiday? It felt like another time. It certainly had been another scene. They had never spent Christmas at the lake, and she smiled as she remembered cross-country skiing Christmas Day after a big breakfast, the turkey in the oven. The pines had been blanketed with heavy snow, and mounds and waves of the white stuff had created a dazzling breathtaking beauty. When she shut her eyes, she felt tears squeezing out from the closed lids and she rolled over on her stomach to sob into the pillow.

"Hey, sis, you all right?"

Kate awakened and turned over onto her back. Light entered the darkened room from the hallway. Gordie let his weight down on the edge of the bed. Her head ached. "Oh sure. Are you all right?" she asked him, propping herself up on a pillow.

"Are you kidding? I'm so angry, Kate. You know what I mean?" His voice shook.

"Yes, I know," she replied, unable to see his face because his back was to the light.

"Move over," he said.

She scooted over to the other side of the double bed, and he lay down. He still had his suit and shoes on, and he crossed his legs and placed his hands behind his head. "There's a ton of food down there," he remarked.

"Should I go down and put it away?" She worried about what should be refrigerated.

"No, it's already done."

"You have nice friends."

"Any one of them could be next."

Except for a clock ticking in another room, an

occasional car in the street below, the room was quiet. Gordie fell asleep first. Kate heard his heavy breathing, and she drifted off into welcome oblivion. When she awakened, cold from lying uncovered and still, Gordie was gone.

In the morning she stayed under the covers as she sorted her thoughts. Looking out the window at a gray sky, she contemplated spending the day in bed. But she forced herself to get up, shower, put on sweats and head for the kitchen to prepare coffee. The door to Gordie's room was closed. Sitting at the table drinking coffee, musing on the future, she decided the best way to handle death was to just continue life as normally as possible.

Gordie shuffled into the kitchen and smiled sadly at her. "Morning, Katie. Glad you're here."

"I'm glad I'm here, too."

"What's it like at the lake?" He poured himself a cup of coffee.

"Ten inches of snow on the ground. It was quite lovely to look at."

"I bet." Gordie dropped his large frame into the chair across from her and met her eyes. His were still bloodshot. "I'm going to stay here as long as I feel all right, Kate. I want to keep busy."

"Of course, Gordie," she agreed. "You do feel okay then?"

"I get tired easily, and I sweat in the night, but I was doing that last summer. Sometimes I'm nauseated but it doesn't last. I've got medication to take; it seems to help. Maybe there'll be a cure before it gets me." He raised his eyebrows and smiled thinly.

Was that supposed to hearten her? She got up and refilled her cup and his.

"How long can you stay?"

"I ought to go back Sunday. I left Arthur with Pat again, and she'll be at school Monday. Gordie, is it time to tell the girls?"

"Any time you want to."

"Thanks," she said ruefully.

Kate parked in Pat's parking lot and opened the door to the glacial evening. The snow crunched under her feet as she hurried into the building.

"Have you eaten?" Pat asked, smiling in welcome.

Kate ran her hands over Arthur, who whined deep in his throat. The weekend had caught up with her. "No, but I'm not hungry."

Pat sized her up with one glance. "You're still skinny."

"You should see Gordie, if you think I'm thin. How's your dad?"

"Doing well." Then Pat inquired hesitantly, "You want to talk about Gordie?"

"I drove all the way here and I don't even remember the trip." They had moved to the kitchen and Kate leaned against the counter. "I wasn't even thinking. Seven hours without a conscious thought." She met Pat's eyes. "Are you going to feed me anyway?"

"I'm going to feed me. Sure you won't join me?"

Kate picked at her food and watched Pat eat. What she wanted was suddenly crystal clear. It swirled out of the fog of her mind. She leaned back in her chair and waited for the opportunity.

Pat looked up from her food and was startled by

the intensity of Kate's gaze. "What is it? You don't like the food?"

Kate shook her head and smiled a little. "It is so good to see you."

"It's nice to see you. Why are you looking at me like that?"

"I'll tell you when you're finished eating."

"I'm through." Pat pushed her plate away.

"I want to . . ." Kate started, her eyes pinning Pat to the chair.

Intuitively, Pat realized what Kate was trying to say and she felt herself flushing with heat from the acceleration of her heartbeat.

"I'd like to do it," Kate continued softly, the words echoing in her ears, sounding loud to her.

"You don't mean that," Pat said after a few breaths of silence. "I'm not taking advantage of your grief."

Kate gave a short laugh, her eyes still holding Pat in place. She noticed the beating pulse in Pat's neck. "I'm ten years older than you, Pat, remember? If anyone's taking advantage, it's not you."

Pat felt glued in place. She was resisting what she had wanted for months, even before she had stopped wanting Gail. She stared into Kate's eyes, mesmerized. "You have the most compelling eyes, do you know that?"

Kate said nothing, but she looked away and her shoulders sagged a little. Maybe she shouldn't be doing this. To think she had once been afraid this woman might seduce her, and now she couldn't get her into the same bed. How ironic and foolish and misplaced were some fears.

Pat watched Kate, noticing the drop in the

167

shoulders, wanting Kate so much it frightened her. Most of all she was afraid she'd lose their friendship. She started to speak and had to clear her throat first. "I'll hold you, Kate. I'd love to hold you."

"And if I want more?"

"We'll see."

Later in the dim light of the bedroom Pat asked Kate how Gordie was. Kate replied, "Angry, sad, bereft but functioning. Except for being so thin, he doesn't look any different from last summer." Pat's arm was around her and Kate turned and kissed Pat softly, teasingly on the mouth.

Pat turned her head away. "Don't do that."

Kate kissed her cheek and neck. "Why not?" she whispered. She moved her lips over the skin, feeling, tasting, smelling — velvety, sweet, clean. Memorizing Pat with her senses.

"Because I won't be able to resist, that's why. Kate, what if this is a mistake? We're such good friends. I don't want to lose that."

"You won't, even if this is a mistake, but it's not," Kate replied, taking Pat's face between her hands, looking into her eyes and then pulling softly on Pat's mouth with her own, running her tongue tentatively around the inside of Pat's lips.

"Jesus," Pat breathed into Kate's mouth, "I'm not a saint."

"So stop acting like one."

Pat turned toward Kate and wrapped her tightly in both arms, burying her face in Kate's hair, still holding back, but the tugging in her groin was taking over her mind. Her hands moved hesitantly over Kate's body and she felt Kate's hands in turn exploring her and knew she had relinquished control of the situation.

Kate thought she might get lost in kissing, thought she might never get away from Pat's mouth, it was so warm and giving. Pat's hands touched her breasts, slid under the undershirt Kate wore, and Kate pulled the shirt off over her head in one quick movement. She fumbled with the buttons of Pat's nightshirt and hesitantly touched the revealed breasts, cupped one gently in her hand.

Pat's dark eyes glowed, the pupils enormous. She smiled slightly, reassuringly, as she rolled Kate onto her back and ran one hand caressingly over her breasts down to the joining of her legs and slid the panties off. Then Pat paused, covering the wiry reddish mound of hair with her hand. She bent and kissed Kate's breast, teasing the nipple with her tongue.

Arching her back, Kate responded with every muscle, every nerve. Her skin quivered and her gaze followed Pat's movements as Pat raised her face to Kate's and urgently covered her mouth with her own. After that, it was all sensation. She felt Pat's fingers slide into her and rose to enclose them. She trembled when the fingers slowly withdrew in a long caress. Her hips lifted higher in trembling response.

Pat murmured something into Kate's neck, her lips brushing Kate's skin, nibbling it, then joining her mouth again, tongue thrusting. "You feel so good."

Kate said nothing. Her fingers were entwined in Pat's hair, and she moaned as she raised her head off the pillow to kiss her, to curl her tongue around Pat's. She felt as if Pat were reaching into her

169

depths toward a center of intensity, and she moved in rhythm to Pat's fingers, pulling inward. Then Kate froze in position, engulfed with pleasure so concentrated her entire being shuddered in response. She felt Pat's hand grow still and cover the wetness between her legs. Kate's muscles relaxed, her body languid and damp and warm. She drew Pat close.

They lay on their sides, holding each other, moist skin touching, hearts pounding in unison. They kissed gently, their passion growing and intensifying as the kisses deepened. Kate pushed Pat onto her back and leaned over her to kiss her breasts, to taste Pat's skin, salty and warm from lovemaking. When she reached into Pat, feeling the silky warm wetness, hearing Pat's sharp intake of breath, her gratification was as great as when Pat had made love to her. She pulled herself up on one elbow and watched the younger woman succumb to her touch.

When sleep overtook them, they were tucked together spoon-like, Pat's arm holding Kate to her.

"Do you have to go home today?" Pat asked in the morning over coffee, the night fresh in her mind. How difficult it had been to get out of that bed.

"No, I've got an appointment with Dr. Jane today. I didn't cancel before I left for Gordie's. My mind wasn't functioning properly."

"Is it now?"

Kate ran her fingers through Pat's thick curls. "I love your hair." She leaned toward Pat and kissed her. "I love your mouth. I can't wait for you to leave."

Pat laughed shakily, her hand on the back of Kate's neck. "What does that mean?"

"The sooner you leave, the quicker you'll be back."

"You're not making any sense," Pat said, panic touching her. This was serious; at least it was to her.

Kate gazed across the desk at Dr. Blevins and wondered whether to bring Pat into their sessions. They had talked Tom into the ground, and she still didn't know what had happened to the marriage. "Brad died. I just returned from Gordie's last night."

"I'm sorry." They looked at each other in silence for a short time. "How do you feel about Brad's death?"

Kate shifted in the chair and shrugged. "How else? Sad for him, for Gordie, for the waste of an intelligent man."

"And you?"

"Sad for me, too. I cared about Brad. I never know how to treat death. I tend to ignore it, if possible."

"Did you ignore it when your mother and father died?"

"When my father died, yes. It wasn't real to me. I didn't see him die. I think it's different when you see death. I watched my mother die and for months I relived it like a captive audience. I didn't see Brad die. I didn't even see him in death. He's just gone." Would she witness Gordie's death? Would it haunt her like her mother's had? She took a deep breath and exhaled a sigh.

171

"What does that mean?"

"What?"

"The sigh."

"You sound like Beth. My sighs make her nervous." Did there have to be meaning in everything? "I have to tell the girls about Gordie. I haven't even told them Brad died yet." And she wasn't looking forward to revealing these facts when they came to ski the weekend after next. "Do you believe in life after death?" she asked Jane.

Jane's warm blue eyes studied her. "I believe in a higher power."

"Are you hedging?"

Jane laughed. "I guess I am. What I believe doesn't matter, you know."

"I'd like you to tell me."

"Then I have to answer I don't know. Do you?"

"I want to, but no, I can't convince myself. It seems the most likely way for us to avoid dying is to invent an afterlife. When my mother died, I really wanted to believe she was still somewhere, but no matter how much I want to believe it, I don't. Why did you say it doesn't matter what you believe?"

"It won't change *your* beliefs, will it? And that's what matters here — what *you* think, what *you* feel, and how it affects *your* life."

Was that what mattered? "Can you change what I think and feel?"

"We can learn to understand it."

"How?" Kate asked, truly curious.

"Well, how you react to events in your life is often based on how you first perceived yourself in your parents' eyes."

Did something happen when she was young to

make her now want a woman, to make her want Pat? "You mean if one of my parents caught me playing doctor with the neighbors' little boy and scolded me, I would have thought something was wrong with sex?" Perhaps she should have said the neighbors' little girl.

Jane smiled thinly. "It would depend on how you thought your parents felt about you. You're being facetious."

"Yes, I guess I am."

"But if they made it clear that what you were doing was somehow indecent, you might feel an interest in another person's body was shameful and never understand why."

"You don't think just growing up and using common sense frees a person of early impressions?"

"Perhaps it does for some. Common sense isn't what guides most people, though. If it were all perfectly logical, I'd be out of a job. I see intelligent, decent, attractive people who have such low opinions of themselves they can hardly function. And then there are those who see me because they are having relationship difficulties and can't understand why, when they're opinionated, boorish, selfish, argumentative. If I could convince people why they're not acceptable to society and themselves, my job would be easy. Instead we have to go back to find out why they function and feel the way they do before we can make any progress toward change or acceptance."

"And we have to do this with me, too?" Kate asked quietly, soberly. How long did something like this take? How much money? She wondered if Sarah was seeing her shrink regularly and making progress.

It didn't seem like they had found any solutions discussing Tom. Did this mean she had to recapitulate her childhood to discover why her marriage had failed? Sarah would have to disclose her childhood and her parents' failings to some stranger. And now there was another turn in her life. She wasn't ready to talk about what had happened last night; she hadn't started to digest it yet herself. "We have to talk about my parents and my childhood?"

Jane cocked her head and pursed her lips. "It's up to you, Kate."

"I thought I was a happy child." A little shy, perhaps, not so sure of herself. Kate was irritated. She thought she had put that all behind her. She didn't want to dredge it up and expose it to light. She realized she hadn't really liked herself as a child. She had attempted to hide her real self from her parents, afraid they wouldn't like her either.

"Think about it, Kate. We can talk about it next week if you like, or we can talk about anything you want."

The hour must be up. "All right," she said with another sigh. "I'll give it some thought."

She shopped for groceries before returning to the apartment. Afterward, she took Arthur for a walk. He was learning to heel, only occasionally forgetting himself. She was impressed with his progress and told Pat so while they prepared dinner.

"Will he come now when I call him?" Kate asked.

"He's just starting to heel and sit on command. Give us a little more time."

"What's this we stuff? You're the trainer."

"You're reinforcing it. That's just as important. How was your session with Dr. Jane?"

"Unproductive. We've been talking for weeks. Correction, I've been talking for weeks and I don't feel as if I understand things any better than when I started. My childhood is next. I'm not sure I want to talk about it, even if it is relevant."

"Why not?" Pat asked.

"I went to her to learn to cope with the future, not the past. I can't change the past. I don't want to rehash it. I just want to get through the next year or two and keep my sanity."

"Come on, Kate, don't quit."

"It seems like a waste of time." But she just didn't want to reveal herself as a child. She was afraid Jane wouldn't like her either. If she had such insight, why did she need to talk to a shrink?

All day Pat had looked forward to the night. Wanting to make love to Kate without inhibition, yet afraid she might offend her, Pat gave words to her desire. "I want to taste you." She spoke into Kate's mouth, their breath and tongues mingling.

"You don't have to ask," Kate replied, sucking in air and moaning a little as she felt Pat's hand moving over her abdomen, sliding between her legs. The fingers felt cool, the touch exquisitely soft and teasing.

Pat removed her lips from Kate's and started a slow, exciting journey over her body, pausing to touch and kiss and taste along the way. She felt Kate's hands on her back, gripping her shoulders, then in her hair as she arched her back and raised herself to meet Pat's mouth. The wetness became a hot shower.

Kate felt the center of pleasure being drawn from her, sucked out of her, down between her legs in a whirling vortex. Moving in a frenzy of desire, she succumbed to her passion. Then it was over and she relaxed her hold on Pat's curls, glanced down her body and met Pat's eyes.

Pat grinned. "You taste good," she said, pulling herself toward Kate's mouth, kissing her body on the way.

Kate hugged Pat to her and rolled over on top of her. She relished the feel of skin on skin, softness on softness. "So smooth," she said, the contact causing desire to stir itself anew. When Kate made love to Pat, she prolonged the act deliberately, enjoying Pat's slow climb to climax.

Afterward Kate said, "It's like a good meal, you hate to end it."

Pat's throaty laugh was a soft, sensuous sound. "But unlike a meal, we may never get full."

"True," Kate said, gently biting Pat's ear lobe.

"How about another course?" Pat tightened her hold on Kate and searched for her mouth with her own.

XI

Kate paced the floor with Arthur on her heels, worry dogging each step. Knowing Arthur would hear the girls first and let her know, she nevertheless looked out the back door window every few minutes for a sign of Beth's car. The fire in the fireplace danced blue and red and orange, a pot full of chili bubbled on the stove and the table was set for three. Then Arthur paused, ears alert, a whine in his throat, and rushed to the door. Kate grabbed her jacket, shoved her feet into boots and went out with

Arthur to greet them. Snow fell softly, large dry flakes piling up on the trees and ground.

"How is Pat?" Sarah asked, setting her suitcase down in the living room and walking over to the fire, stretching her hands toward the heat.

"Good," Kate said casually. Should she feel guilt over this new relationship with Pat? She didn't. She couldn't have told them how she felt, but she knew she wouldn't be able to explain what had transpired.

"Something smells good," Sarah commented. "I'm famished."

"How's Gordie doing, Mom?" Beth asked a short time later while digging into another bowl of chili.

"Not so well, actually," Kate replied tentatively. Should she tell them now and spoil the meal, especially when the girls were relishing their food so much? "We'll talk about it later."

Sitting in front of the fire after dinner, Kate pondered how to tell them. It was so peaceful and cozy and pleasant with the radio playing a Brahms symphony, the snow falling outside. Why charge the atmosphere with bad news?

"What about Gordie, Mom?" Sarah asked finally.

"Well, Gordie has AIDS," she said in a low tremulous voice. She cleared her throat and continued, "But he's feeling well right now. I went down to Gordie's after Christmas because Brad died. He had what's called AIDS dementia; it affects the brain, causes seizures."

Watching their faces carefully, she knew it hadn't been fair not to warn them earlier, but how could she have known Brad would die so quickly? She understood the meaning of shocked silence as it filled the room. She waited for one or both of the girls to comment or accuse her of withholding information. They looked at each other and then at their mother. They appeared aggrieved. Kate attempted to explain: "Gordie didn't want you to know any sooner than necessary. If Brad hadn't told me about Gordie, I don't know if I'd know myself."

"Brad died?" Beth said with disbelief.

Tears coursed silently down Sarah's face. She got up to search for a box of Kleenex.

Kate said, "I'm sorry I didn't tell you sooner."

"How can Gordie be all right?" Beth questioned.

"He's thin, he's bitter, he's sad, otherwise he's in pretty good shape." Kate took Sarah in her arms. The three of them were crying now, and Arthur put his head in Kate's lap and whined.

"Let's go skiing tonight," Beth suggested, blowing her nose.

To commemorate life. Kate understood.

The snow fell on them, obscuring their vision, coating their shoulders and heads. The only sounds were the swishing of skis. A great horned owl swooped on immense soundless wings across their path as they wound single file along the trail leading out of their yard. When they glided back home an hour later, Kate felt cleansed. They shook the snow off their skis and stuck them in a drift along with the poles.

Kate built up the fire, while Beth heated water for hot chocolate. They'd said very little to each other.

"What are you thinking?" Kate asked when Beth handed her a cup.

"I wish you had trusted us enough to tell us," Beth said.

179

"Gordie asked me not to." But she should have told them, she knew. She could have sworn them to silence.

"How long have you known?"

"Since last fall when I went to Indianapolis the first time. That's why I went."

"How do you live with all this shit, Mom?" Sarah asked abruptly.

Kate smiled grimly. "You do what you have to do. I'm not so bad off. I have you kids. But Gordie doesn't want anyone else to know. Neither Dad nor Jeff nor Scott need to know yet."

"They wouldn't understand, would they?" Sarah asked.

"They would probably say he asked for it," Sarah added.

"But it's not just confined to homosexuals, you know. You have to be careful, too," Kate warned them.

"We know, Mom," Beth replied tolerantly.

"Do you?" Kate asked.

"We do," Sarah assured her.

"Condoms and spermicides," Kate continued, still unsure they understood the dangers inherent in sexual relations these days.

"Yes, Mom." Beth set her mother's mind temporarily at ease. "But I'm just with Scott, you know."

"That goes for you, too, Mom," Sarah remarked, a glint of humor in her eyes.

Kate squeezed her hand and smiled. "I know." But surely not with Pat. How did women protect themselves from each other? By abstinence? There was no incidence of AIDS among strict lesbians, was

180

there? Maybe she was a danger to Pat. What would you say to someone? "Wait, have you had sexual relations with anyone who might have AIDS?" What a cooler to passion. It would wipe it away. Did you justify such a question by reminding the other person that you were sleeping with all of his or her sex partners when you had sex with that person? But so was that person when he or she slept with you. Could Bert have been suspect? She thought not. How about Tom? Her children seemed in more danger than she was and she knew she would worry about them.

Pat had spent many weekends in Fond du Lac since her father's bypass surgery. Her dad was giving her mother a hard time, sneaking out to his workshop whenever possible to escape her hovering worry. He was impatient with his slow recovery. And he was dipping snuff to replace his addiction to cigarettes. Pat had very nearly asked him if he still wanted to give himself the choice of how to die — cancer or heart disease — but she had held her tongue. His carelessness with his life caused her distress, too. She couldn't imagine life without his reassuring presence.

She hadn't seen Kate since their weekend together. What had happened between them was becoming unreal to Pat, and she questioned whether Kate had regrets. She had been waiting for Kate to call. She herself had placed the past two calls, the last one a week ago. Kate had said she needed time alone — to digest everything was how she had put it. Pat sensed she was on shifting ground. Were she and

Kate still friends? Was Kate pushing her away? She reached for the phone just as it rang. Hope sprung in her heart.

"Pat, how's it going?" Karen's voice was hesitant.

"Pretty good," Pat replied, struggling to keep the disappointment out of her voice. "I was just going to call you." A lie, but a white one.

"Really? I thought maybe we could go out tonight. We haven't seen each other for such a long time."

In fact they hadn't seen each other in nearly four weeks. "Sure, where do you want to go?" What should she do about this? Karen must think she had been used and discarded. She would like to keep Karen's friendship without sex, without offending her. Pat felt as if she were in limbo, waiting for Kate to make a decision, and this annoyed her.

"I don't care. Anywhere."

"Want to go to dinner?"

"Sure."

She couldn't tell Karen she had rebounded from Gail to her and now that she was over Gail she didn't need her anymore. Besides she did need her in a way. And what was wrong with a little physical affection between friends? If she couldn't have Kate, at least she could have Karen. Not nice, not nice at all, but who had said she was nice? Kate had. Well, Kate didn't really know her.

She reached for the phone again and then decided to wait for Kate to call. She should have resisted, kept their friendship as it was, she thought, as she started toward the shower. What could Kate be doing that she hadn't called, hadn't been to town to see Jane? Surely she would have called if she'd been in town. Maybe not. She couldn't get the goddam woman out of her mind. What if she'd broken her leg skiing alone and was frozen in the woods somewhere? That thought sent Pat back to the phone.

"Kate?" she asked uncertainly, sounding like Karen, probably feeling like Karen.

"Pat, how are you?" Kate asked.

Reassured that Kate was all right by the sound of her voice, Pat's irritation asserted itself. "Why haven't you called?"

"But I have. You're never home when I call."

"When did you last call?" Pat inquired with disbelief.

"I don't remember. A few days ago."

"You haven't been in to see Jane?"

"No, I haven't," Kate replied. She had cancelled her last appointment and had been unable to force herself to call for another. Since the girls' departure she had been in seclusion, unwilling to communicate with anyone.

"Why?" Pat persisted.

"I just haven't."

"What have you been doing?"

"Do you do this with all your friends?" Kate asked, annoyed and amused.

"You aren't just one of my friends, Kate. And I've made all the phone calls since we last saw each other," she said accusingly, thinking bitterly that she had believed there had been something more between them. "I thought maybe you'd gone skiing and been hurt and frozen." Kate laughed and Pat smiled at the sound, wishing she were with her. She resented the mind games going on between them.

"I have been doing a lot of skiing. I've been doing a lot of thinking, too, Pat. Remember, I said I needed time when we last talked? Can you be patient with me?"

"Sure," Pat said, her worry somewhat assuaged. How much time? she wondered.

Kate went on. "I talked with Gordie. I'm going to stay with him for a while, but don't worry, I'll take Arthur with me."

Disappointment nauseated Pat. They listened to each other breathe into the receivers.

"You still there, Pat?"

"You know I am." She felt outraged. "You were going to leave without even calling me?"

"Of course not. I just told you I've tried to call."

"Will I see you before you leave?"

"Why don't you come this weekend? I'm leaving next week sometime. I haven't decided which day. There's so much to do first."

She wanted desperately to see Kate, but here it was Friday night and she had had to call and force an invitation out of her. How could she go under these circumstances? "I'm having dinner with Karen tonight."

"Come tomorrow morning then."

Again silence filled the line between them. Finally Pat accused, "I have to call for you to ask to see me? You would have left without seeing me?"

"Please come," Kate said. She had thought she was getting along well without Pat, without anyone, until she heard Pat's voice.

"Why, Kate?" Pat demanded.

"Because I really need to see you now."

"Now, why now? Why not last weekend?"

"We'll talk tomorrow. Okay?"

"Okay." Pat reluctantly, almost sullenly, relented.

"Bring your skis."

Hanging up, Kate knew she had been unfair. She should have called until she had reached Pat, should have invited her for this weekend. She didn't understand this self-imposed exile. She had made few attempts to contact anyone since her weekend with the girls. She sensed she had wronged them somehow. Now she was unsure about all her motives. What did she think she was doing anyway? First Bert, now Pat. Had she been using them? Wasn't that the compelling factor that drove everyone? Didn't we all use others to gratify our needs? She liked Bert, and she cared for Pat even more. Then why had she waited for Pat to contact her? That had been cruel and she knew it. But just as she hadn't been able to force herself to go back to Jane, she hadn't been able to voluntarily reach out to anyone.

The decision to go to Gordie's house had been his. He had asked if she'd like to spend the winter with him, and she had agreed to do so without knowing why. She would write her columns there and send them through the mail, just as she already did for the *Chronicle*. She had phoned Dan Mills this morning about the address change. Monday she would go into Waushara and give Gordie's address to her editor at the *Journal*.

The next morning, while Kate filled her bird feeders and tasted guilt because no one would be feeding the birds when she was in Indianapolis, Pat drove up in her Honda. Kate waved; bare-headed, she squinted against the glare of sun on snow. The day was warm for the end of January, the temperature hovering around the freezing mark, the snow sticky.

Pat walked toward Kate along the packed snow

185

path leading from the barn to the feeders, hands thrust in her pockets, smiling to hide the frustrated anger consuming her. She felt awkward and unsure of her welcome. Last night she had slept very little and she was tired and on edge.

Dinner with Karen had been a diversion, but her mind had been on Kate, and she was sure she had been poor company. Karen had asked her what had gone wrong between them, and Pat had been at a loss to answer. Kate was between them, she could have said but hadn't, because she didn't know where Kate was. She needed to know where she stood with Kate but was afraid to ask.

"Nice day," she said noncommittally.

"Isn't it?" Kate replied with a wispy smile. "I should never have started feeders this winter. What will happen to the birds when I leave next week?"

"Want me to come up and fill them on weekends?" Pat asked.

"No, I don't want that."

"Don't any of the resident neighbors feed the birds?"

"Probably. I think the Davidsons do."

Whining deep in his throat, his body trembling, Arthur planted himself in front of Pat.

"He's glad to see you," Kate remarked.

"*Are* you?" Pat rubbed the dog's head and shoulders.

They stood in the snow, looking at each other. Pat wondered what would happen this weekend. Nothing physical, she was sure, not if she could help it.

"I'm glad to see you, of course. I can't tell you how glad."

186

"Then tell me why you haven't made an attempt to see me or talk to me?" Pat had sworn to herself she wouldn't ask Kate this again, and here she was demanding an explanation.

"I told you I needed to be alone. Let it go, Pat. I don't know why. I've been hiding from everyone," Kate said in a soft voice.

"Why?"

"Let's go inside."

Arthur leaped up the steps in front of them. Pat pulled him back and opened the door, and for some reason this action annoyed Kate. In the living room the fire was burning low in the fireplace. "Shall I build it up?" Pat asked.

"No, not now, after we ski." Kate thought: This is my place, don't come in and take over.

"Will you tell me why you've been hiding? I can understand the need to be alone, but a phone call now and then would be nice. Just to let me know you're all right, if nothing else."

Kate met Pat's eyes. They looked dark, angry, bruised. How easy it would be just to reach for her, but she wouldn't do it, couldn't do it. She told herself it wasn't fair to Pat, when she didn't know if what she felt was more than temporary. She wouldn't do to Pat what she had done to Bert. Besides, she could never tell her kids about Pat; she could never tell anyone, except Gordie. "I would tell you if I knew."

"Then isn't it time to go back to Dr. Jane?"

"Don't tell me what to do, Pat."

The hurt was there for Kate to see. Her heart lurched for Pat, for them both, but still she kept her distance. A little pain now was better than a lot later, wasn't it? "I need the space right now," Kate heard herself say, more of a plea than a statement.

Pat lifted her shoulders and attempted to let Kate go in her mind. What happened between them wasn't going to happen again. "Are we still friends, Kate?"

"We'll always be friends. Let's go skiing."

The warm snow stuck to their skis, making it impossible to glide, forcing them to pick up the skis to move forward.

"How was your weekend with the girls?" Pat asked.

"Not good. They're very unhappy with me because I waited till Brad died to tell them about Gordie and Brad. The more they thought about it the madder they got." She picked up a ski and tried to knock off the snow packed in a tight glob.

"They'll get over it." Pat took a ski off and used a pole to scrape the white stuff loose, but then it was stuck to the sole of her ski shoe.

"It's no good today. Too warm. Let's go back." Kate was sweating and couldn't shed any more clothes. She called Arthur, who was far ahead out of sight, and they turned back. "I suppose they will. I don't know if they'll trust me again."

"How can they not trust you? You keep confidences well."

"Too well."

"Why are you going to Gordie's?" She was also sweating in the warm day, struggling with the heavy snow on her skis.

"He asked me to come."

"That's the reason?"

"It's as good as any."

"When are you coming back?"

"Probably in the spring."

At the back door they stuffed their skis and poles in the snow. Inside Kate put more logs on the fire as the sweat dried on her and she became chilled. She rested on her heels in front of the fire. Sensing Pat's gaze on her, she met it.

"I'll miss you, Kate."

It was a flat statement, but the pained longing was there in Pat's voice and eyes. Kate looked away. "I'll miss you, too, but I'll be back. Maybe Gordie will come with me. We'll have another summer."

Pat perched on the edge of the davenport and took Arthur's head between her hands, scratching behind his ears. "You're sorry, Kate?"

Kate silently shook her head. "Not sorry, just sorting feelings. I don't want to do to you what I did to Bert."

"I see," Pat replied quietly. "And what about my wants?"

"What do you want?"

"You."

"I knew this would happen."

"No, it won't. I'm leaving. Give my best to Gordie, Kate. Let me hear from you now and then."

XII

Driving to Gordie's after spending a night at Beth's, Kate was still stunned by Pat's sudden departure. But until Kate found answers, she had to let her go. First she had to know what she wanted, if anything. Maybe she should just enjoy each day as it came. What was wrong with that?

Arthur surprised her by barking at a dog in a passing car. She jumped and the Taurus swerved. "Bad dog," she scolded, angry from the scare.

Gordie welcomed her with a grin and a kiss. He grabbed a couple of suitcases and hurried into the house. Carrying an overnight bag and leading Arthur, Kate followed him inside where stifling heat hit her like a wall. Gordie, breathing heavily, collapsed on the davenport. From carrying two suitcases fifty feet or so?

She frowned at him. "I could have carried them, Gordie."

"You can take them up the stairs, Katie." He gestured toward the stairway, one hand on his chest.

"Are you like this all the time?"

He nodded, still struggling for breath. "I'm okay if I don't lift stuff or walk up too many steps or try to run. Sit down and stop staring at me like that."

"Like what?"

"Like I'm dead meat."

"Come on, Gordie, don't talk that way. God, it's hot in here."

"Think so? Complaining already, I see."

"You're not hot?" She walked over to the thermostat. "Eighty degrees."

"Leave it," Gordie said. "Take some clothes off. Walk around naked but leave it alone. Right now I'm cold."

Still scowling, she observed him. He was wearing a heavy sweater and jeans. How was she going to bear this? She had only brought winter clothes with her. She pulled off the sweater covering her shirt. "So how are you, besides short of breath and cold?"

"Sometimes I'm hot and turn it way down. Looks like we're going to get along splendidly, Katie."

"You always were difficult to live with," Kate commented.

"So what's new?"

"The girls are furious with me."

191

"They'll get over it." He patted the cushion next to him. "What have you been doing?"

Arthur whined. He had investigated the living room and kitchen and now he looked at her imploringly. Water, she thought, watching him pant, in this heat he had to be thirsty. "He probably needs a drink, Gordie." She put a pan down on an old newspaper for him and returned to the other room.

"I see he's going to be a pain in the ass," Gordie said.

"You bought him," she countered.

"So I did. Never thought I'd get stuck with him, though." He smiled. "I'm teasing, Katie. Does he have some manners now?"

"Yes, Pat taught him all the necessary behavior for a well-mannered dog."

"How is Pat?"

Kate looked away. "Unhappy, I'm afraid."

"Why?"

"I don't want to talk about it right now."

"Aw, come on, sis. Don't start something and not finish."

In a low voice she related what had transpired between Pat and herself.

"How could you leave?" He grinned devilishly.

Then she explained as best she could the past two weeks, when she had become so reclusive and how she and Pat had parted.

The smile had long since faded away. "What's with you, Katie?"

"I don't know. I thought some distance might put everything in perspective."

"You even quit seeing your shrink?"

"Yes and I don't think I'm going back. I'm not going to review my childhood. Living through it once was enough."

"You didn't have a happy childhood?" He feigned surprise.

"Let me recant. I didn't have a happy teenhood."

"Do you know someone who did?"

"I didn't really like myself when I was a kid, Gordie. Did you?"

"Not when I discovered I was a pervert."

She laughed. "Oh, Gordie, you weren't a pervert."

"Well, I thought I was."

"That was after you climbed into bed with Junior Massengale, wasn't it?"

"That was when I discovered what my prick was for. I mean I used to beat off at every opportunity, and Dad found out about that, too. I bet he beat off as much as I did, but he told me I shouldn't do it so much."

"You're kidding?"

"Nope."

"How did he know?"

"My sheets probably. We had a little talk once about too much masturbation. A little was okay. Too much was bad for you, according to Dad, and please do it in the shower. Don't tell me you didn't do it, Katie?"

She howled at the "please do it in the shower." She said, "Of course I did. I remember when I first discovered myself and released all that tension. It was a mind-saver."

"And you still do it, right?"

"Yes, once in a while. Don't you?"

193

"Sure. It's a little boring now, but it was a great discovery then, wasn't it? What's really wrong, Katie? How could you do that to Pat?"

"I don't want to do to her what I did to Bert."

"Bullshit, Katie, she's not Bert. You don't feel about her the way you felt about Bert."

"How do you know what I feel, Gordie? I don't feel anything much anymore, that's the problem."

"Because of me, I suppose."

She glanced sideways at him. Arthur lay at her feet and licked himself.

"What is he doing?" Gordie asked in disgust.

"Don't, Arthur," Kate commanded, and Arthur lifted his head for only a moment before resuming his licking. "He's doing what all dogs do. Just ignore it. Gordie, we had a dog when we were kids. They lick themselves. Get used to it."

"Must I?"

"Yes."

"Answer my question. Is it because of me?"

Kate sighed deeply. "I don't know. I just want to hide — or I did then."

"You can't hide from the future, no matter how unpleasant it is."

"I could never tell the girls or Jeff."

"Excuses, Katie."

"I don't need to make excuses, do I? I don't need to do anything."

"No, you can vegetate if you want. You don't have to love anyone. That person might die or leave you."

Kate felt shock and pain. Was that why she had backed off from Pat? "Why do I need a shrink, Gordie? I've got you."

"And I need a nap. Move, sis."

She got up and he stretched out on the davenport and covered himself with an afghan. Taking her suitcases she went up the stairs.

She set up her typewriter in the bedroom. She could see the top of a leafless maple from the window, its bare branches swaying in the wind. She cracked the window and breathed the fresh air. Arthur put his nose to the opening and sniffed as if he were in the car.

The days took on a certain routine. First thing mornings she took Arthur for a short walk. Then she made coffee and waited for Gordie to come downstairs. He did only free lance work now and some consulting for the firm he had worked with for nearly twenty years. He had assured her he had enough money put away and his health insurance was in effect. These were genuine worries, because she only made enough to support herself. On Mondays the *Chronicle* letter packet arrived and she worked on the contents Monday and Tuesday. On Fridays the *Journal* packet was in the mail and she spent that day and sometimes the weekend on those letters. She walked to the store every other day for groceries, did all the cooking and the laundry and cleaning. She wrote weekly letters to her children and Pat.

Dan had suggested she consider selling her column to more newspapers. She had given the idea serious thought and was undecided as to whether she wanted the additional work. There was enough to keep her busy.

At first she had watched Gordie like a hawk, much to his annoyance, but now she accepted his lack of energy. His frequent naps became the norm. She talked to the neighbors, especially the ones who walked their dogs. Gordie's friends dropped by and she sat in on the conversations. Actually, she was less alone than she had been at the lake, yet she was lonely. A feeling of displacement made her strangely restless.

February was a difficult month for Pat, nearly as bad as August. She told herself she should be grateful — her dad continued to improve. Dr. Hiller had given him the green light to return to his life as it had been before the heart attack and surgery, but he'd already jumped the gun and was doing what he wanted to do. At least the doctor's okay had relieved her mother's mind, she had been able to stop trying to restrict his activities. Pat went home at least once a month. Her friends and students dominated the rest of her life.

The weekly letters from Kate provided a tenuous link. Pat thought she should break this bond but found she could not. She haunted the mailbox. And there were the phone calls. Kate called one week, Pat the next. After Pat hung up, she often couldn't recall much of the conversation. Did Kate miss her as much? She had no idea. Once she called when Kate was out and talked to Gordie. She remembered that conversation well.

"Sorry, Pat," he had said. "Kate's grocery shopping. How are you?"

"Fine, Gordie, and you?"

"Getting by. Kate misses you, you know."

She snorted in disbelief. "I don't know. How do you know?"

"I think she's afraid of what she feels for you. We've had some long talks. I'm the resident shrink here."

Pat's heart jumped in hope. "She talks about me?"

"She's afraid of the relationship, Pat. She's not ready for anything lasting and doesn't want to hurt you and it's still an impossible thing to her — loving a woman. Mostly, I think she doesn't want to be hurt herself, but she doesn't know that."

The whole business depressed Pat. She was not sorry they had made love. How could she regret something she had enjoyed and wanted so much? But she did feel remorse for the way it had sabotaged the friendship. She had been afraid it would. Now when they met it would stand between them — but it had been between them before as an unrealized desire. Perhaps Kate didn't know they could be friends and lovers without telling the world, without informing anyone. But she sensed it was more complicated, that Kate's sensibilities were rather raw right now.

Barb appeared in the doorway of her classroom. It was almost uncanny the way Barb showed up when she needed her. "Missed you Saturday night," she said.

"I was at my parents'. I'll come next Saturday."

Pat smiled. Barb's cheerfulness rubbed off. "Did you have enough people for a game?"

"Oh yeah, Karen was there, and Joy."

Pat didn't understand. "Joy was there without Gail?"

Barb nodded. "You don't know, do you?"

"Know what?"

"Gail and Joy broke up."

"Really?" Pat had an impression of being layered, and Barb's information took time to work its way to her brain. "No, I didn't know." Why didn't she feel something, anything? "Why Karen and Joy?"

"I think they're taking each other up." Barb fiddled with the paperweight on the desk.

"What's Gail doing?" she asked, still finding this difficult to believe.

"Maybe you should call her. She may be having a hard time." Barb turned the paperweight over, making snow fall on the little village inside.

"You think I should? She might think I'm gloating or something. Why don't you call her?"

"I did. She's not doing well."

"I'll call her tonight." Perhaps by then she would feel something besides this numbness. Her future loomed bleakly ahead of her, empty of Kate, Karen and certainly Gail. She'd never love Gail again, and she only wanted Karen for a friend, didn't she? This solved that problem.

"Gail? Pat here." She felt foolish, sure that Gail hadn't forgotten her voice.

"How are you?"

Pat had expected to be rebuffed and had prepared herself, so she was pleasantly surprised by Gail's receptiveness. "Barb stopped by my room today."

198

"She told you?"

"Yes. I haven't seen Karen lately, so I didn't know."

"I think I was meant to live alone." Gail gave an abrupt laugh.

It sounded harsh to Pat. "Me, too," Pat lied, knowing she wanted to live with Kate. "Are you going to Barb's for poker Saturday night?"

"I'll go if you go."

"Okay. I'll call you Saturday." Of course Gail wouldn't want to go alone. Joy and Karen might be there.

"Thanks for the call."

Pat turned out the lights, poured herself a glass of wine, and lay on the davenport. Kate crept into her thoughts and she picked up the phone, then put it back down. It was Kate's turn to call.

March. Winter had temporarily thrown off its cloak. Gordie warned the good weather wouldn't last: "You know, in like a lamb, out like a lion." The warm spell had nurtured a crop of flu and colds, but Kate relished this promise of spring. She and Arthur took long walks, sometimes driving out to Eagle Creek Park to walk those trails.

Gordie's free-lancing had nearly turned into full-time work. Lulled by his renewed good health Kate tended to forget the risk factor he faced with the public. So when she let herself and Arthur into the house after walking to the grocery store late one Monday morning to find him lying on the sofa, one arm thrown over his eyes, she was startled into

199

reality. She stared at him in fright, thinking this was it, he was so pale and thin.

"Why are you staring at me, Katie?" he demanded without uncovering his eyes.

"You said you'd be home late this afternoon."

"Well, I feel rotten, so I came home late this morning." His thin chest rose and fell in an exaggerated effort to breathe.

"How do you feel?"

"Clammy, weak, nauseated, sick. Don't get too close. I think I've got the flu. Everyone else has."

But he was not everyone. He couldn't afford to have the flu. "No, Arthur," she said, holding the dog's collar. Arthur was attempting to lick Gordie's face. "Let's get a yummy." The dog followed her to the kitchen. Her heart had plunged to gut level and was on its way to her feet. Should she insist on calling the doctor? She returned to Gordie's side, where Arthur got in a quick slurp on Gordie's cheek before curling up next to the couch.

"Goddam dog," Gordie said, turning on his side toward the back of the davenport.

"I should call the doctor," Kate suggested.

"Not yet, Katie. I feel too sick to go anywhere. I just want to sleep. You could get me a bucket in case I puke."

Gordie vomited all afternoon, and when she saw what appeared to be blood in the pail, she told Gordie that was it. She called the doctor, who insisted she take Gordie to the hospital. Gordie didn't argue.

Talking to Dr. Steincrohn — a kindly man, tall and spare with inch-long hair, giving her the

200

impression he was all business — Kate listened carefully, waiting for reassurance. He offered none. He told her Gordie had Kaposi's sarcoma, which was news to her, and verged on pneumocystic pneumonia. They stood in the hallway outside Gordie's room in the AIDS wing of the hospital. The door was closed but Kate still saw the IV dripping into Gordie's arm, the oxygen tubes in his nose.

"I didn't know, I didn't see any marks. He didn't tell me he had symptoms of Kaposi's sarcoma." Sensing doom, she sagged and her voice faded. It was just like Gordie not to tell her.

The doctor patted her on the shoulder. First he knocked her down with the unvarnished facts, then picked her up with hopeful possibilities. "He'll probably pull out of this. Physically, he's still pretty strong and medication will help."

"Do you think so?" she asked, looking at him with hope.

"I think so." He smiled at her with his mouth. His eyes were elsewhere, most likely where his mind was.

When Gordie told her to go home, that he wanted to sleep, she returned to the house to feed and walk the dog. She was so deep in depression she could barely function. This wouldn't do, she thought. She had to put on an encouraging face for Gordie. If she was so glum, he'd think the doctor had told her he was going to die. The relentlessness of the disease threatened to crush her, its reality brought home by Gordie propped up in the white bed, nearly as pale as the sheets. Too defeated to turn on the lights or fix herself something to eat, she sat in the dark with

Arthur parked at her feet. The sound of the phone startled her, and she bumped into the kitchen door and cursed before finding the light switch.

"Kate? How is everything?"

"Do you really want to know, Pat?" Kate asked, her voice low and carefully controlled, desperately wishing she were at the lake and that none of this had happened.

"Yes, of course," Pat replied, alarmed. Actually, she had called needing to hear Kate's voice.

"Things aren't going well for Gordie." She told Pat about the afternoon. Then: "It just became real to me, Pat, that he might die. I can't ignore it anymore."

"I wish I were there, Kate," Pat said after a pause.

"Oh God, I wish you were, too. I'm sorry, Pat."

"What do you mean you're sorry?"

"I'm sorry I behaved the way I did before I came here. I was sticking my head in the ground, like an ostrich with its behind exposed. Stupid."

"What were you doing when I called, Kate?" Pat asked, concerned about the dejection in Kate's voice.

Kate's laugh caught in her throat, sounding like a sob. "Sitting in the dark with Arthur, not even thinking."

"Have you eaten?" Pat shot a look at the clock: 9:25 p.m.

"Not yet, I'm not hungry." Kate kicked at the chair rung and smiled a little, because she knew what was coming next.

"Will you promise to eat something now?"

"Is that a cure-all? Reminds me of the Waltons. If

anything went wrong, some adult always advised food. I'll be all right, Pat. I'm glad you called, though."

"How long will Gordie be hospitalized?"

"I have no idea. I'd like to take him to the lake when he gets out, but I guess that isn't practical. The medical facilities are here."

"Does that mean you won't be coming home?" Damn, damn, damn. Soon she would be as depressed as Kate.

"Maybe you could visit, Pat?" Kate suggested, hoping. "But it's seven hours each way and you only have weekends free," she said, offering Pat an easy out in the next breath.

"You mean that, Kate? You'd like me to come?"

"Oh yes." Kate realized she was holding her breath and covered the receiver with her hand while she exhaled.

"I could fly, maybe even take a day off."

"You'd do that?"

"Of course. I love you, Kate."

Silence as they pondered this statement.

"I love you, too," Kate replied quietly.

Didn't she? Wasn't that why she was afraid? And she thought about how she wanted to express this love, wondered why she had insisted on making love, why she had given in to the attraction and then had backed away from the implications. Life had shown its hand. Its brevity was uppermost in her mind, allowing no time for refinements. She wanted to plunge back into the thick of it, to embrace it, to feel pain and joy instead of this numbness.

* * * * *

203

The plane bumped the runway twice and braked to a long stop before taxiing to the terminal. Kate, having broken all her previous city speeding records attempting to reach the airport in time, exhaled a sigh of relief upon reaching the gate before the first passengers appeared. The sight of Pat was like a breath of home.

They grinned at each other. Kate hugged Pat. Nothing like a long separation to sweeten reunion. "I think it's okay to hug in airports," she said, her smile growing of its own accord. Attraction was like a magnet between them. Kate backed off a couple feet to look at her.

"You look good, Kate," Pat said, lifting her eyebrows, smiling happily.

"So do you."

In the car, Pat opened her window, watching Kate, refilling her memory. The blue-green eyes laughed at her, the reddish hair shone in the sun, the mouth was drawn wide in a smile, causing Pat herself to smile. Kate's hands on the steering wheel were small with slender tapering fingers, and Pat recalled with a faint thrill of pleasure the feel of them on her. How could she have walked away the last time they had been together? "How's Gordie?"

"Home and being difficult." She started the engine. "He wanted out of the hospital, now he wants out of the house. He's hard to please." Kate noticed the difference in her body, as if it were awakening from sleep, anxious to greet a new day, glad to be alive. How long since she had felt this way?

"And Arthur, is he behaving himself?"

"He'll be delighted to see you, just as I am."

204

"If I'd known that, I'd have been here long ago."

"Really?" Kate asked with interest.

"Really," Pat replied.

"Could have fooled me the way you left last time." She hadn't meant to say that, had she? The car in front of them suddenly braked at a yellow light. "Idiot," Kate said.

Pat smiled. Behind the wheel Kate was always in a hurry. Then she said, "I didn't realize how long it would be before I saw you or how difficult it would be not to see you." There, it hadn't been so hard to say.

Kate scanned her, a little startled by the honesty. Tiny freckles marched across Pat's cheeks and nose, the soft brown eyes gleamed. Her colors blended nicely, Kate thought, glancing at the sandy hair curling over the smooth forehead, her eyes focusing briefly on Pat's mouth. She ran her tongue over her lips and returned her gaze to the road. The stop light had changed to green. "Neither did I."

She anticipated Pat's departure in a few days and fought off depression at the thought. "Wish I could go home," she said wistfully. She backed off the gas pedal. There was no rush to get to the house.

"I wish you could, too. Is there no way to bring Gordie to the lake?"

"I don't know." How could she stay here through the spring? Her depression would smother them both.

Gordie greeted them from the davenport, where his long frame took up most of the length. Arthur waited joyously inside the door, his body wagging, his teeth bared slightly in a grin.

"About time you came for a visit," Gordie commented, laying down his book. "We needed a good cleaning. You'd think the Queen Mother was visiting." He grinned at Kate.

Pat gave a shaky laugh, her hands occupied with patting a quivering Arthur. "Glad to know I'm so welcome." Gordie's appearance shocked her, even with Kate's warning of his weight loss, his paleness. It was his eyes, deep set and haunted, that appalled her.

"Stay as long as you want, Pat. You're always welcome."

"This is a wonderful house, Gordie. It's beautiful."

"Thanks, it's my creation."

"Come on, I'll show you upstairs." Kate took Pat's suitcase and started up the stairway with Pat and Arthur on her heels. She set the suitcase down in her room, then turned and lightly touched Pat's arm.

"This is your room, Kate?" Pat asked hesitantly, staring at the double bed.

"Yep, there are only two bedrooms. Do you mind sleeping with me?" she asked, running her hand up and down Pat's arm. Tiny hairs stood on end under her fingers.

Pat's heart shifted and picked up speed. She covered Kate's hand with her own and made a stab at lightness. "If it's a choice between you and Gordie, I'll sleep with you." She squeezed the hand.

"I could take the couch," Kate replied with a lopsided smile, looking into the soft dark depths of Pat's eyes.

Pat shook her head, blood thumping in her ears as she reached for Kate. She buried her face in the bright hair, ran her hands down the small back pressing Kate against her.

The sensation of smoothness, the smell of skin and hair filled Kate's awareness. She kissed the warm velvety neck, the rounded chin, working her way to Pat's mouth.

Pat responded with fervor. Her tongue met Kate's, and she lowered her to the bed.

Arthur whined and they ignored him. He thrust his wet nose in their faces. They rolled away. He barked.

Pat murmured, "Maybe he has to go outside?"

"Probably. Damn."

"We can finish this later."

"Something to look forward to." Kate smiled, then turned serious. "Living the way we do, Pat, is unnerving. It takes its toll. You may be sorry you came."

"I doubt it."

Kate looked toward the window and heaved a sigh. The maple branches bent before the wind under a gray sky. "All right. Let's take Arthur for a walk."

Gordie hadn't been outside since coming home from the hospital and then only long enough to get from the car to the building, yet he kept closer tabs on the weather than when he had faced it every day. He warned them to don warm jackets, told them the temperature was plummeting.

Afterward, they carried in logs and built a fire in the fireplace, and Gordie waxed enthusiastic over their efforts. "Now we can have popcorn later." But Kate knew he wouldn't stay up long after dinner.

Pat helped Kate in the kitchen. This scene, the two of them preparing food, was so familiar it was comforting. How many times had they done this in different locations?

207

When Gordie had gone to bed and Arthur had been taken on his final walk of the evening, Pat and Kate sat on the couch, hands lightly clasped. The flames behind the glass doors died into coals as they watched. They had exchanged information on each other's lives, catching up on events since they had last been together.

"Ready for bed, Pat?"

"Any time." Pat stared into the fire, hypnotized by the pulsing coals and short flames leaping to life and dying down.

"Think I'll take a quick shower. Do you want one first?"

"I just want to be with you," she said quietly, begrudging Kate's absence even for a shower. "I'm great at back rubs." She ran her hand up the middle of Kate's back. "Why are you tense?"

"I don't know," Kate replied, chills of pleasure traveling up her spine with the touch. "Why don't we do this in bed?"

"We don't have to do anything, you know. It's enough just to be with you." Pat's hand dropped to her side.

"Come on," Kate said softly. "It'll never be enough."

The street lights cast shadows in the bedroom. They heard the wind rattling the windows. Kate leaned back a little, in order to see Pat's eyes, which became one when they were so close. "I learned a lesson, one I should have known already."

"What lesson?" Pat asked, thrilled with the turn of events.

"Not to be afraid to live. Life is a short gift. You

know? I don't want to be sorry because I didn't do something."

Pat drew Kate closer and buried her face in her hair, inhaling the scent. She asked, "Is this the something you don't want to be sorry you missed?"

"Yes."

Their lovemaking that night began slow and tender, became comforting and healing. They kissed and tasted gently and lingeringly — eyelids, facial contours, lips, throats, breasts. Their hands caressed with controlled passion, moving over each other to the joining of their legs, where they stroked each other to climax.

Falling into the depths of sleep with lips touching, they awakened in the night to renewed desire. Disappearing under the covers, Kate moved with difficulty down Pat's length. Wadded in a ball at the end of the bed, she tasted the hot wetness and found it fed her desire. Reacting to Pat's responses, together they tore the bedding loose.

XIII

Smiling wistfully, Kate listened to Pat's voice on the phone Tuesday night. Gordie called hello from the couch. It had been a long two nights and days for Kate since Pat had left. When Pat had walked through the gate to the plane, she had taken the breath of home with her. Kate had busied herself with Monday's letter packet in an effort to stave off the depression threatening to settle over her. "I miss you, too, Pat," she responded in kind.

"You sound so down, Kate," Pat said.

Kate snorted into the receiver. "I *am* down but

what good does that do?" She replied quietly so Gordie couldn't hear. "I want to be home and I can't be." Her growing need hinged on Gordie's death, an unthinkable contingency.

"I love you, Kate." An inappropriate response perhaps, but Pat had no answer to Kate's problem.

"That only makes me want to come home more."

"Is that all you have to say?"

"I love you, too. You know that."

"I like to hear it."

When Kate returned to the living room, Gordie asked, "Well, how is she?"

"Good," Kate replied.

Gordie studied Kate. "How about a vacation, Katie?"

"What?"

"Let's fly to the Caribbean and take in the sun. It's that time of year."

"We ought to fly to Florida and visit Jeff. He's been begging me to come."

"Then let's do it."

"How can we do it?"

"I can afford to take us both, Katie."

"You'll become too tired."

"I think I'll be all right. I need a change of scenery from this couch."

Kate panicked. "And if you get sick?"

"The alternative is lying on this couch. I think I prefer lying in the sun. I'd love to see the ocean again," he said wistfully. "When we get back, maybe it will be spring and we can go to the lake."

Kate was startled. Was he reading her mind? A protest rose to her lips and died there. Why not?

"Don't frown, Katie. You'll get more wrinkles. Make arrangements tomorrow."

The arrangements took her a full day. There were no seats on flights to Florida because it was spring break for some schools. She had a choice between Aruba, an island off the Venezuelan coast, and Ixtapa, a resort in Mexico on the Pacific. She knew nothing about either place but Ixtapa was closer. She spent additional time on the phone calling her editors and finding a suitable kennel for Arthur. Kate was excited. She called her kids in the evening to tell them where and how long they'd be gone and then she talked to Pat.

"Good, Kate. It'll do you both wonders."

"It'll take wonders. I am worried about Gordie getting sick in Mexico. Maybe it's foolish to go."

"If you're going with one of those travel groups, they'll take care of you."

"And we're only going to be gone ten days. I haven't told the doctor yet. He might make us cancel the whole thing."

Surprisingly, the doctor thought it was a good idea for Gordie to get away. He prescribed medication to protect them from unsafe food and water but warned Kate to eat and drink carefully. If Gordie showed any signs of relapse, the first hint of diarrhea or nausea or cold, they were to fly out immediately.

On the Boeing 747 Gordie lay back in his window seat and closed his eyes, hoarding his strength. The stewardesses were breaking out champagne and mixing drinks for the passengers, and it was only nine a.m. The partying began in earnest. Kate opted for tomato juice.

212

Four and a half hours later they descended onto the only landing strip at the Zihautanejo airport. The plane's wings hung over the runway as the aircraft bounced and then braked and taxied up to the small, clean airport building. The passengers disembarked, some already drunk. Gordie's face was gray, and Kate stood in line to hold a place for him when it came time to check their birth certificates and proofs of American citizenship. The building was cool, but the heat of the dry season hit them as they stepped outside.

When they were finally checked into a third floor room of the Hotel Krystal, Gordie sank onto one of the two double beds. Kate couldn't wait to put on her suit and go to the beach. The pounding surf drew her to it, and she opened the glass door to the balcony overlooking the ocean. A warm breeze smelling of sea softly lifted the hair sticking to her face and neck.

"Never mind me, sis. You go on down. I'll go out on the balcony and catch some rays in a little while. Maybe you can sneak me up a lounge chair from around the pool."

The sand was blistering hot and Kate ran the hundred or so feet to the water, where she cooled her feet in the waves. Walking on the packed wet sand, the undertow tugging at her legs, Kate experienced a surge of joy. Ten days of this and then the prospect of moving back to the lake dangled like incredible promises.

When Kate returned to their room, Gordie called to her from the bathroom. "I'm getting ready for dinner, Katie." He stuck his head out the open door, his face covered with soap. "How's the beach?"

"Wonderful, not a rock on it, just marvelous sand. And look at the ocean, it's so blue. Are you rested, Gordie?" she asked, hoping for the best.

"I feel terrific. This is just what I need." He wiped his face clean and padded into the room on bare feet. "You look like a sunburst, Katie."

"I know." Kate grimaced at herself in the mirror above the dresser. She touched her face and shoulders, leaving white marks in the red. Her eyes were brilliant, set in the sunburn of her face. "I'll have to be more careful. It doesn't hurt, though."

"Where do you want to eat tonight?"

"I don't know." She studied the list of safe restaurants. "There's one down the beach."

"Okay. Can we walk?"

"I can. Can you?" she asked him.

"Sure, I didn't come here to lie in bed."

Their days settled into a pattern: Kate walked the beach early mornings and evenings, met Gordie for the outdoor breakfast buffet in the hotel compound, went shopping or sightseeing after breakfast, while Gordie returned to the room. In the afternoon they sunned and read, she where she could swim, he on the balcony. Each evening they ate at a different restaurant and always outside. Sometimes Gordie swam after dark when no one was in the pools.

One morning while Kate was devouring green scrambled eggs, he asked her, "Bored, Katie?"

"You're kidding, aren't you? I'm having the time of my life. I love it. I'll never forget this. Really."

The plane lifted into the air and carried them back to Chicago, where they were met by rain and temperatures in the low forties. By the time the 707

214

landed in Indianapolis Kate was frantic for Gordie, who was quiet and pale from exhaustion.

Please let him be all right, she begged silently. Gordie had said they would return to the lake in May. "April in Indiana is beautiful," he had told her. "Then we'll go to the lake for the summer." But they couldn't go if he was in the hospital.

He made it to the couch and fell on it.

She turned away. Ixtapa was a dream. This was reality.

Watching the calendar, waiting for the days to pass, had become a way of life for Pat, and she was not pleased with it. Kate and Gordie were probably back in Indianapolis by now, she thought, glancing at the clock. If Kate didn't call by seven, she'd call her. The prospect excited and disturbed her. If she could just get her relationship with Kate in a proper place and keep it there, she would be more at ease with herself. She didn't want anyone dominating her life as Gail once had. And this was worse, because of the distance that separated them, because communication could only be by phone and letter. While Kate and Gordie had been in Mexico she had kept as busy as possible. Being totally out of touch had made her a little desperate.

She laughed thinking of her conversation with Gail yesterday. She had stopped by Gail's apartment on a whim. Gail had joked about gaining weight, had said there was an easy way to burn calories but you must need a partner, because if you didn't she'd have worn a size six. Had she been making a convoluted pass at Pat? If she had, Pat had missed it and only wondered about it later.

She peered out the apartment window at blowing snow. Well, soon it would be April, maybe one more snowstorm before summer. She could stand that. Grabbing a jacket she went out into the cold. Hands in her pockets, she leaned into the wind, walking quickly but with no planned destination. The cold made her head feel numb and her nose run. She discovered herself standing in front of Barb's house.

Barb opened the door and reached out to pull her in. "What's wrong, babe?"

"I need to blow my nose." The warmth closed in on her, making her nose run harder.

"You came all this way to blow your nose? I'm honored. The tissues are in the bathroom. You know the way."

Pat looked at her reddened face in the mirror. What the hell was she doing? She should be home calling Kate.

"You need a hat," Barb said when Pat emerged from the bathroom. "It's colder than a witch's tit out there. Sure everything's all right? Why don't you sit and talk. Sandy's gone. I could use some company. How about a beer?"

Pat removed her jacket and sat on the sofa. "Kate should be back from Mexico tonight."

Barb handed her a Miller Lite and opened one for herself. "Missed her, didn't you?"

Pat nodded and compressed her lips. "Too much."

Barb perched on the edge of a chair across from her. "What does that mean?"

Pat frowned and met Barb's solemn gaze. "That means I'm in love with her and I don't want to be. I just got over Gail."

"You're finally admitting it," Barb said.

"You knew?"

"Sure. I could see it when she was here playing poker."

"You knew before I did then."

"No, I didn't. You've been fooling yourself is all."

"I saw Gail yesterday. She's doing all right — not happy, but who is?"

"I am, Sandy is."

"You two are the exceptions, Barb. Most of us just search for what you have." Pat tasted the cold beer running down her throat. "Most of us never even get our acts together. We spend our lives hiding what we are from our families and co-workers and end up losing our identities. I admire you, Barb."

"Why? I don't have any ads out on me and Sandy." She got two more beers and threw the empty cans in the wastebasket.

"You haven't lost yourself."

"Neither have you, Pat."

"Haven't I? I feel as if I'm living in a cocoon, emerging when Kate is around. Marking time. I don't like that, Barb. I resent it. But I don't know what to do about it."

"Was it that way with Gail?"

"I saw Gail every day."

"When is Kate coming home?"

"Who knows? Maybe in May."

"Why don't you go down during spring vacation?"

"I probably will. Think I'll go home and call her."

"Let me drive you." Barb stood up.

"No, I need the exercise, but thanks, Barb, for being such a good friend."

She walked home kicking snow in front of her. Tree branches and bushes bent under the weight of it. The night was hushed by the falling snow.

"I've got to see you, Kate," she blurted after asking about the trip and Gordie's health.

Kate expelled a deep breath in a sigh. "I need to see you, too," she admitted.

"When?"

"Spring break? When is it?"

"Three weeks."

"I'll come to the lake this weekend, if Gordie's all right," Kate said, deciding impulsively. "I ought to check on the house anyway, and it's Bert's wedding. Maybe we should go."

"You're really coming home?"

"For a few days."

"Better than no days at all, Kate."

The drive was even enjoyable, so glad was Kate to be heading north. There had been a hint of spring in Indianapolis. The forsythia and magnolias had been budding, the daffodils and jonquils getting ready to bloom, the grass greening as the days warmed toward the end of March. As she drove north, all signs of spring vanished, but she knew they were there, hidden, a few weeks behind. And she didn't care. The sun was out, the air was warm, and she was impatient to see Pat, to reach the lake.

Eight hours later she stood on the shore while a

warm brisk wind blew her hair into tangles. Arthur raced along the water's edge, small piles of ice still littered the beach, the sun glinted off the waves, and Kate savored her surroundings. She pulled herself onto the stacked pier sections and lay back next to Pat.

"Want to go inside?" Pat asked.

"Can't we do it out here in the sun?" Kate said with a grin.

"That would be nice but maybe a little uncomfortable."

"And somewhat blatant."

In the bedroom the sun streamed through the glass and streaked the beds and walls with light. "Do you ever wish you were a man?"

"No, Kate, do you?"

"I did when I was a kid. The boys got all the breaks, you know. The girls were allowed to be cheerleaders. It wasn't fair."

"They also got the girls. It's better now," Pat replied, removing Kate's shirt and unzipping her jeans.

"You're in a hurry, aren't you?"

"You bet."

Kate emitted a satisfied sigh. The windows were darkening and cold seeped in. She heard Arthur padding around the house. "The best thing about making love with a woman is it can go on and on. You don't have to worry about erections. You can do it all day and night."

"I know," Pat replied. "Let's start a fire."

219

"Do we have to? I'd just as soon stay in bed."

"A little food and wine and a nice fire don't appeal to you?"

"You appeal to me, and there's so little time. We have to go to that damn wedding tomorrow."

Pat wrapped a robe around herself and pulled on her socks. "It'll make it sweeter next time."

"Do you think that's possible?"

Saturday morning the sun and the smell of coffee wakened Kate. She poured herself a cup of coffee and joined Pat in the shower.

After the wedding at the United Methodist Church in Waushara, Kate told Pat she felt fortunate to have escaped a second marriage. "If I hadn't met you, if Gordie hadn't shown up, perhaps I'd have married him."

"You're giving me and Gordie the credit?"

Kate smiled. "I liked her, did you?"

"Bert's new wife? Yes, I did. Attractive, isn't she?"

"Do you suppose she'll help in the funeral business? I never would have."

"No telling."

Back at the house Pat insisted on a walk. "We can't spend all our time in bed."

"Why not?" Kate asked, but she enjoyed the walk. She took off her shoes, put a foot in the lake and quickly removed it. "Ice water."

"It's not even April. I can't wait for you and Gordie to move back."

"Will you move in with us?"

"For the summer if you want me."

"Can we go back to bed now?"

Pat laughed. "Sure."

"Do you want to?"

"Of course. I never get enough of you."

"Never is one of those words you should never use."

"I know."

When Pat next arrived in Indianapolis it was in mid-April. Pink blankets of fallen flowers encircled magnolia tree trunks. Redbuds and crab apples and dogwoods bloomed in a haze of red and pink and white blossoms. Petals fell at their feet as Pat and Kate walked Arthur along the streets. Always thrilled with spring, Kate found herself acutely aware of the season as the air became pungent with new growth and one plant species after another assumed its few days of burgeoning beauty. She had looked forward to showing Pat this dream world of botanical delight, and Pat was duly impressed. But she was so happy to be with Kate, she would have been pleased with slums and a few scraggly tulips.

"Are you really coming home next month, Kate?" Pat asked when they were alone in Kate's bedroom.

"I've got my fingers crossed." Kate's face was alight with pleasure. She looked no further than the present anymore. "It's good to see you."

"I know what you mean. Even two weeks can be a long time. I've been busy, though. That helps."

"Tell me about it," Kate said.

Pat brought her up to date on the happenings in

her life, including the disturbing news of the gifted thirteen-year-old in her class who, she had heard, was pregnant.

"Her family knows," Pat said. "You've got two girls — is there anything I can do for her?"

Kate shook her head sorrowfully. "She'll come to you if and when she's ready. When the kids were young and even now, I wanted to keep them from making mistakes. You can't do it. Everybody learns on their own and in their own way."

Then Kate looked at her. "You went out with Gail?" she asked, focusing on that revelation.

"We're becoming friends again."

"Really? Just friends?" Was she jealous? Surely not, but she admitted to herself she was hunting for a little reassurance here.

"Just friends. Come on, Kate. We like to do the same things."

"Good," Kate said, hoping she meant it.

"Tell me about Gordie."

"It was like the trip took everything out of him, but he's made a good recovery. The doctor said he's seen many AIDS patients make remarkable comebacks. I suppose that was meant to be reassuring."

That night at dinner Kate suggested they leave for the lake when Pat returned home, and Gordie said, "I can't go yet, Katie. I've still got a job to finish." He sampled the steamed asparagus and closed his eyes in appreciation. "Mmm, good." Then he glanced from one to the other. "Why don't you leave, Katie, and I'll follow in a few weeks? I don't know why you just didn't stay when you were there at the end of March."

Kate stared at Gordie. Did he really mean what he had just said? It hadn't been necessary for her to return? "You didn't even suggest I not come back."

"You thought you had to stay with me, Katie? Shut your mouth. You look dumb. I can get along without you, believe it or not. Maybe I'll turn this place into a home for friendless AIDS men. Wouldn't the neighbors love that?" He laughed. "I would if I could stand sick people. As it is I can hardly bear myself."

"You mean you might not leave for the lake in May?" She was ashamed at how excited she was at the prospect of going home.

"I'll come as soon as I can get away. I'm feeling well right now."

"But what if you become sick and you're alone?"

"Telephones, Katie, help is only a fingertip away."

Kate continued to gape at Gordie, her dinner forgotten.

"Eat, Katie. Show Pat a good time and then go home. I'll follow in May or June. If you have to, you can always return."

"You can drive that far? Why don't you fly?"

"I want my car. I'll stop if I'm tired, stay in a motel or something."

Kate remarked later to Pat, when they were lying in bed, "It's such a good feeling not to be indispensible. Do you really think he'll be okay?" Arthur was scratching somewhere in the darkness.

"You know that better than I do," Pat replied. "Why don't you talk to the doctor?"

"Stop scratching, Arthur," Kate commanded. The scratching ceased and was replaced by a licking sound. "Goddammit, Arthur, don't lick. I'm going to

223

put him in the hall. No one should have to sleep with a dog."

Pat propped herself on an elbow, an amused smile on her face, as she watched a naked Kate walk Arthur across the room and shove him out the door.

"I felt trapped, Pat, and felt guilty for feeling that way." Kate climbed back in bed and snuggled under the covers. The warm sweet smells of spring drifted in the open window.

"I know, Kate. Come here."

"I've been thinking about us, too," Kate said. She saw the highlights of Pat's face, her cheekbones and forehead. Her eyes were shadows.

Pat's heart gave a warning leap. "Oh?" Lying back and putting her hands under her head, she waited for Kate's next words.

"I think we should meet this way more often, don't you?"

"Damn it, Kate, don't scare me like that." She wrapped Kate tightly in her arms.

Pulled out of a deep sleep by Gordie's calls and a brief shake from Pat, Kate jumped to her feet, snatched a shirt off a chair and ran to Gordie's room. He was jerking spasmodically on his bed. Not knowing what to do, attempting to hold him still, Kate grabbed his arms in panic. Pat called for the rescue wagon. They heard the siren in a matter of minutes, just time enough for Pat and Kate to take turns dressing, while one stayed with Gordie. Gordie's eyes were wild with fear, with despair. Kate sat on the edge of the bed and brushed his short sweat-dampened hair back in a futile gesture of comfort. She knew his thoughts. They were hers: Was he going to die like Brad?

"Soon as I'm released from the hospital we'll go to the lake, Katie," he whispered when he could talk, as the medical attendants packed him on a rolling ambulance cot.

"Sure, Gordie. I'll follow with Pat."

In the hall one of the attendants asked her, "He has AIDS, doesn't he?"

"Does it make any difference? Just get him to the hospital. He's sick."

"I need to know, ma'am."

"Yes," she replied in an angry hiss. And what she was thinking through her panic was she wouldn't be able to go home now, hating herself for the thought, almost hating Gordie for being the cause of it.

Speeding behind the ambulance through the night traffic, Pat concentrated on keeping the rescue wagon in sight. She didn't know where they were going. Both women were mesmerized by the flashing red lights and the piercing siren, which eclipsed all other sounds. Kate's teeth and hands were tightly clenched. She felt almost catatonic — unwilling to think, to talk, to admit to this setback.

Pat snatched glances at Kate whenever she could take her eyes off the road for a few seconds. She would like to reassure Kate but how could she? How could someone apparently so all right, as Gordie had been that evening, suddenly be felled? If it scared the shit out of her, what must it do to Kate, not to mention Gordie?

In the hall outside the emergency room Pat attempted to put a comforting arm around her, not

225

something she would normally do in public, but Kate pulled away. Resentment, fear, concern, anger were what Kate felt, and she stood uncertainly on the blue and beige carpet struggling with her emotions. Her entire body ached with tension, and after forcing herself to relax her jaw and open her hands, she stared at the half-moon indentations left in the palms of her hands by her fingernails.

"I'm sorry, Kate," Pat said softly, attempting to break into Kate's misery, to make contact with her.

Kate smiled bitterly. "So am I," she said inclining her head slightly. "So much for going home."

Pat's heart dropped like a stone.

But Dr. Steincrohn was encouraging. "We'll keep him here a few days. Then if you want to take him north with you, go ahead. Just be certain you have a doctor who can care for him. He may live another year, maybe longer. Who knows. If he wants to go, why not? He might as well enjoy the time he has left. Right?"

Kate fixed her gaze on Dr. Steincrohn's departing back as if he were the good fairy exiting, then turned to Pat and smiled wryly. They were actually going home.

XIV

The lake moved and glittered, a restless blue-green. Dressed in jeans and a sweatshirt despite weather in the eighties, Gordie read on the porch. He laughed aloud at an amusing passage and Kate, just entering the room, smiled.

"I want to read that next," she said.

"I promised it to Pat first," he replied.

She looked at the lake with longing. When she finished the latest letter packet, she would get to the water. It beckoned to her as the day heated up. "Want to sail later?"

"Maybe," Gordie said, burying himself in the book again.

She returned to her typewriter. She knew he wouldn't sail. He rarely even walked down to the lake. He was always cold and tired. With a sigh she opened another letter and scanned it, her expression registering horror. It read in large, childish print: *Send that filthy queer with his filthy disease back where he come from or we'll have to take action.*

The envelope was postmarked Waushara. Anger seized her and for the space of a minute her vision blurred and vomit rose up her throat, forcing her to swallow repeatedly. She set the letter aside to show Pat and then felt fury with Pat for teaching summer school and not being here right now. Tearing open another letter she read it two or three times before it registered through her distress.

Dear Jane,

I know this is a foolish thing to let bother me, but it's driving me nuts. I can't stand watching my husband eat. His face is inches from his plate and he shovels the food in as if it's going to jump off the fork and escape between the plate and his mouth. I hate to eat out because I'm embarrassed by his bad manners. Food dribbles down his chin and he makes rude noises. In all other ways he's a gentleman. What can I do about this?

Dear Disturbed,

I don't consider this a foolish problem. Good table manners are often necessary in conducting business and enjoying a satisfactory

228

social life. Have you talked to him about your feelings? Suggest tactfully that he upgrade his table manners. In the end he will be grateful.

She tossed the letter and answer in a pile and put on her swimsuit. She and Pat had taken Gordie's old bedroom upstairs so he could be on the first floor. The windows were all open, admitting a hot breeze. Perhaps she would be able to forget the threatening letter if she worked off some energy in the water.

"Want to go with me?" she asked Gordie, as she passed through the porch.

Glancing up from his book he shook his head. "If it warms up some, maybe I'll come down." His beautiful deep set eyes were streaked with red.

Kate knew he didn't sleep well. He frequently woke soaked in sweat and shaking. She often heard him in the night as he wandered around downstairs. Sometimes she joined him. Knowing it wasn't going to get warm enough for Gordie if it wasn't warm enough now, she said, "Okay. Do you want anything before I go down to the beach?"

"I'll get it if I do, Katie. Think I'll take a nap in a little while anyway."

Kate strolled down to the lake, dove off the end of the pier and pulled herself along underwater, then suddenly surfaced to send water spraying in all directions. Facing the shoreline, enjoying the feel and smell of the water, she floated on her back. The day lilies were blooming along the path leading to the lake.

Next weekend her children would be here for ten days. Jeff had a week off. Pat had offered to stay at her apartment during their visit, but Kate wouldn't hear of it. "They may wonder why I'm living here," Pat had remarked. "Let them wonder," Kate had replied. Sooner or later they were going to form opinions anyway. Maybe they would make inquiries, maybe they wouldn't. She hoped they wouldn't and didn't know how she would respond if she was confronted with direct questions. She swam in and waded to the sailboat, which floated around a couple gallon plastic bottles anchored to the bottom.

Raising the bright sail, she watched it flap in the wind. The sun shone through the colors, highlighting them against the blue sky. Then she recalled the threatening letter and wondered if the writer or writers were watching her now. She looked furtively around the lake and put her imagination on hold before she began to invent mysterious fires or explosions in the night.

Pat was lunching with Gail and Barb at a restaurant in Northland. Her attention strayed to the window and the sunshine. The branches of trees across the parking lot stirred in a silent breeze, which reminded her she could be sailing. But she had made this lunch date with Barb a week ago. She didn't feel right neglecting her old friends. She knew too well she needed them.

"How's Natalie?" Barb asked unexpectedly. "I heard . . ." She trailed off.

Pat pulled her eyes and thoughts away from the window and the sunshine to think wrenchingly about the sad, no-longer-innocent face of the gifted thirteen-year-old girl in her class. She nodded at

Barb. "She had an abortion. She seems okay, considering." Perhaps she would be able to invite Natalie to the lake for a day. She'd talk to Kate about it. "Are you renting at the lake again this year?" she asked Gail.

"Barb and Sandy and I are." Gail cast a fleeting smile at Barb.

Meaning Gail was still living alone. Pat studied Gail. Such an attractive woman. Too bad she couldn't seem to sustain a relationship. "We'll have to get together there."

"You're going to be at the lake?" Gail asked.

Pat nodded. "I'm staying with Kate this summer."

"Nice," Gail commented, raising an eyebrow. She brushed blonde strands away from her forehead.

Pat recognized this gesture as one of annoyance, and she smiled at the irony of how her lifestyle had changed and developed. From her misery when breaking up with Gail last summer to her happiness in this new association with Kate. "Isn't it? When have you got the place rented?"

"For a month starting the Saturday after July Fourth."

On the way to the lake Pat considered a visit to her parents the following weekend in order to give Kate time alone with her kids. But when she had suggested being absent during Jeff's visit, Kate had been adamant about her not leaving. Maybe if she had a good reason, like going to see her folks, Kate wouldn't object. She was concerned about Jeff's reaction to her living with Kate.

The door to Gordie's room was closed when Pat walked into the house. She headed upstairs to change into her suit before taking the path to the lake. The

231

sailboat was gone from its mooring, and she stood on the pier to scan the lake for the bright sail. She spotted it coming toward her close to shore, heeling in the wind, Kate leaning back using the sheet for support. Pat dove into the water, grabbed the boat as it surged past and slipped over the side, slid off again and again hauled herself onto the slippery hull.

"Neat trick," Kate commented, maneuvering away from the pier and handing Pat the sheet.

"I've been waiting to see you all day," Pat said, clasping the hand which had helped pull her into the boat. She relished the hot wind and cool spray. Releasing Kate's hand after a squeeze, she smeared lotion on her legs and arms.

"You didn't have to teach summer school." Kate took the suntan lotion from Pat and rubbed some of it into the warm skin of Pat's back. She touched the tanned freckled shoulder lightly with her lips.

"Thanks. You want some on your back?"

"Please," Kate said and then cringed at the cool liquid on her hot skin.

Pat worked the lotion in slowly, ending near Kate's waist, hugging her with one arm. "I was already committed to teaching before I knew I'd be spending the summer here or I wouldn't have done it. God, this is nice. Something to remember when the cold rain falls."

"Where have you been?" There was an edge to Kate's question.

"Having lunch with Barb and Gail, wanting to be here the whole time. Last week I told you I had a lunch date with Barb today. Why?" She glanced at Kate, wondering about the sharpness in her tone.

"You said nothing about Gail," Kate remarked.

She was picking and she knew it. The letter had made her edgy.

"What's wrong, Kate?"

"I'll tell you later. I'll show you."

"Show me what?"

"A letter I received today, an obscenity."

Pat frowned. "What did it say?"

"Coming about." Kate turned the boat and changed sides. The boom whipped over their heads as Pat shifted sides, too. "It said in essence to send that filthy queer with the filthy disease back where he came from."

Pat stared at her while unpleasant chills rippled down her body. Some self-righteous bigot, no doubt, who thought it was his right to impose his beliefs on everyone. The lovely day was tarnished. She leaned back and dipped the back of her head in the water. "Going to let this creep spoil your day?" she challenged Kate.

Kate's return gaze was at first angry, then she shook herself and forced a smile. "No."

"Good." Pat started to tell her she wanted to go home next weekend and decided to save it for later. She didn't want to upset Kate further by arguing with her.

In bed she broached the subject. "Think I'll go visit the folks next weekend," she said into Kate's hair.

Kate had given this more thought and had come to the conclusion that perhaps it would be best if Pat was not here the first weekend. "When are you coming back?"

"I have to be back Monday, but I'd like to stay in town that week until the weekend."

Kate shook her head. "No, it's better you come back here. They have to get used to you."

"Why?" Pat's lips brushed Kate's cheek and moved to her neck. "Jeff is hardly ever here. Why does he have to get used to me?"

"The girls do." Kate turned onto the side facing Pat.

"The girls already have. It'll give you some time together alone," Pat murmured into Kate's mouth.

"Mmmm," Kate responded, feeling the passion grow, holding it off a while longer.

"Does Jeff know about Gordie?"

"Yes." The threatening letter and worry over her children's reactions to her lifestyle faded as desire pushed thought aside. Now there was just the sensation of touch — lips and tongues and hands.

"God, I love you," Pat whispered.

"Don't feel like the Lone Ranger," Kate replied.

"What does that mean?" Pat asked, momentarily disconcerted.

"It means you're not alone."

"Then say it."

"I love you," Kate said, as Pat pushed her gently onto her back.

Pat spent Saturday with her dad in a boat on Lake Winnebago. Rocking with the swells, the sun beating down on the aluminum eighteen foot bass boat, Pat felt as if she were on broil.

"Better cover up, girl. You're going to burn."

"You know I don't burn, Dad."

"I remember you burning."

She did, too, and recalled how miserable she had been. She picked up her shirt and slipped it on over her swimsuit.

Her dad spit into the lake.

"Still dipping, Pop? You know what that does to your mouth?"

"No lectures, kiddo. Remember who's the dad here."

Something tugged on Pat's line and she jerked it and reeled in a crappie. As she brought it into the boat, she thought fleetingly of Kate, and while she removed the hook and put the fish on the stringer, she wondered if it felt pain like she would have. "That makes eight. How about a contest, Dad? The one who catches the least fish gets to clean them."

"You're on."

Pat stared over the glassy rolling water, spotted a sailboat in the distance and squinted at it. She had told Kate she was planning to stay at her apartment until Wednesday when she'd return to the lake.

"Hey, look at this one." Her dad held up the largest crappie yet caught that day. "How about the one who catches the biggest fish gets off from cleaning them."

"Nope, the most fish," Pat insisted, grinning at him, pleased with the way he looked — tan and robust.

"What do you think, girl. Is this the biggest crappie you ever seen?"

"It's pretty big, Pop, but I've caught bigger."

He snorted, removed the fish from the hook and put it on the line with the others. "Too bad your mother couldn't come with us."

"Has she been fishing?" Pat asked with surprise.

"Sure, somebody has to fish with me now that all you kids are gone."

"That's great." They lapsed into silence. Pat pictured her mother fishing, sitting where Pat was now. Her dad probably baited the hook for her and removed the fish.

"Remember when you were a little kid and we went fishing?" her dad reminisced.

"Sure, we'd have a whole boat full of kids in orange jackets. Man, I'd like to get in the water."

"You'll scare the fish away."

"I know but I don't care right now."

"Want to go home? We got plenty of fish for dinner tonight. Your mother would like to see you some, too."

"Let's." She reeled in her line, removed the minnow, stripped off her shirt and dove in. The water was only slightly cooler than the air.

"Warn me next time," her dad shouted, holding both sides of the rocking boat.

"I thought I did. Come on in. It's like a bathtub." She treaded water, grinning a challenge, knowing he wouldn't accept it. The water was yellowish with tree pollen. Pat grimaced with distaste and struggled back into the boat.

Puttering around the familiar kitchen, helping her mother prepare dinner that evening, put Pat in mind of her childhood. "How are the kids, Mom?"

"The grandkids?"

"What other kids are there?"

"They'll be here over the Fourth. Are you going to be here then?"

"Nope. Sorry. I'll be at the lake."

"Who is this person now?"

"You mean Kate? A friend. We met at the lake last summer. Maybe you and Dad could come for a weekend." Here she was inviting guests to Kate's cottage without even asking Kate, but she knew Kate wouldn't mind. Then she envisioned Gordie. Would they know what was wrong with him?

"I'd rather visit your apartment sometime."

"You'd love the lake, Ma, really, but if you'd rather you can come to my apartment. Dad'll be bored there. I hear you've been fishing with Dad."

"Oh yes, it's kind of fun."

Pat passed near her mother and gave her a hug. Her mother stiffened, then responded with a pat on her daughter's back. Pat wondered what Kate was up to.

Playing volleyball in the water with her children, two to a side, reminded Kate of last summer. She recalled Pat and Gail joining them and then later Gordie and Brad. Her heart lurched at that memory. Gordie lay on the pier watching them, calling out encouragement to Beth and Sarah who were sided against Kate and Jeff.

Jeff's face had registered shock when he had first seen Gordie. He attempted to hide his distaste and she hoped it was not as apparent to Gordie as it was to her. She had looked again at Gordie, after watching the girls' expressions, and had seen him through their eyes — thin and hollow-eyed with visible lesions, which he couldn't completely hide with

237

make-up. He was still witty, and Kate had grown somewhat accustomed to his appearance — it no longer startled her.

He stretched out in the sun in his customary garb, sweatshirt and jeans. She found it hard to believe he was not hot. "Don't you want your swimsuit, Gordie?" she asked as the ball flew over her head.

"Pay attention, Mom," Jeff said.

"I couldn't reach it anyway and it's just a game," she retorted, annoyed with his attitude toward Gordie and the game. And then she was sorry, because she was so seldom with him and because she didn't really like what he had become. What had happened to the compassionate little boy? He had to be in Jeff somewhere.

"We need more players," Sarah panted, ducking down in the water. "When did you say Pat is coming?"

"Wednesday."

"Who is Pat?" Jeff asked. "One of the dykes, right?"

Kate halted in the water, her heart beating rapidly. "Don't call her that, Jeff. Okay? She's a very good friend of mine. Most of the summer she lives here." She glanced at Gordie and caught a grin, sort of an angry grimace. She shook her head, begging his silence.

"You're an asshole sometimes, Jeff," Sarah said.

Kate looked at Beth and met her questioning gaze. So Beth wondered about Pat.

"She's a fun person," Beth volunteered.

Jeff shrugged. "Hey, I'm sorry. I didn't mean

238

anything." He tossed the ball across the net to Beth. "Your serve."

Kate's anger faded. He was her son. She mused on this for a few minutes. No matter what they did or said she forgave them because they were her children. Why? If one murdered another, would she forgive that? There was little logic where her kids were involved.

Gordie got slowly to his feet and walked toward the house. Kate knew he was leaving in order to control his tongue, before he told Jeff what was on his mind. She felt pain in her stomach. Sometimes the pain reached right through to her back.

The weekend was hot and windy. Jeff and the girls had a lot of fun with Pat's sailboat, which she had obligingly left for them to use. Sitting on the porch at night they discussed their lives. Beth would be starting graduate courses in the fall. Sarah would be in law school. And Jeff would still be in Florida.

"Why don't you look for a job in the midwest, Jeff?" Kate asked during a card game one night on the porch.

"Because I hate winters." He threw the queen of spades on Sarah's trick.

"You jerk. That's the third time you gave her to me. Why don't you pick on Mom or Beth? They've got the low scores."

He shrugged. "Got to get rid of her when I can. Besides, you passed her to me."

"I couldn't help it. I didn't have any spades."

"I thought you loved to ski," Kate said to him.

"What? Oh, you can't ski in the midwest, not really. I wouldn't mind living in Colorado but I like

Florida, especially in the winter. It's just the opposite from living here. You stay inside in the summer and out in the winter."

Kate thought of Gordie's comments to her before he had hit the sheets an hour ago. "He's a goddamn bigot, Katie — your son, my nephew. How did this happen?" She had replied in defense of Jeff, "I think he was just talking without thinking." The stomach pain gripped her again. She realized with a pang of guilt she'd be glad when Jeff returned to Florida.

"You can't really catch what Gordie's got, can you, Mom?" Jeff asked worriedly. "I like Gordie," he added quickly. "I'm just worried about you."

Kate frowned at him and swallowed an angry retort. He was no doubt genuinely concerned for her.

"Don't be a dope, Jeff," Sarah said before Kate could reply. "It's not like measles or polio. You should know that with all the publicity."

"But if he cut himself and it got into the food," Jeff persisted, ignoring his sister and meeting his mother's angry gaze.

"He doesn't cook," Kate answered shortly.

"Okay, Mom, I won't bring it up again."

"Dad's a little worried about you, too, Mom," Beth said suddenly.

Kate's heart made an unpleasant jump. "A little late to be worried about me, isn't it?" she asked sharply. What was this anyway? An insult to her intelligence, an assault on Gordie.

"Oh, Mom, he still cares about you," Beth remarked.

Again Kate swallowed her anger. Pain grabbed her stomach in a vise. She winced but no one noticed. "Does he?" she asked coldly. She didn't care whether

240

he did or not. Her life with him seemed an eternity ago. "How is he anyway?" She looked up from her cards. Three pairs of eyes were on her. She laughed a little. "It's okay, kids. I'm not bitter. I'm satisfied with my life now. I certainly don't hate him." Actually, she was grateful to him for ending their marriage.

"He's fine," Beth replied stiffly.

"And Nancy?"

"She's fine, too."

"Good. I'm glad they're happy." She sounded facetious, she knew, but she wasn't. She was happy, too, in spite of Gordie's condition. "Honestly," she added for emphasis, trying to read conviction in the young eyes studying her in silence.

In bed that night she swallowed rapidly to keep from vomiting. Listening to the night sounds she heard Gordie prowling downstairs and joined him, padding quietly down the steps. The night was close and hot with only a slight breeze off the lake to ease the heat. She found Gordie sitting on the porch in the dark and sat near him. "Can't sleep?" she asked lightly. "Is Jeff a noisy sleeper?" Jeff was in the other bed in Gordie's room.

"He tosses a lot. I just woke up is all."

She could make him out now in the dark. He wore a bathrobe over his pajamas. She had thrown a short terry cloth robe over her nakedness before descending the stairs.

He rolled a joint and lit it, sucking deeply then holding his breath as long as possible before exhaling in a rush. "Want a drag?" He held it out to her.

She shook her head, smiling slightly in the dark and settling back in the chair. Objects slowly became discernible as her eyes adjusted. "I'm sorry about Jeff," she said hesitantly, hating to apologize for her son.

"Don't worry about me, Katie," he replied staring toward the lake and taking another deep pull on the joint. When he expelled his breath, he said: "I've come up against Jeffs everywhere."

The pain returned. She wanted him to like Jeff, she wanted to like Jeff herself. "Maybe I should talk to him."

"Naw, let it go, Katie. It doesn't matter."

"It matters to me, Gordie," she said with anguish. "He's my son. I love him. I don't enjoy not liking him."

"He's just young, is all. You know how the young are."

"How are they?" she asked, her arms crossed over her stomach.

"They're intolerant."

"The girls aren't."

"The girls learned to know and like me before this happened. If this happened to you, he'd be understanding. Let it go, Katie. It's not like he's going to be around. Why are you clutching yourself like that?"

Letting her arms drop to her sides, she said, "I didn't realize I was."

She climbed the stairs to her typewriter, which rested on a desk under windows overlooking the lake. She had worked on Friday's mail over the weekend and nearly finished it. Deciding to complete it now, she opened one of the last letters and froze as she read: *I warned you, Lady Jane. I won't warn you no more. Send that queer back where he come from or be*

242

reddy for what you get. Her stomach clenched into a fist and she rubbed a hand over it. Now what the hell should she do? Show the letters to the sheriff or something? She needed advice. She tiptoed downstairs again, put coffee on to perk, and phoned Pat's apartment.

Pat answered sleepily, wondering who would be calling so early. Maybe her dad had collapsed after she had left.

"I'm glad you're home," Kate said with relief.

Pat threw a glance at the luminous digits on her clock radio telling her it was four-thirty a.m. "What the hell, Kate, not that I'm not glad to hear your voice, but do you know what time it is?"

"I couldn't sleep and was working on Friday's letters and came across another threatening letter. I don't know what to do, Pat. What if whoever it is acts on the threats? Should I go to a lawyer or what?"

"What does it say?" Pat asked.

Kate read it to her.

"Yes, go see a lawyer. Get some legal advice. I don't know what else to do, Kate. Do you want me to come up?"

"Yes."

"All right, I'll be there after school."

"I'm sorry I woke you."

"It's all right. I'll just go back to sleep." But she knew she wouldn't. She'd worry, that's what she'd do, and when it was time to get up and shower she'd be nervous and tired.

XV

When Pat turned the car into the driveway at the lake and the pine trees closed around her, she only wanted to sleep. Finding Gordie on the porch she sat with him for a few minutes.

"Pardon me for saying this but you look bushed," Gordie commented. "I thought you weren't coming up until Wednesday."

"I wasn't but Kate called and asked me to come today. So here I am." She raised her hands and let them drop. "And yes, I'm tired. Think I'll take a nap. How's it going?"

"As expected."

"And what does that mean?"

"It's okay. Could be better but then it could be worse."

"Could you be a little more specific?" Pat asked. Gordie grinned impishly but on his cadaverous face it looked devilish. "You'll see. They're all down at the lake, except Katie, who went to town for something or other. Glad you're back, Pat."

"Thanks." She got to her feet and climbed the stairs to take a nap. Lying on the bed she heard voices drifting up from the lake. Her mind separated Sarah's voice from Beth's; Jeff's sounded vaguely familiar and took her back to a year ago. Hot weather always made her sleepy, and she slipped into sleep in a haze of heat. Sensing someone's presence she awoke from a dream. Her consciousness reached for the dream but it was gone.

Kate was perched on the side of her bed, one leg drawn up. "I am so glad you're here."

"Been sitting there long?" Pat asked, a little groggy from being awakened.

"Only a few minutes. I went to my divorce attorney. She — did I tell you it's a she? — suggested showing the letters to the local police or sheriff or whatever, but she didn't know what could be done about them without knowing who wrote them. Cost me fifty dollars to find that out."

Pat stretched as she listened. "Did you go to the sheriff or whatever?"

"No, not yet. I will, though. I don't know what he can do, but we can't take unnecessary chances with the kids here and Gordie and us. I'll probably have to tell him about Gordie. She asked if I had a dog." Kate laughed thinking of Arthur, the friendly guard dog. "How can we just sit and wait for whatever's coming?"

"Maybe it's all talk," Pat said. "Come here. I haven't seen you for days." She pulled Kate down next to her on the bed. "How are the kids?"

"Okay." Kate lay still while Pat pushed the hair away from her face and caressed her cheek.

"I missed you," Pat said quietly. "You look so troubled."

"I am. I missed you, too." She ran her fingers through Pat's hair and kissed her. "We can't do this, you know. We might get caught." But she felt incapable of getting up. She wanted to sleep, to hide from everything.

"I know," Pat agreed, "but they're down at the lake. I can hear them."

"How was your weekend at home?"

"Good. I had a nice time. Went fishing with Dad. Tell me about yours."

"Nothing to tell really. We need you for volleyball. Actually, we need you and someone else."

"Jeff and Gordie hit it off?"

"Well, not exactly," Kate hedged. Her stomach clenched and she grimaced.

"Tell me." She had known something was wrong. She assumed the grimace reflected the problem.

"Well, Jeff was shocked when he saw Gordie. I could see it in his face. He's been trying to hide what he feels, but he's young, maybe a little intolerant, and worried about me catching AIDS. There's a tenseness, you know."

"That's understandable." It was what Pat had expected. "And the girls?"

246

"They were shocked, too. They hadn't seen Gordie for so long, but they both care for him. Their shock was sympathetic."

"Hmmm," Pat murmured, squeezing Kate and kissing her forehead.

Kate frowned as the pain returned.

"Why the face?" Pat asked, realizing she had been seeing these expressions a lot lately, usually connected with Kate's hand on her stomach. She glanced in that direction and, sure enough, Kate's hand was there. "What is it, Kate?"

"Nothing."

"Tell me."

Kate moistened her lips with her tongue. "I've got these pains in here — my stomach, I think. They come and go."

"Time to see the doctor," Pat said, placing a hand over Kate's hand.

"It's time anyway. I'll make an appointment for after the kids are gone. Want to go down to the lake?"

"Sure." She didn't though. She'd have liked to lie here with Kate and drift off to sleep again.

In the kitchen, the whoomp of the grill lighting reached Kate's ears. She glanced out the back door to make sure Jeff hadn't burned off his facial hair.

He turned the gas down and took the back steps in two leaps. "Got the brats ready, Mom?"

"They're boiling on the stove." She nodded at the pan and continued cutting up potatoes for potato salad. "What's the hurry?"

247

"I'm going fishing with Pat after supper."

"Oh — did you get a fishing license?"

"Yeah, when I went to the store. Nice lady." He started opening drawers.

"Who? And what are you looking for anyway?"

"Your friend and the foil," he replied.

"All my friends are nice and under the sink," she said, hiding her pleasure. His liking Pat meant more to her than she had thought it would.

"But your other friends don't play volleyball like that. Do you suppose she is a dyke?" The question was almost conversational.

"If you say that one more time, I'm going to slug you, Jeff. What does being good at volleyball have to do with something like that?"

"Hey Mom, sorry." He backed off, raising his hands. "Just curious, that's all. I like her."

"Then don't insult her." The pain tightened and her hand moved to the source. She tasted vomit and swallowed quickly.

"You all right, Mom?" Jeff's arm encircled her shoulders.

"Yes, I'm fine," she reassured him, leaning into the hard young arm supporting her.

"You looked sort of glazed for a minute."

They ate on the porch and talked inconsequentially about anything that came to mind. Gordie cut the bratwurst on his plate into tiny pieces and tasted a few, then tried a little potato salad. Kate watched him in silence. She ate three times as much as he did.

"Sarah and Beth can clean up the dishes. You want to go fishing with us, Mom?" Jeff said.

"We don't need you to tell us what to do, Jeff." Beth bristled. "We know when you cook we clean."

"I should help clean up then, too," Pat commented.

"No, we're going fishing, remember?" Jeff protested. "You know where the fish are."

"I hope I remember," Pat replied. "You coming with us, Kate?"

"Why not? I'll row or something." She met Gordie's eyes. He smiled at her.

Arthur followed them down to the lake and padded out onto the pier. The days had been so hot he spent most of his time lying in the shade. "Sorry, Arthur, the boat is full." Kate patted his large head. He panted at her and showed his teeth in a small grin.

The dog stood on the pier observing the boat's progress along the shoreline, then jumped in the shallows and followed it. "Go home, Arthur," Kate hollered at him. He stopped, lapped some water, watched them uncertainly, then sat in the lake.

Jeff howled with laughter. "Look at him. He's a nice dog, Mom."

Arthur barked a couple times, stood and sloshed out of the lake and disappeared up the hill.

The evening brought last summer to Kate's mind when she had gone fishing with Pat and left Bert on the pier. She had seen Bert the other day in town, in the grocery store. He had looked happy. She seldom thought of him. The sky was a deep red, almost purple in the west, the colors reflected in the lake, and in the east puffy clouds glowed pink. The wind had died to a breeze, causing a rippling effect on the lake.

Kate pulled on the oars and then rested, moving the boat at the speed Pat requested. A whippoorwill started its monotonous call across the water. They rounded the lake at this speed and darkness closed in on them before they reached the pier again. Bass and mosquitos were biting. Kate sprayed them all with Off, and Jeff and Pat each reeled in two decent-sized bass. Bats dipped and swooped around them. A new moon floated in the west.

When they reached the house, Gordie waited on the porch in the darkness, an outline in a chair. "You all right, Gordie?" Kate asked.

He cleared his throat and Kate sensed all was not well. "I'm all right but Arthur isn't. The girls rushed him to the animal hospital. They haven't come home yet."

"What happened?" Kate asked.

"He started puking and convulsing like he was poisoned or something."

Kate and Pat exchanged glances. It was too dark to see the horror in their eyes. The letters, the threats. Arthur was the first victim.

Kate called the animal hospital. "But is he going to be all right?" they heard her ask. "Yes, leave him there overnight at least."

The overhead light cast a yellow glow over Jeff and Pat and Gordie. June bugs and moths battered themselves against the screens. She and Pat could see each other now and Kate knew they were both having the same thoughts. Kate would go to the sheriff tomorrow. But how to protect the dog or any of them? Should Gordie be warned? Kate didn't want to tell him about the letters nor did she want to inform the kids. She wanted desperately to pack the kids off where they would be safe, but she knew they wouldn't leave if they thought she was in danger. Instead, they would insist on her leaving.

Her stomach rebelled and she rushed to the bathroom to vomit. What a crummy way to end a beautiful day. Anger at this unknown person or persons took hold as Kate stared at the toilet bowl while spilling her stomach contents, spattering the sides. She studied the mess for signs of blood and was grateful to see none. Splashing cold water on her face she saw Pat's reflection in the mirror. Kate attempted a sickly smile as Pat closed the bathroom door behind her.

"What did you throw up?"

"Dinner, what else?"

"That's all? No blood?"

Kate shook her head. "I'm not handling this well, am I?"

"Sooner or later something had to give, Kate. I'm surprised it took this long."

The next morning Pat found her tires slashed. She leaned her forehead against her car and sighed into the early morning.

Kate joined her and stared at the flat tires. "Oh God, what next?" she asked tiredly.

"I'll have to drive your car," Pat said resignedly. "Call the garage in town, will you, Kate, and have them change the tires." Pat climbed in behind the wheel.

It was okay to leave Kate now, but when the kids were gone how would she feel about Kate and Gordie being alone with this crazy person or persons around? Maybe she had better bring her rifle back with her just in case. And do what with it? Shoot someone?

251

You couldn't just take aim at a human being, even if that person tried to kill your dog and slashed your tires. But what was next? A fire in the night maybe? An explosion? She'd bring the gun back.

Kate returned to the house and carried two cups of coffee out to the porch for herself and Gordie. How would she explain the slashed tires? How would she hide them?

"Okay, sis, what are you hiding from me? Time to confess."

She told him and then listened to the long silence. Blue jays screamed in the pines and their babies muttered for attention. Chattering squirrels leaped from branch to branch, knocking pine cones to the ground with their acrobatics. A chickadee called loudly. Two speedboats chased each other around the lake, their white wakes rolling into green waves.

"I've been thinking about going home," Gordie said quietly, sipping his coffee.

"You're going to let this crazy person chase you away?" Kate asked with disbelief.

"Not because of me, Katie." He turned his ravaged face toward her. His eyes burned with an angry intensity that betrayed his feelings, concealed by his quiet voice. "Look, you're not used to this shit. I am, and this bozo is carrying out his threats. For Christ's sake, he nearly killed the fucking dog."

"I shouldn't have told you," she said. "Please don't leave, Gordie. I'm going to the sheriff today."

"That'll do a whole hell of a lot of good. Then the entire town will know, and we'll be bombarded with requests to rid the community of my threatening presence."

"What's going on?" Beth stood in the doorway,

her hair rumpled during sleep. She ran a hand through it and yawned.

"Nothing," Kate assured her. "There's coffee on the stove."

"You guys want some?" Beth asked.

Then under her breath when Beth disappeared in the house: "You leave and I'll have to go with you."

"No, I don't want you to, but maybe you're right. I shouldn't let someone like that send me running."

"Of course I'm right."

By moving Beth's car between Pat's and the house Kate shielded the slashed tires. She urged Jeff to fish when he appeared, disheveled and barefoot, on the porch. The girls headed toward the pier after breakfast. With luck no one would notice the man from Wally's Garage. Around ten Kate drove to town to see the sheriff. By then the tires had been replaced and no one was any wiser.

Waushara baked in the morning sun. Kate parked in front of the courthouse. How was she going to break this so the sheriff would side with her?

"Sit down, Mrs. Sweeney. Aren't you new in the area?"

"As a permanent resident I'm a year old," she explained, studying the large friendly looking man sitting behind the desk. She removed the letters from her purse, breathed deeply and told him about the dog and the slashed tires, then waited while he read the letters.

A puzzled frown appeared between his eyes. "What do these mean?" he asked.

"My brother is very sick, actually he has AIDS. The letters refer to him." She met his eyes candidly, hoping to find sympathy.

"Oh," he said as if at a loss for words. He handed her back the letters. "You think this person poisoned the dog and slashed the tires?"

"Well, the threats in these letters and then those things happening. What would you think?"

"You're probably right. There are some crazy people around here." He sighed audibly and frowned more deeply, as if in thought. "I'll come out this afternoon and nose around a bit."

"Please don't say anything about this to my kids. They're visiting and they'll try to get me to leave and they'll worry, because I'm not leaving."

The sheriff stood, as he had when she entered, and reached across the desk. Her small hand disappeared in his large one. He smiled around the scowl. "I honestly don't know if I can help any, Mrs. Sweeney. I don't have much manpower or time. If you just had a clue as to what he's driving, maybe I could find him. Then I could stop him."

"Thanks. Maybe I can spot him."

"That would help, ma'am."

She drove to the grocery store to shop for dinner. This feeding six people was expensive, but everyone pitched in. By the time she reached the animal hospital to retrieve Arthur the day was unbearably hot. Arthur tugged against the leash, anxious to leave the clinic behind, while she talked to the veterinarian. He told her Arthur would be weak for a few days. She glanced at the dog. He didn't appear weak to her, as he choked himself trying to reach the door. "Sit, Arthur," she commanded and he rested on his haunches.

In the car he stretched out on the back seat and

panted, saliva dripping off his long tongue onto the floor. Kate turned on the air conditioner and opened the window a crack to give the heat an escape route. Her mind spun in place. The sooner the kids left the better; until then she'd keep them close at hand. And what would she do with Arthur now? Never let him out of sight? This was not only terrifying, it was annoying, an inconvenience. Arthur's hot breath bathed her neck.

At home she led him to the front porch. "Well, look who's back, the intrepid hound," Gordie commented from his chaise lounge. "I suppose I'm delegated to keep an eye on him while you're elsewhere, Katie."

"I'll be at my typewriter for at least a couple hours. I have to work on Monday's packet."

The days passed in a spell of heat, accompanied by the sounds of fireworks. The lake was a zoo on the weekend with motorboats everywhere. Arthur didn't mind the confinement, because he feared the firecrackers which drove him under Gordie's bed.

Saturday evening beach fires dotted the shoreline and nearly every fire was accompanied by a display of some sort of fireworks, lighting the sky with color and sound. The girls, Jeff, Pat and Kate were on the beach around their fire, while Jeff set off the few fireworks he had brought with him. Gordie had refused to leave the porch, and Arthur only emerged from under the bed to relieve himself.

Another letter had been in Friday's packet. It had been a little wary: *I seen the sheriff sneaking around there. It won't stop me. Move the queer or I'll be back.* Fucker, she had thought, goddam fucking madman.

255

The name had taken hold. She had almost called him that when she'd told Sheriff Haines about this latest letter.

Surprised and pleased with the efforts the sheriff had put out, Kate thought he might actually catch the culprit. All the local mailmen and women had copies of the madman's envelopes and had been asked to look for envelopes addressed to the newspaper in the mail they picked up. Kate wondered if this was legal. But if the letters were mailed at the post office, it would probably be impossible to nail the madman this way.

All week Kate had been riding her bike with one of the kids at her side or behind her struggling to keep up. She had seen a battered green Chevy truck near her driveway twice. It had looked suspicious to her but everything and everyone looked suspicious to her these days. Once she had nearly run into it as she'd pulled out of the driveway. Her impression had been that it had been parked near the drive and moved forward when she and Jeff had ridden out on the blacktop. She hadn't been able to get a good look at whoever was behind the wheel.

Catching this person had become an obsession with her. There had been no more efforts to sabotage or destroy anything since the slashed tires, perhaps because they'd been so observant, leaving outside lights blazing all night. But it had only been a few days since the tires had been cut.

Sitting cross-legged on the beach, she sensed Pat's eyes on her and met her gaze across the fire. A smile passed between them.

"Mom, where are you? It's like you're miles away," Beth said.

"Sorry, honey. Did I miss something?"

"Do you want to light some of these rockets?" Jeff asked.

"No, you go ahead. Where's Arthur? Under some bed?"

"Gordie'll keep an eye on him, Mom," Sarah said.

"I think I'll just go check. Be right back." She started up the path, turned to look at the fire and the dimly lit figures around it, heard their voices. The moon was low in the west, the sky bright with variations of colors. Tomorrow the water would be floating with debris.

"You really are psychic, Katie," Gordie said. He stood on the darkened porch.

"What do you mean?"

"Arthur escaped out the back door. I was just coming to tell you. I called but the stupid mutt is gone."

"Shit," Kate muttered. "Goddamn dog. He's probably hiding in the woods out back. I'll have to go look."

"Katie, don't go alone," Gordie called, but she was already gone. The door slammed behind her.

The driveway spooked her with the white pines looming darkly on either side. She called for the dog several times, while trying to maintain her anger to ward off fear.

When the man grabbed her arm, she nearly wet her pants. She found she could not make any sound. Even though she tried to scream, it stuck in her throat. This couldn't be happening to her. Things like this didn't happen to her. She smelled his breath, it reeked of garlic. She'd tell the sheriff to look for someone with garlic breath, she thought, and a small

257

hysterical giggle escaped her. The sound enabled her to make others. She screamed once and a large hand covered her mouth.

"Don't scream, lady. I ain't hurting you this time, just telling you to take that queer and go wherever you come from."

She bit at the hand but couldn't get her teeth into it. Then she stomped on his foot, but he had boots on. He twisted one arm behind her back until she bent forward and gasped from the pain.

Arthur burst out of the trees to dance and bark around them. They were both so startled the madman let go of her and she forgot to scream. Arthur never liked his people to get physical, it alarmed him. Kate realized the man was reaching into his pocket and sensed the gun before she saw it. She shoved his arm, threw her whole body against it, and the shot went wild. So did Arthur. He turned tail and disappeared in the woods, his yelps getting fainter as he put distance between them. Kate erupted in fury, freeing herself and diving into the woods after the dog.

She heard voices calling her — Pat, Jeff, the girls. She turned and ran toward the sound. Thinking the madman was behind her, she sprinted for her life and ran headlong into Jeff in her blind terror to escape.

"Mom, what's the matter?" Jeff asked, holding her trembling body in his arms.

"I thought I saw a bear." It was the first thing that came into her mind. She couldn't let him know. "I think Arthur thought he saw one, too." She laughed shakily.

"Where is Arthur?" Pat asked, staring at Kate, wondering what the hell really had happened.

Kate waved an arm at the woods. She hugged Jeff for safety. "He ran off after scaring the bear."

"I thought I heard a shot," Beth said, taking a tentative step toward the woods.

"Just a cherry bomb or something," Kate said, her voice quavering.

"I'll go look for Arthur," Jeff volunteered.

"No," Kate protested, still hugging him. "He'll come back." Arthur wasn't going to let anyone strange near him tonight. "You'll never find him in there."

The girls called Arthur's name. Then Pat called him but there was no response. Her gaze kept straying to Kate, noticing Kate's eyes huge in a pale face, but since Kate hadn't volunteered the information it must have had something to do with the threats. The back door banged and Gordie joined them in the yard.

"All this for a dog?" he asked.

"For Arthur," Kate replied. "He saved me."

"Quite by accident, I'm sure," Gordie said dryly, but he shouted for Arthur a few times, too.

"I'll go put out the beach fire," Jeff said when it was apparent the dog wasn't going to respond to their pleas to return.

"I'll go with you," Kate said quickly, unwilling to let anyone go anywhere alone.

"I'll go with him," Pat said quietly, her eyes still on Kate.

"Okay, what happened out there?" Pat asked later in bed.

Kate told her, nestling against her. She needed to feel another human being. She had felt so alone and helpless in the driveway.

259

Pat held her, burying her face in Kate's hair, and listened with growing alarm, chills racing each other up and down her skin during Kate's recital, tightening her hug until Kate complained. "Sorry, I just can't stand the thought of somebody hurting you."

"I don't think he was trying to hurt me tonight, just warn me, but he was going to kill Arthur." She pulled away a little.

"What are you doing?"

"Going to see if Arthur's out there."

"We'll both go."

"Thank God the kids will be gone tomorrow and they'll be safe and we won't have to hide this anymore." Kate covered herself with a terry cloth robe, as did Pat.

"I think maybe we should all move to my apartment until this blows over," Pat suggested.

"When is it going to blow over? Tell me that," Kate objected.

"You're right, Kate, but tonight it really became serious. It was bad enough when he poisoned the dog, but grabbing you was too much." Pat shivered at the thought.

"He's getting too bold. He'll be caught."

When they descended the stairs Gordie's dark figure gave them a start. He was pacing the downstairs with the lights off. "You two can't sleep either?"

"We thought we'd see if Arthur is back," Kate whispered.

"I just looked. He's not."

Kate and Pat exchanged grins at Gordie's concern.

"What happened out there, Katie?"

Kate related again the terrors of the night. Every time she told it she relived it in her mind and felt the mindless fear and helplessness that had enveloped her.

"You're a tough cookie, Katie," Gordie remarked grimly.

"I was scared shitless," Kate said.

"You tried to bite him and stomped on his foot and you shoved his arm so he couldn't shoot Arthur. You even got away. I'm proud of you."

"Really?" Kate asked in surprise. In retrospect her witless fear embarrassed her.

On the porch in the dark they watched the moon set. A whine and scratch alerted them to Arthur's return. With a small cry of relief and joy Kate opened the door to him. She ran her hands over the large dog, feeling for wounds. Pat turned on the overhead light, and they inspected him thoroughly while he panted and licked their faces with happiness at the attention. Kate gave him a dog treat and he settled at their feet.

Gordie said, "Well ladies, got any ideas about what we do now?"

"I'll call the sheriff after the kids leave tomorrow," Kate said.

"Do either one of you know how to shoot a shotgun or a rifle?" Pat asked, thinking she'd better borrow her dad's shotgun.

Kate stared at her.

"I'm ready to learn," Gordie replied.

"We'll start target practice tomorrow."

The next morning, short-tempered and frazzled from lack of sleep, Kate vowed to make an appointment to see the doctor Monday. She had spent the night with her arms wrapped around her midriff in a futile attempt to quell the pain. Her back ached, contributing to a general feeling of malaise.

"No coffee, Mom?" Beth asked Kate at breakfast.

"No thanks, honey."

"You always drink coffee, Mom," Sarah said, pausing with a spoonful of Wheaties halfway to her mouth.

"I've given it up," she replied, buttering a piece of toast.

"You don't look well, Mom," Beth persisted.

"I'm fine," Kate answered, trying not to snap, reminding herself the kids were leaving this morning.

"The bear scared the sleep out of you, huh?" Jeff asked, grinning at his mother.

So he had believed it. Kate returned the smile with a tired one. "Yes, it sure did. It's going to be quiet without you."

Sitting across the table from Kate, drinking a cup of coffee, hair unbrushed and unruly, Pat met Kate's eyes and raised her eyebrows. Was this the way to say goodbye to one's children, telling them it was going to be quiet without them?

"What does that mean, Mom? Does that mean you're going to miss us?" Sarah asked.

"Of course. I'm going to miss you something fierce." But more than anything she wanted them safe, and the only way to accomplish that for them to leave. She had to deal with the fucking madman and whatever was the matter with her insides and she didn't want interference. Pressure from the kids could be disabling.

When the young people were gone, Kate returned to bed with Pat and sections of the Sunday paper.

They wrapped their arms around each other in their first free expression of love since Kate's children had arrived on the scene.

"God, I'm so tired," Kate said into Pat's neck.

"Want to sleep?"

Kate emitted a throaty laugh. "Are you kidding? I've been waiting for this for nearly two weeks. I want you."

"Why didn't you sleep last night?"

"Because of the night's happenings."

"That's part of it. Let's have the rest."

"You know why. I'm calling the doctor tomorrow. I promise." She concentrated on kissing Pat's neck. "You have the most delicious neck."

Pat laughed and tightened her arms around Kate.

XVI

His face registering dismay, Sheriff Haines let Kate finish her story before asking questions. "Did you get a look at him?"

"It was too dark," she replied, shaking her head. "He's not young, he's heavy set, he smelled like garlic. I think I'd recognize his voice if I heard it again. I was so scared I had trouble concentrating on anything but getting away and keeping him from killing the dog."

Poor, innocent Arthur. Next time she'd shoot the fucking madman. She knew how to load the rifle and shotgun and she'd use them. Absently she rubbed her hand over her mid-section. The doctor had scheduled an appointment for her at the hospital Tuesday afternoon. Pat would have to take her, because he had said she wouldn't be able to drive home.

"Let's rig more lights in the yard," the sheriff suggested. "At least he won't get close to the house without being observed."

"Unless we're sleeping," she added.

"I wish I knew what else to do." He appeared tired and discouraged.

"I know you're doing your best," she said. But it wasn't good enough.

"It's frustrating to always wait for him to make the first move, Mrs. Sweeney."

It was as if he were talking to someone else when he called her Mrs. Sweeney. She no longer thought of herself that way. "Call me Kate, please."

"Okay." He smiled at her. "My name is Doug."

"Sheriff Doug," she said with a grin, liking him and needing him on her side.

When she got home Gordie was still in bed. She leaned on the door frame to her old bedroom and talked to him. He looked gray and his breathing was labored. Pneumonia? "Not feeling so well, Gordie?"

"Tired, sis. I think I should have gone with you to the doctor."

"I'll call him," she said.

On the way to the hospital, having left a note for Pat, Kate worried about Arthur. She had never locked the house when going into town. Knowing Pat was without a key and Arthur was inside, she didn't lock it this time. If someone set it on fire, no one could get him out but she didn't dare leave him outside to be poisoned again. It made her furious to have to worry about things like this when Gordie, slumped beside her, was struggling to breathe. The tires squealed around the curves.

"I'll be okay, sis. Don't kill us trying to get there a few minutes faster."

She glanced at him. He was leaning forward supporting himself with his arms, thin chest heaving under his shirt. She took her foot off the gas pedal and the speedometer dropped to fifty. "That all right?" Better not let him know how bad he looked. Pretend she was not worried.

He nodded and smiled thinly and even that looked like an effort.

Her heart went out to him. What a shitty way to die, bit by bit, looking worse all the time. His hair was thinning and he looked at least ten years older than he was, gaunt and marked. What had happened to her handsome brother? Tears of frustration and anger temporarily blinded her. She brushed them away with the back of her hand and felt Gordie's hand patting her leg, something she wouldn't have dared do to comfort him. She smiled tremulously at him.

"I'll be glad when it's over, sis." His smile was sad. His voice changed. "Don't you start bawling now."

Instead of crying she laughed a little and then more. He joined her and soon they were laughing so hard and desperately that Kate drove off the road and parked. Gasping, tears running down their faces, they slowly regained control. What had prompted that bit of hysteria, Kate wondered as she resumed the drive to the hospital.

266

That night, afraid for Pat to join her because it meant leaving the house and Arthur alone, Kate waited in Gordie's room and wandered the hospital corridors until the doctor sent her home. "We'll call you if there's any need." "But he looks bad." "He is bad. He's very sick and he may die, but he doesn't even know you're here. Get some sleep. You have tests tomorrow." It was true Gordie didn't know her. His condition had deteriorated once they had reached the hospital. He had experienced a slight seizure and drifted into a comatose state. "Call me if there's a change, if he wakes up, please?" she begged the nurse at the station. The nurse eyed her warily. Kate realized she was not happy to have Gordie for a patient. "He's my brother," Kate explained. "I don't want him alone if he gets worse." She didn't want him to die alone.

Except for its humiliating finality death hadn't seemed so terrible for her mother. She hoped Gordie's death would be like that — apparently painless, one minute alive, the next dead. Driving home along the dark ribbon of blacktop with woods on either side, preoccupied with thoughts as dark as the night, she slowly became aware of headlights closing in behind her.

"Pass, you jerk," she said, squinting in the rear view mirror, the interior of the car awash with light. Amazed, disbelieving, she felt the Taurus leap forward, pushed from behind. Her head snapped and her heart doubled its beat. Kate floored the accelerator, and the car responded by surging into the beam of its headlights, leaving the tailing vehicle as if it were in park. But not for long, she knew. Tires protesting and rear end swerving, the car rounded the next curve. Easy, don't panic and end up in the ditch, she warned herself. Thinking what that could mean caused adrenalin to flood her system and her mouth to go dry as dust. The lights reappeared in the mirror. She concentrated on the road and outdistancing the vehicle. When her driveway appeared, a black gap in the pines, the road behind was dark and empty.

Shaking, she parked in the yard and ran to the house. Arthur's bark, deep and resonant, was comforting to hear. He and Pat met her on the back porch.

"How's Gordie?" Pat asked.

Kate had forgotten all about Gordie in her panic to reach home. "Let's go inside," she said, shutting the back door.

Pat watched her lock the bolt. "Now what's happened, Kate?"

"He followed me, rammed my car from behind." Kate hurried to the front door, closed and locked it.

"What?" Pat gasped.

Kate nodded. "He did. I think it was a truck. The headlights were too high for a car." Her gaze moved nervously to the open windows. She wanted to shut and lock them, but it was too hot.

"Call the sheriff, Kate. Now." Pat walked to the phone and lifted the receiver off the hook, handing it to Kate. "But first tell me how Gordie is."

"Not so good," Kate replied. How quickly she had forgotten everything and everyone else in her fear.

She felt a fleeting shame. "I asked the nurse to call if he gets any worse. She didn't call, did she?" New anxiety grabbed at her stomach. Kate stood in the kitchen, the receiver in one hand, dial tone buzzing. Pat shook her head no, terror for them all gripping her. What could they do to protect themselves when they couldn't even identify the danger?

In bed that night with Arthur lying on the floor, occasionally scratching, they jumped at every sound. Both were acutely aware this could not continue but neither was able to think of a solution. Lying tensely in each other's arms, they finally made love to relieve the strain. It was a distracted lovemaking, leaving both dissatisfied and more drained than before they had started. Hot from the physical effort they moved apart and lay on the edges of the bed.

"Pat, it's not fair to ask you to stay here."

"What does that mean, Kate?" Pat asked, irritated. "Do I just forget I love you? Why did you say that?"

"I don't know. I guess I feel guilty."

"Let's just go to sleep. None of this is your fault."

They fell into exhausted sleep, punctuated by unpleasant dreams, and woke tired and nervous to a cloudy, muggy, oppressive day. Neither wanted to get up, but Arthur's urgent need to relieve himself forced Kate outdoors. She stood on the back steps, calling the dog when he strayed toward the pine woods. It was daylight and she was still afraid. Would she never feel safe again? It was easy to castigate herself for the terror when in a safe place. It was impossible to rid herself of it when she felt vulnerable and exposed.

"Thought I was a goner, didn't you, sis?" Gordie asked as she entered the room. He looked emaciated, his hair stood in thin spikes, his skin with the exception of the marks was the color of the sheets, and he greeted her with a grin which looked ghoulish.

But all Kate experienced at seeing him conscious was relief. The wolfish smile appeared beatific to her and her whole face lit up in reply. "Don't do that again. You enjoy scaring the piss out of me, don't you?"

"It's a big thrill," he replied dryly.

"When did you wake up?" She sat near the window, glancing out at a small lake bordering the lawn. Not a bad view, if one had to be in the hospital, better than looking out at traffic and other buildings.

"This morning. Didn't know where the hell I was. The nurse had to tell me. She stood in the doorway, wouldn't come any closer." He lay back on the pillows as if exhausted.

There were three boys wading in the lake, walking west along the length of the hospital. Kate watched them dawdle along the edge and smiled a little as she remembered her own youth at the lake, days spent with Gordie exploring the shallows.

"What?" Gordie asked.

"Just looking at those boys out there by the lake. Nice little lake, isn't it? Nice view."

Gordie nodded and watched the boys' progress. "We used to do that, Katie."

She smiled again. "We did. There weren't so many cottages then." She felt a pang for those days, but to go back would be to experience again the bad along with the good. Would she do it? If she could do it differently, would she? She would have had to marry Tom or none of the kids would be alive. Silly to even think about it, since it wasn't possible. No Tom, no kids, an interesting thought. What would she have done?

"Hey Katie, are you here? What are you thinking about?"

She compressed her lips. "Would you do your life differently, if you could?"

"Probably not. My nature wouldn't let me. I would have to come back to see Dad, try to make it right with him. And there was one guy — Jeremy was his name — I would have tried harder. He was just before Brad. I think he's dead, though . . ." He raised his eyebrows in question. "Would you?"

"I don't know. To do it differently would be to deny my kids. I can't do that."

Pat met her in Gordie's room around one-thirty and stayed with Gordie while Kate went to the emergency room for testing. "Tell them to call me here when it's over, Kate, or do you want me to come?"

"No, I'm a big girl."

As she climbed onto one of the examining tables in the emergency room, the doctor said, "If anything

271

shows up on the X-rays, we'll be administering Valium intravenously. First the X-rays, okay?"

Afterward Kate sat in a wheelchair listening to the doctor talk to Pat. Why wasn't he talking to her, she wondered. Did he think she was incompetent just because she had an ulcer? He smiled at her and put a hand on her shoulder. She looked up at him.

"You'll be fine, Kate. Take the Tagamet, no liquor, no caffeine. We'll have to look at the stomach again in three months. You'll probably be all healed." He gently pushed her back in the wheelchair when she tried to stand. "Someone will take you to the car."

Kate didn't argue. She was conscious, she heard everyone, she even talked, but the Valium was in her bloodstream. She was not quite there.

Pat drove Kate home in her Honda. "How are you feeling?" she asked, waiting to pull out of the parking lot. The Honda idled roughly. She'd have to take it in, she thought with annoyance. If it wasn't one thing it was another.

"Good. He shoved this tube down me and looked at the inside of my stomach. I didn't even care, except my throat hurt a little. Next time I'll ask if he has a smaller tube."

"Gordie was cheerful. He said he may come home tomorrow. Let's stop at the drugstore and fill this prescription. Okay?"

"Arthur," Kate said.

"He'll be all right a little longer." Pat glanced at Kate, who appeared to be perfectly lucid, even though the doctor had said she was under the influence of Valium.

At home, after taking a Tagamet, Kate parked herself on the porch with a book in her lap. She cared about nothing, not Gordie, not her health, not even the fucking madman. It was kind of nice not to worry about anything. Thunder rumbled in the distance. Her eyelids felt heavy.

"Why don't you go to bed?" Pat suggested, sitting near her. She sipped coffee, staring at the lake, hoping for rain to break the oppressive heat.

"Good idea."

Rain beating on the roof and the persistent ringing of the phone woke Kate. The phone was abruptly silenced, probably answered by Pat, and the drumming of the rain created a rhythm. A damp breeze blew over her and she reached down to draw the top sheet over her naked body before drifting back to sleep.

Pat slipped between the sheets and drew Kate to her. She slid an arm under Kate's head and cradled it. Her tears wet Kate's forehead and Kate reached up to wipe away the dampness as she again wakened.

"What, Pat?" Her body stiffened, as she felt Pat's arms tighten around her. "Gordie?" she asked, not really believing. She turned in an attempt to see Pat better.

Pat inclined her head slightly.

"The nurse said she'd call." Kate denied it, disbelief still in her voice.

"There wasn't time to call. He had a seizure and died."

"That was the phone call?"

"Yes."

"I was sleeping while he was dying. I didn't even

273

know it." Kate frowned, waiting for the facts to take root in her mind. She lay quietly but felt nothing except a strange emptiness. Where was the pain?

"Kate, you have to tell the hospital where to take him. Do you want me to call Bert?" Pat asked gently.

"What? Can't they wait? I'm going for a walk." She freed herself from Pat's arms and reached for her clothes. "I'll take Arthur."

"Let me come with you."

"I think I want to be alone." Kate tried to smile but it didn't come out right. It looked more like a painful grimace.

Pat panicked, thinking of the madman.

"Go ahead and call Bert." Kate pulled on shorts and a shirt and put on tennis shoes.

Pat sat up and clasped her knees, fear and concern for Kate showing. "You haven't forgotten it's not safe out there, have you?"

"I'll be safe. He's the one who better watch out," Kate said savagely.

In a drizzle, water drenching her whenever she brushed a branch, she prowled the woods with Pat trailing her. Arthur kept pace with Kate, then Pat, traveling the distance as a tenuous link joining them. Finally, Kate stopped and waited for Pat to catch up. Silently they passed the afternoon fruitlessly searching for the man who had made their lives a misery these past weeks.

The next morning Kate resumed her search. She slipped out of bed early and alone. Pat had taken a sleeping pill the night before and only stirred when

274

Kate left the room. Later they would have to go to Bert's funeral home to see to arrangements for Gordie, but now she let herself and Arthur out the back door and walked toward the road. She, too, had taken a sleeping pill but still she had awakened in the night several times.

Arthur barked at the battered truck parked on the road near her driveway and the man leaning against it. It was unlike Arthur to bark at humans and Kate took hold of his collar and silenced him.

Squinting at her in distrust, his clothing worn, his face lined with age, the man looked very ordinary to Kate. Certain he was the madman she asked, "What are you doing here?" Her heart beat loudly in her ears. Anger converged on her and she wanted to jump him, to claw and kick and spit.

"He's dead, ain't he?" The man straightened.

"Yes." She recognized his voice. He apparently had made it his business to know Gordie's whereabouts. So what was he doing here?

"That's good. I seen you out looking for me yesterday. You can't prove nothing, you know," he said in a flat voice.

"You son of a bitch," she said.

Then she heard Gordie talking in her mind, his own brand of humor: *He's not worth your anger, Katie. Just shoot him.* She almost smiled.

The man shrugged and started around toward the driver's side of the truck.

That was it, like a dirty epitaph. And suddenly she wanted nothing to do with him, wanted to be as far away as she could get from this poor excuse of a man. She turned and started back through the woods. Behind her the truck's engine sputtered to life.

275

At the lake she took a long swim, scrubbing her skin to a dark red. Pat found her in the water and sat on the pier. Mist floated across the water as the sun warmed the new day, streaking the eastern sky with hues of red.

"Where've you been, Kate?" she asked when Kate offered no information.

"I found him or he found me. I don't think he'll bother us any more."

"You shouldn't have gone without me."

"I didn't want to bother you." Kate stood next to the pier, waist deep in water. She wrapped a towel around her shoulders and started up the path toward the house.

"Kate, I can't help if you won't let me," Pat said despairingly. It was as if a wall had been built between them since yesterday, since Gordie's death.

"I'll be all right," Kate said, drawing into herself where she felt safe.

Kate and Pat left the lake a week after the funeral, when they were once again alone. Looking at the water caused Kate such distress she wasn't able to stay, not even in the heat of summer. She started packing early one morning, knowing only that she had to leave, at least for a while. She drove to Northland with Pat, stayed with her a few days, and then rented an apartment in the same building.

"Why don't you stay with me?" Pat asked despondently.

"I can't just move in on you. There's not enough room."

"We'll get a bigger apartment," Pat suggested.

"I need time alone," Kate said. "Give me a month or two. Okay?"

Unable to bridge the distance between them apparently caused by Gordie's death, Pat accepted the voluntary estrangement with a shrug. Her face resembled a thundercloud. Feeling as if her heart would break, she helped Kate move. Then she began her own withdrawal from Kate.

XVII

One warm Saturday in September Kate returned to the lake. The sun made shadows of the pines as she walked through them and she stepped from shade into light and back again, the rays flickering over her in rapid succession. Arthur ran ahead of her, disappearing and then reappearing to assure himself of her presence. Coming out on the north side of the woods to a field of corn, she stood listening to the wind rattling through the drying stalks and turned her face to the sun and wind as if to dry it.

She was just there for the day, and Arthur

relished the freedom. Maybe she should move back to the lake, but the darkness was still here. She couldn't shake it. Next summer perhaps. She sat on a nearby rock. Huge rocks, which must have been removed with great effort at some time, bordered the field. Jumping down she started back through the pines to the lake.

Emerging in the back yard, she avoided the house and walked down to the lake. Arthur galloped past, excitement in every move. The pier stood as she had left it, an extension of land in the lake. She removed her shoes and sat on the edge, dipping a toe in the water, testing it. Still warm. She lay back and closed her eyes to the sun. She had learned not to think aimlessly. Thoughts needed direction. Still, sometimes they strayed.

She deliberately directed them at the work she had left behind today. She had taken on two more newspapers, syndicating her column.

"Hey lady, want some help taking down this pier?"

Kate started at the sound of Pat's voice. She turned, smiling warmly. "Following me?"

"You look friendly enough. I brought my suit."

"I never heard you."

Arthur parked himself at Pat's feet and whined.

"I'm sneaky," Pat replied, rubbing the dog's head. "How are you, Arthur?" Then: "He misses me."

"He does see you rather often. We do live in the same building." Kate's smile broadened and she patted the pier. "Sit with me."

Pat let herself down next to Kate, took off her shoes and put her feet in the water. "Why didn't you tell me you were coming today, Kate?"

"It was a spur of the moment thing."

"It's nice to be here. I miss the lake. Don't you?"

"Yeah, I do."

Pat's heart thudded rapidly, warming her. "I miss living with you."

Kate heaved a sigh. "I know. I miss it, too."

"Do you still need to be alone?"

Kate shook her head. "I was talking about that with Dr. Jane the other day." They had discussed Kate's relationship with Pat, its evolution. With trepidation Kate had confronted her feelings for Pat or, more to the point, her attitude toward those emotions. Kate had never seen Jane surprised or disapproving over her revelations. She had gleaned some insight into why she had been so zealously guarding her independence. But mostly she had decided to go with the feelings, and she hoped it wasn't too late.

She scissored her feet in the water and glanced at Pat. "Did you mean it?"

Pat was trying to decide if the head shake meant Kate didn't need to be alone any more. "What?"

"When you asked me if I needed help taking down the pier?"

"Of course I meant it. I don't want to take it down in October when it's fifty degrees out or worse."

Taking the pier down was easier than putting it in. Pulling the sections off and stacking them on the shore, unbolting the crosspieces and removing them from the poles, and then unscrewing the poles only took them an hour. At the end of the time the tension was gone. It seemed natural to be together again.

"Remember when you first helped me put this in?"

"I'll never forget," Pat replied, grinning.

"I didn't know what to make of you." Kate's face sobered.

"I know you didn't. I was running away from Gail. I never thought I'd fall in love with you." Pat suddenly was deadly serious. "What happened, Kate? Why couldn't you let me help you after Gordie died?"

Kate hauled the last pole up on the beach and set it down next to the others. "I don't know. I think I was punishing myself. I wasn't fit to live with anyway."

Pat came up behind her and ran a hand down her back. "Do you still care for me?"

Kate did not move away from the touch. "Very much. Let's go change."

"How about a swim first."

Treading water, watching the shore with its ever-changing array of flowers, the dark pines, Kate knew a sense of loss so poignant it was a physical pain.

Pat floated nearby, lost in her own memories, wanting only to preserve this time with Kate, if possible to lengthen it, to salvage some of their love for each other. Gordie's death and Kate's withdrawal afterward were nightmares. She had seen Kate often but had not attempted any physical intimacy with her since leaving the lake. She had been terribly hurt when Kate had taken her own apartment. Recently she had decided not to let the hurt cause a permanent rift between them. Her eyes moved from the deep blue overhead to the glittering of sun and wavelets. God, what a gorgeous day. There was not another soul on the lake as far as she could tell. She floated closer to Kate. "Did you ever turn the madman in?"

Kate shook her head, all that was visible of her above the water. She spit out a long stream of water and breathed in the smell of lake and pines to remember through the winter months. She should have told Sheriff Haines, she realized. Instead she had talked it out with Jane Blevins.

She turned and felt Pat against her, face inches from her face. She smiled into the familiar dark eyes, looking so seriously into her own. On impulse she reached for Pat and kissed her, both women kicking hard to stay afloat.

When they ended the kiss and stared at each other, Pat raised her eyebrows in response. "Want to go in?" she inquired, hope taking hold.

"Let's." Kate's eyes were alive, excitement surging. She had thought her sexual desire had vanished. She should have known better.

"Upstairs, downstairs?" Pat asked, once inside.

"Doesn't matter. Downstairs." Kate stripped off her wet suit, watching Pat do the same.

When they came together the length of their bodies touching, cool and wet, hands moving gently over each other, it was as if it was all new. Kate took a deep, ragged breath and listened to Pat do the same as their mouths met — pulling, tugging gently, tongues flickering over lips and teeth, probing softly. Legs weak, they fell on the nearest bed and lay quietly for a minute or two, eyes locked, passion growing.

"It's about time," Kate commented gravely.

"I thought it might be over," Pat said.

"I'm so glad you came up today." Kate covered Pat's breast with a hand, caressing the nipple with her thumb, then bent to kiss it, to tease it with her tongue. Her hands moved down over Pat, followed by her mouth until she reached the joining of Pat's legs where she tasted and touched the silky warm wetness, her fingers sliding in the wake of her tongue. Hearing the sharp intake of breath, she smiled and sighed a little, knowing her turn would follow, enjoying the effect she was creating. She wanted Pat to remember this, to separate it from the rest of their lovemaking.

When it was over, they lay breathing heavily in each other's arms, hugging tightly to shut out the world.

"Nice," Kate commented, hearing her heart pound against Pat's. "Want to spend the night?"

"Love to. I'd like to spend the rest of my life with you." She hadn't meant to admit that. Making love was one thing, making a life together was another. Pat held her breath.

"So would I."

A few of the publications of
THE NAIAD PRESS, INC.
P.O. Box 10543 • Tallahassee, Florida 32302
Phone (904) 539-5965
Mail orders welcome. Please include 15% postage.

CHESAPEAKE PROJECT by Phyllis Horn. 304 pp. Jessie &
Meredith in perilous adventure.   ISBN 0-941483-58-4 $8.95

LIFESTYLES by Jackie Calhoun. 224 pp. Contemporary Lesbian
lives and loves.   ISBN 0-941483-57-6   8.95

VIRAGO by Karen Marie Christa Minns. 208 pp. Darsen has
chosen Ginny.   ISBN 0-941483-56-8   8.95

WILDERNESS TREK by Dorothy Tell. 192 pp. Six women on
vacation learning "new" skills.   ISBN 0-941483-60-6   8.95

MURDER BY THE BOOK by Pat Welch. 256 pp. A Helen
Black Mystery. First in a series.   ISBN 0-941483-59-2   8.95

BERRIGAN by Vicki P. McConnell. 176 pp. Youthful Lesbian–
romantic, idealistic Berrigan.   ISBN 0-941483-55-X   8.95

LESBIANS IN GERMANY by Lillian Faderman & B. Eriksson.
128 pp. Fiction, poetry, essays.   ISBN 0-941483-62-2   8.95

THE BEVERLY MALIBU by Katherine V. Forrest. 288 pp. A
Kate Delafield Mystery. 3rd in a series.   ISBN 0-941483-47-9   16.95

THERE'S SOMETHING I'VE BEEN MEANING TO TELL
YOU Ed. by Loralee MacPike. 288 pp. Gay men and lesbians
coming out to their children.   ISBN 0-941483-44-4   9.95
                                       ISBN 0-941483-54-1   16.95

LIFTING BELLY by Gertrude Stein. Ed. by Rebecca Mark. 104
pp. Erotic poetry.   ISBN 0-941483-51-7   8.95
                         ISBN 0-941483-53-3   14.95

ROSE PENSKI by Roz Perry. 192 pp. Adult lovers in a long-term
relationship.   ISBN 0-941483-37-1   8.95

AFTER THE FIRE by Jane Rule. 256 pp. Warm, human novel
by this incomparable author.   ISBN 0-941483-45-2   8.95

SUE SLATE, PRIVATE EYE by Lee Lynch. 176 pp. The gay
folk of Peacock Alley are *all* cats.   ISBN 0-941483-52-5   8.95

CHRIS by Randy Salem. 224 pp. Golden oldie. Handsome Chris
and her adventures.   ISBN 0-941483-42-8   8.95

THREE WOMEN by March Hastings. 232 pp. Golden oldie. A
triangle among wealthy sophisticates.   ISBN 0-941483-43-6   8.95

RICE AND BEANS by Valeria Taylor. 232 pp. Love and
romance on poverty row.   ISBN 0-941483-41-X   8.95

PLEASURES by Robbi Sommers. 204 pp. Unprecedented
eroticism.   ISBN 0-941483-49-5   8.95

EDGEWISE by Camarin Grae. 372 pp. Spellbinding
adventure.   ISBN 0-941483-19-3   9.95

FATAL REUNION by Claire McNab. 216 pp. 2nd Det. Inspec.
Carol Ashton mystery.   ISBN 0-941483-40-1   8.95

KEEP TO ME STRANGER by Sarah Aldridge. 372 pp. Romance
set in a department store dynasty.   ISBN 0-941483-38-X   9.95

HEARTSCAPE by Sue Gambill. 204 pp. American lesbian in
Portugal.   ISBN 0-941483-33-9   8.95

IN THE BLOOD by Lauren Wright Douglas. 252 pp. Lesbian
science fiction adventure fantasy   ISBN 0-941483-22-3   8.95

THE BEE'S KISS by Shirley Verel. 216 pp. Delicate, delicious
romance.   ISBN 0-941483-36-3   8.95

RAGING MOTHER MOUNTAIN by Pat Emmerson. 264 pp.
Furosa Firechild's adventures in Wonderland. ISBN 0-941483-35-5 8.95

IN EVERY PORT by Karin Kallmaker. 228 pp. Jessica's sexy,
adventuresome travels.   ISBN 0-941483-37-7   8.95

OF LOVE AND GLORY by Evelyn Kennedy. 192 pp. Exciting
WWII romance.   ISBN 0-941483-32-0   8.95

CLICKING STONES by Nancy Tyler Glenn. 288 pp. Love
transcending time.   ISBN 0-941483-31-2   8.95

SURVIVING SISTERS by Gail Pass. 252 pp. Powerful love
story.   ISBN 0-941483-16-9   8.95

SOUTH OF THE LINE by Catherine Ennis. 216 pp. Civil War
adventure.   ISBN 0-941483-29-0   8.95

WOMAN PLUS WOMAN by Dolores Klaich. 300 pp. Supurb
Lesbian overview.   ISBN 0-941483-28-2   9.95

SLOW DANCING AT MISS POLLY'S by Sheila Ortiz Taylor.
96 pp. Lesbian Poetry   ISBN 0-941483-30-4   7.95

DOUBLE DAUGHTER by Vicki P. McConnell. 216 pp. A Nyla
Wade Mystery, third in the series.   ISBN 0-941483-26-6   8.95

HEAVY GILT by Delores Klaich. 192 pp. Lesbian detective/
disappearing homophobes/upper class gay society.
                                ISBN 0-941483-25-8   8.95

THE FINER GRAIN by Denise Ohio. 216 pp. Brilliant young
college lesbian novel.   ISBN 0-941483-11-8   8.95

THE AMAZON TRAIL by Lee Lynch. 216 pp. Life, travel & lore
of famous lesbian author.   ISBN 0-941483-27-4   8.95

HIGH CONTRAST by Jessie Lattimore. 264 pp. Women of the
Crystal Palace.   ISBN 0-941483-17-7   8.95

OCTOBER OBSESSION by Meredith More. Josie's rich, secret
Lesbian life.   ISBN 0-941483-18-5   8.95

LESBIAN CROSSROADS by Ruth Baetz. 276 pp. Contemporary
Lesbian lives.   ISBN 0-941483-21-5   9.95

BEFORE STONEWALL: THE MAKING OF A GAY AND
LESBIAN COMMUNITY by Andrea Weiss & Greta Schiller.
96 pp., 25 illus.   ISBN 0-941483-20-7   7.95

WE WALK THE BACK OF THE TIGER by Patricia A. Murphy.
192 pp. Romantic Lesbian novel/beginning women's movement.
                                          ISBN 0-941483-13-4   8.95

SUNDAY'S CHILD by Joyce Bright. 216 pp. Lesbian athletics, at
last the novel about sports.   ISBN 0-941483-12-6   8.95

OSTEN'S BAY by Zenobia N. Vole. 204 pp. Sizzling adventure
romance set on Bonaire.   ISBN 0-941483-15-0   8.95

LESSONS IN MURDER by Claire McNab. 216 pp. 1st Det. Inspec.
Carol Ashton mystery – erotic tension!.   ISBN 0-941483-14-2   8.95

YELLOWTHROAT by Penny Hayes. 240 pp. Margarita, bandit,
kidnaps Julia.   ISBN 0-941483-10-X   8.95

SAPPHISTRY: THE BOOK OF LESBIAN SEXUALITY by
Pat Califia. 3d edition, revised. 208 pp. ISBN 0-941483-24-X   8.95

CHERISHED LOVE by Evelyn Kennedy. 192 pp. Erotic
Lesbian love story.   ISBN 0-941483-08-8   8.95

LAST SEPTEMBER by Helen R. Hull. 208 pp. Six stories & a
glorious novella.   ISBN 0-941483-09-6   8.95

THE SECRET IN THE BIRD by Camarin Grae. 312 pp. Striking,
psychological suspense novel.   ISBN 0-941483-05-3   8.95

TO THE LIGHTNING by Catherine Ennis. 208 pp. Romantic
Lesbian 'Robinson Crusoe' adventure.   ISBN 0-941483-06-1   8.95

THE OTHER SIDE OF VENUS by Shirley Verel. 224 pp.
Luminous, romantic love story.   ISBN 0-941483-07-X   8.95

DREAMS AND SWORDS by Katherine V. Forrest. 192 pp.
Romantic, erotic, imaginative stories.   ISBN 0-941483-03-7   8.95

MEMORY BOARD by Jane Rule. 336 pp. Memorable novel
about an aging Lesbian couple.   ISBN 0-941483-02-9   9.95

THE ALWAYS ANONYMOUS BEAST by Lauren Wright
Douglas. 224 pp. A Caitlin Reese mystery. First in a series.
                                          ISBN 0-941483-04-5   8.95

SEARCHING FOR SPRING by Patricia A. Murphy. 224 pp.
Novel about the recovery of love.   ISBN 0-941483-00-2   8.95

DUSTY'S QUEEN OF HEARTS DINER by Lee Lynch. 240 pp.
Romantic blue-collar novel.   ISBN 0-941483-01-0   8.95

PARENTS MATTER by Ann Muller. 240 pp. Parents'
relationships with Lesbian daughters and gay sons.
                                          ISBN 0-930044-91-6   9.95

THE PEARLS by Shelley Smith. 176 pp. Passion and fun in
the Caribbean sun.   ISBN 0-930044-93-2   7.95

MAGDALENA by Sarah Aldridge. 352 pp. Epic Lesbian novel
set on three continents.   ISBN 0-930044-99-1   8.95

THE BLACK AND WHITE OF IT by Ann Allen Shockley.
144 pp. Short stories.   ISBN 0-930044-96-7   7.95

SAY JESUS AND COME TO ME by Ann Allen Shockley. 288
pp. Contemporary romance.   ISBN 0-930044-98-3   8.95

LOVING HER by Ann Allen Shockley. 192 pp. Romantic love
story.   ISBN 0-930044-97-5   7.95

MURDER AT THE NIGHTWOOD BAR by Katherine V.
Forrest. 240 pp. A Kate Delafield mystery. Second in a series.
                                      ISBN 0-930044-92-4   8.95

ZOE'S BOOK by Gail Pass. 224 pp. Passionate, obsessive love
story.   ISBN 0-930044-95-9   7.95

WINGED DANCER by Camarin Grae. 228 pp. Erotic Lesbian
adventure story.   ISBN 0-930044-88-6   8.95

PAZ by Camarin Grae. 336 pp. Romantic Lesbian adventurer
with the power to change the world.   ISBN 0-930044-89-4   8.95

SOUL SNATCHER by Camarin Grae. 224 pp. A puzzle, an
adventure, a mystery — Lesbian romance.   ISBN 0-930044-90-8   8.95

THE LOVE OF GOOD WOMEN by Isabel Miller. 224 pp.
Long-awaited new novel by the author of the beloved *Patience
and Sarah.*   ISBN 0-930044-81-9   8.95

THE HOUSE AT PELHAM FALLS by Brenda Weathers. 240
pp. Suspenseful Lesbian ghost story. ISBN 0-930044-79-7   7.95

HOME IN YOUR HANDS by Lee Lynch. 240 pp. More stories
from the author of *Old Dyke Tales.* ISBN 0-930044-80-0   7.95

EACH HAND A MAP by Anita Skeen. 112 pp. Real-life poems
that touch us all.   ISBN 0-930044-82-7   6.95

SURPLUS by Sylvia Stevenson. 342 pp. A classic early Lesbian
novel.   ISBN 0-930044-78-9   7.95

PEMBROKE PARK by Michelle Martin. 256 pp. Derring-do
and daring romance in Regency England.   ISBN 0-930044-77-0   7.95

THE LONG TRAIL by Penny Hayes. 248 pp. Vivid adventures
of two women in love in the old west. ISBN 0-930044-76-2   8.95

HORIZON OF THE HEART by Shelley Smith. 192 pp. Hot
romance in summertime New England.   ISBN 0-930044-75-4   7.95

AN EMERGENCE OF GREEN by Katherine V. Forrest. 288
pp. Powerful novel of sexual discovery.   ISBN 0-930044-69-X   8.95

THE LESBIAN PERIODICALS INDEX edited by Claire
Potter. 432 pp. Author & subject index.   ISBN 0-930044-74-6   29.95

DESERT OF THE HEART by Jane Rule. 224 pp. A classic; basis for the movie *Desert Hearts.*   ISBN 0-930044-73-8   7.95

SPRING FORWARD/FALL BACK by Sheila Ortiz Taylor. 288 pp. Literary novel of timeless love.   ISBN 0-930044-70-3   7.95

FOR KEEPS by Elisabeth Nonas. 144 pp. Contemporary novel about losing and finding love.   ISBN 0-930044-71-1   7.95

TORCHLIGHT TO VALHALLA by Gale Wilhelm. 128 pp. Classic novel by a great Lesbian writer.   ISBN 0-930044-68-1   7.95

LESBIAN NUNS: BREAKING SILENCE edited by Rosemary Curb and Nancy Manahan. 432 pp. Unprecedented autobiographies of religious life.   ISBN 0-930044-62-2   9.95

THE SWASHBUCKLER by Lee Lynch. 288 pp. Colorful novel set in Greenwich Village in the sixties.   ISBN 0-930044-66-5   8.95

MISFORTUNE'S FRIEND by Sarah Aldridge. 320 pp. Historical Lesbian novel set on two continents.   ISBN 0-930044-67-3   7.95

A STUDIO OF ONE'S OWN by Ann Stokes. Edited by Dolores Klaich. 128 pp. Autobiography.   ISBN 0-930044-64-9   7.95

SEX VARIANT WOMEN IN LITERATURE by Jeannette Howard Foster. 448 pp. Literary history.   ISBN 0-930044-65-7   8.95

A HOT-EYED MODERATE by Jane Rule. 252 pp. Hard-hitting essays on gay life; writing; art.   ISBN 0-930044-57-6   7.95

INLAND PASSAGE AND OTHER STORIES by Jane Rule. 288 pp. Wide-ranging new collection.   ISBN 0-930044-56-8   7.95

WE TOO ARE DRIFTING by Gale Wilhelm. 128 pp. Timeless Lesbian novel, a masterpiece.   ISBN 0-930044-61-4   6.95

AMATEUR CITY by Katherine V. Forrest. 224 pp. A Kate Delafield mystery. First in a series.   ISBN 0-930044-55-X   8.95

THE SOPHIE HOROWITZ STORY by Sarah Schulman. 176 pp. Engaging novel of madcap intrigue.   ISBN 0-930044-54-1   7.95

THE BURNTON WIDOWS by Vickie P. McConnell. 272 pp. A Nyla Wade mystery, second in the series.   ISBN 0-930044-52-5   7.95

OLD DYKE TALES by Lee Lynch. 224 pp. Extraordinary stories of our diverse Lesbian lives.   ISBN 0-930044-51-7   8.95

DAUGHTERS OF A CORAL DAWN by Katherine V. Forrest. 240 pp. Novel set in a Lesbian new world.   ISBN 0-930044-50-9   8.95

THE PRICE OF SALT by Claire Morgan. 288 pp. A milestone novel, a beloved classic.   ISBN 0-930044-49-5   8.95

AGAINST THE SEASON by Jane Rule. 224 pp. Luminous, complex novel of interrelationships.   ISBN 0-930044-48-7   8.95

LOVERS IN THE PRESENT AFTERNOON by Kathleen Fleming. 288 pp. A novel about recovery and growth.   ISBN 0-930044-46-0   8.95

TOOTHPICK HOUSE by Lee Lynch. 264 pp. Love between
two Lesbians of different classes.   ISBN 0-930044-45-2   7.95

MADAME AURORA by Sarah Aldridge. 256 pp. Historical
novel featuring a charismatic "seer."   ISBN 0-930044-44-4   7.95

CURIOUS WINE by Katherine V. Forrest. 176 pp. Passionate
Lesbian love story, a best-seller.   ISBN 0-930044-43-6   8.95

BLACK LESBIAN IN WHITE AMERICA by Anita Cornwell.
141 pp. Stories, essays, autobiography.   ISBN 0-930044-41-X   7.95

CONTRACT WITH THE WORLD by Jane Rule. 340 pp.
Powerful, panoramic novel of gay life.   ISBN 0-930044-28-2   9.95

MRS. PORTER'S LETTER by Vicki P. McConnell. 224 pp.
The first Nyla Wade mystery.   ISBN 0-930044-29-0   7.95

TO THE CLEVELAND STATION by Carol Anne Douglas.
192 pp. Interracial Lesbian love story.   ISBN 0-930044-27-4   6.95

THE NESTING PLACE by Sarah Aldridge. 224 pp. A
three-woman triangle—love conquers all!   ISBN 0-930044-26-6   7.95

THIS IS NOT FOR YOU by Jane Rule. 284 pp. A letter to a
beloved is also an intricate novel.   ISBN 0-930044-25-8   8.95

FAULTLINE by Sheila Ortiz Taylor. 140 pp. Warm, funny,
literate story of a startling family.   ISBN 0-930044-24-X   6.95

THE LESBIAN IN LITERATURE by Barbara Grier. 3d ed.
Foreword by Maida Tilchen. 240 pp. Comprehensive bibliography.
Literary ratings; rare photos.   ISBN 0-930044-23-1   7.95

ANNA'S COUNTRY by Elizabeth Lang. 208 pp. A woman
finds her Lesbian identity.   ISBN 0-930044-19-3   6.95

PRISM by Valerie Taylor. 158 pp. A love affair between two
women in their sixties.   ISBN 0-930044-18-5   6.95

BLACK LESBIANS: AN ANNOTATED BIBLIOGRAPHY
compiled by J. R. Roberts. Foreword by Barbara Smith. 112 pp.
Award-winning bibliography.   ISBN 0-930044-21-5   5.95

THE MARQUISE AND THE NOVICE by Victoria Ramstetter.
108 pp. A Lesbian Gothic novel.   ISBN 0-930044-16-9   6.95

OUTLANDER by Jane Rule. 207 pp. Short stories and essays
by one of our finest writers.   ISBN 0-930044-17-7   8.95

ALL TRUE LOVERS by Sarah Aldridge. 292 pp. Romantic
novel set in the 1930s and 1940s.   ISBN 0-930044-10-X   7.95

A WOMAN APPEARED TO ME by Renee Vivien. 65 pp. A
classic; translated by Jeannette H. Foster.   ISBN 0-930044-06-1   5.00

CYTHEREA'S BREATH by Sarah Aldridge. 240 pp. Romantic
novel about women's entrance into medicine.
                                ISBN 0-930044-02-9   6.95

TOTTIE by Sarah Aldridge. 181 pp. Lesbian romance in the
turmoil of the sixties.   ISBN 0-930044-01-0   6.95

THE LATECOMER by Sarah Aldridge. 107 pp. A delicate love
story.   ISBN 0-930044-00-2   6.95

ODD GIRL OUT by Ann Bannon.   ISBN 0-930044-83-5   5.95

I AM A WOMAN by Ann Bannon.   ISBN 0-930044-84-3   5.95

WOMEN IN THE SHADOWS by Ann Bannon.
                                       ISBN 0-930044-85-1   5.95

JOURNEY TO A WOMAN by Ann Bannon.
                                   ISBN 0-930044-86-X   5.95

BEEBO BRINKER by Ann Bannon.   ISBN 0-930044-87-8   5.95
        Legendary novels written in the fifties and sixties,
            set in the gay mecca of Greenwich Village.

VOLUTE BOOKS

JOURNEY TO FULFILLMENT   Early classics by Valerie   3.95

A WORLD WITHOUT MEN   Taylor: The Erika Frohmann   3.95

RETURN TO LESBOS   series.   3.95

These are just a few of the many Naiad Press titles — we are the oldest and
largest lesbian/feminist publishing company in the world. Please request a
complete catalog. We offer personal service; we encourage and welcome
direct mail orders from individuals who have limited access to bookstores
carrying our publications.